No Secrets Allowed

A SWEET
AND LIGHT-HEARTED
ROMANTIC SERIES,
BOOK 2

KANA WU

www.kanawuauthor.com

Ordering Information:

Quantity sales. Special discounts are available on quantity purchases by corporations, associations, and others. Orders by US trade bookstores and wholesalers. For details, contact the publisher at the address above.

Editing by The Pro Book Editor
Proofreading by Fine Fuse Editorial Services
Interior Design by IAPS.rocks

ISBN: 978-1-7357676-3-5

1. Main category—FICTION / Women
2. Second category—FICTION / Romance / New Adult
3. Third category—FICTION / Romance / Clean & Wholesome

First Edition

Chapter 1

A CRISP, EARLY WINTER MORNING GREETED me as I left my aunt's house. Vapor rose in the air from my breath. Gazing up, I noticed the color of the sky matched the gray sidewalk, although the Weather Channel had predicted a bright, sunny day in Boston. Well, so much for expecting a warm day today.

As I turned onto the main street, the hustle and bustle of the city surrounded me. The sound of passing cars and the groaning and hissing of the city bus when it halted at the nearby bus stop overwhelmed the chatter and footsteps of people rushing to and fro. Twenty feet from me, a man yelled and waved his fist as a biker swirled past him on the sidewalk. It was against the law to ride a bike on the sidewalk, especially where it was prohibited by signs, but sometimes, people did it anyway. I chuckled and shook my head.

When I moved to this city four months ago, I hadn't liked its hustle and bustle. Too noisy. However, I was used to it now and felt something inside me come alive every time my ears picked up the familiar sounds.

I sped up a bit, speed-walking toward the O'ahu Café for my favorite winter drink, a mint-flavored mocha latte. Another nearby café had the same drink, but the one from the O'ahu was better and not too sweet. The best part was the location of the café near the bus stop, which allowed me to take shelter from the frigid weather while waiting for the bus.

My idea wasn't as brilliant as I'd thought because, looking through the big window, I saw a long line waiting inside the café. My favorite table near the window and facing the street was already occupied. When the café wasn't too crowded, I enjoyed sitting at that particular table while drinking my coffee, watching pedestrians pass by on the sidewalk.

Seven people were waiting in line, but thankfully, my bus wouldn't be coming for a while.

The bell above the café door made a soft ding as I pushed it open. A couple of customers near the door turned to see who had entered, as well as a young man in a beige apron behind the counter, whose brown skin made many people jealous of his natural tan. His long hair was tied up in a bun and hidden beneath his black beanie. I felt a twinge of envy over his long, shiny, black hair.

Standing next to a girl with a pixie haircut, who was currently taking the customers' orders, he waved to acknowledge me, and I waved back at him.

As I approached the counter, he signaled the cashier to change places with him so he could ring up my order.

"Good morning, Aurorette Arrington," he sang. "You look great this morning with your red nose like Rudolph." He tapped at his own nose.

"Good morning, Tyler Sheridan James Kahale," I teased him back. "You look great too, with your long hair that makes me jealous hidden under your beanie."

The wide grin on his face faded. Ty, as he wanted people to call him, had never liked his long name. He always said that he wanted to change his name to "Tyler James," making it short but cool. However, after his dad passed away, he decided to keep it.

"No more free espresso for you, since you called me by *that* name." He pouted, but his eyes twinkled with good humor. He rang up my usual order, a small mint mocha latte.

"I can deal with that." I smiled sweetly, tapping my card on the reader.

Ty scoffed and closed the register. He asked the girl with the pixie haircut to ring up the next order. The girl switched places with him, seemingly used to acting on the whim of the owner's son.

"Where have you been? You haven't come around lately," Ty said, pumping two shots of mint syrup into a cup. "My mom has been asking about you."

His mom, Dot, was my aunt's closest friend in Boston. After her husband had passed away, Dot had begun managing the café with Ty, her daughter, Brie, and three workers. My aunt came and helped out sometimes when the café was extra busy or if one of the workers couldn't come in.

"Busy, busy, busy." I sighed dramatically. "It's almost Christmas, and my office has been super hectic since October. I haven't had a chance to stop by because I've been exhausted by the time I get home. Please tell Dot that I'll stop by after work for her delicious chicken pesto panini tonight."

His mom's panini was one of the café's specialties. Made fresh, people loved the crunchy texture and delicious pesto sauce. Usually, I texted Dot to put aside one or two that I'd pick up later after work.

"Yeah, I'll tell her. By the way," Ty said as he poured an espresso shot into my cup, "I heard from her that your aunt got a new coffee machine for her birthday last month, but she doesn't drink coffee, does she? Now, tell me, why would someone give her a coffee machine? I'll bet the giver isn't a very thoughtful person. Just saying," he added, giving me a meaningful smile.

In return, my smile was sour. The giver was Peter Ryder, my long-distance, British-born boyfriend, who lived in California. He'd known that my aunt loved tea more than coffee and bought an

3

English tea set for her birthday. He also bought a coffee machine for me from the same store. Somehow, the store had messed up the orders and sent the coffee machine in beautiful wrapping paper to my aunt instead of the tea set. My aunt was upset and thought Peter wasn't a thoughtful person. When I told him, Peter freaked out and complained to the store. My aunt felt better after he apologized and explained it to her. Later on, the store called for clarification and sent her another tea set by way of compensation.

"It wasn't his fault. The store messed up the order," I said quickly. "Besides, my aunt now has two beautiful new English tea sets while I got the coffee machine."

"Ha! I knew you'd defend that useless guy," Ty said, pointing at my nose. A proud smile plastered his face. "Aurorette, you should date me, not a guy who lives far away in California. Since I live close to you, I wouldn't make a blunder like that. Three years younger means nothing in this century. Besides, I think I'm more mature than him. And where does he work now?" Leaning toward me, he placed his hand behind his ear.

"Yeah, yeah, yeah. I've heard that before." I waved a hand. "And instead of dating *me*, you should find a girl your age. Besides," I leaned toward him and whispered in his ear, "you're working for your family business too." I gave him a wink.

His mouth opened slightly and then closed again. "But this is only temporary until I finish colle—"

His words were cut off when a large, tall woman, her gray hair wrapped in a hairnet, came from the kitchen. "Ty! I'm busy, and the milk company will be here soon. I need you to receive the delivery." Her dark brown eyes widened as our eyes met. "Oh, hey, Rory. Sorry, I didn't notice you there. Where have you been, dear?"

"It's been crazy at work," I replied. "I'm glad I saw you today, Dot."

Dot smiled and nodded. "Well, enjoy the coffee. I have to get back to the kitchen again. Do you need some panini today? One or two?"

"Two would be great, and I'll pick them up after work. Have a good day, Dot."

"Thank you. I'll save you two panini."

Dot retreated to the kitchen, and Ty handed me my order. "Come again tomorrow. I'll give you a free shot of espresso," he said, his voice lowered so the other customers wouldn't hear.

"Okay, but I can't promise anything," I said.

He pouted.

I grinned widely before taking my drink to the condiment bar to retrieve additional chocolate powder and a lid.

As I turned, a young boy rushed toward the door and bumped my elbow, spilling the hot drink onto my hand. I shrieked and jumped sideways, losing my grip on the cup.

The next events seemed to happen in slow motion.

Mocha splashed onto the man waiting nearby for his order before the cup hit the ground, sending the rest of the hot liquid everywhere.

The man gave a tiny yelp and tried to shake the coffee from his light blue sweater. The brown stain was already spreading down his chest.

"Oh my God!" Ty screamed, grabbing a roll of paper towels from the counter before rushing toward us.

"I'm sorry," Ty and I said almost in unison.

"You should be careful next time, young lady," a voice said from behind me.

I turned and saw a bald guy standing near the condiment bar.

"He could have been scalded by the hot coffee," he continued.

"That's not my…" I glanced at the bald man before turning to my mocha victim. "The kid bumped my elbow and—"

"At the very least, you can take him to the doctor to treat his burns, and pay for his dry cleaning," the bald guy interrupted.

I took a breath. It was clear this guy loved making trouble. "Yes, that's what I'm going to—"

Before I finished, the mocha victim turned to the bald guy. "Hey, man," he said, "thanks for your concern. The coffee wasn't too hot, anyway, and I don't need a doctor. And this young lady"— he pointed to me—"didn't do it on purpose. That means she doesn't need to pay for my dry cleaning."

The bald guy mumbled and moved toward the door with his nose in the air. A few customers murmured and glanced at him as he left the café.

Sighing, the mocha victim turned to Ty. "Please show me where the restroom is, so I can clean my shirt." He pointed to me. "Would you mind watching my luggage while I change my clothes?" He indicated the luggage at his feet.

I nodded. "No problem at all."

"The restroom is this way." Ty ushered him down the narrow hallway. "I can give you our café sweater for free, too," I heard him say.

"Is your hand okay?" asked Dot, who must have heard the commotion from the kitchen.

I picked up a beige jacket from the floor, assuming it belonged to the mocha victim. One sleeve of the coat had a coffee stain on it.

"Yes, I'm fine, Dot," I said, searching for the young boy who had caused the ruckus. When I didn't see him, I assumed he must have run off.

"I've never seen that boy or the bald guy before," said Dot, following my gaze to the front door. "Let me replace your drink, dear."

Before I could decline her offer, she'd already walked behind the counter and apologized to the customers for the commotion.

Shortly after, Ty and the mocha victim came out of the restroom. The man now wore a bright pink sweater with the words "I need my coffee now!" printed above the cartoon picture of a sullen lady in pajamas with rollers in her hair. Ty had drawn the cartoon, and every time I saw it, I smiled.

But not this time.

As our eyes met, I mouthed to Ty, "Pink?"

Ty shrugged.

The mocha victim seemed relieved as I handed him his jacket. He put it on quickly, buttoning it up to conceal the sweater.

"I'm sorry we don't have any other color, sir," said Ty apologetically. "Our new order will be here in two days. If you don't mind waiting, I could go upstairs and lend you one of *my* sweaters."

The man shook his head. "That's okay. I have no time to waste as I have a plane to catch."

"How about me paying for the laundry service?" I offered, using the chance to look at him clearly.

He was a head taller than me, sturdy but slim. Behind his glasses, his eyes were blue with a hint of green. His light brown hair was neatly cut with clean edges, making him look like the classic gentleman. I guessed he couldn't be over the age of thirty-five.

"Don't worry about that. I was here for my business trip, hence I can charge my company for a new, expensive sweater," he said, half joking. "Thanks, but it's unnecessary. Besides, I got a free pink sweater." He grinned after saying the last sentence.

"But—"

"It's okay." He shook his head again. "Accidents can happen anywhere. And this wasn't your fault."

Before I could say more, Dot brought me a new mint mocha latte. After thanking her, I turned to the man, but he was already gone. I exhaled, waving at Ty, who was busy mopping the floor to prevent people from stepping on the spill. I tried to put the event behind me and walked to the bus stop.

ALL THE WAY TO WORK, I couldn't shake thoughts of what had happened earlier.

The poor guy.

He was here for a business trip, and on the day he had to fly back home, his sweater and coat were ruined by a mint mocha latte.

I'll bet he bought a new sweater at the airport rather than wearing that bright pink one.

I pressed the red stop button as the bus rolled closer to my destination and waited until it came to a halt. Once the door opened, the fresh air rushed in, wrapping its cold fingers around me.

Walking slowly along the sidewalk toward my office, I pulled my beanie down to cover my ears and adjusted the scarf around my neck. The tip of my nose was growing numb from the frigid wind. I missed the mild winter season in Southern California. After living there for more than five years, I'd been spoiled by year-round warm and sunny weather.

Boston was beautiful, but I would have liked it more if the winter wasn't so harsh and the summer wasn't so humid.

No one had forced me to live in Boston. After I graduated from college, my aunt had suggested that I move in with her, but I loved California and was happy when I got a job as an accountant at Myriad Food and Beverage. I'd thought I was ready to settle down there. Many things had happened in August, including the horrible car accident after I resigned from Myriad. My aunt was my only kin, so after the accident, I decided to move and stay with her.

I entered my office building and took the elevator to the tenth floor, where I got off at Veles Capital, a financial holding company possessing a diversified line of community banking and commercial finance. I'd worked there as a senior analyst in the risk department for almost four months. My boss, Sally Kranda, was the nicest boss compared to my bitchy, bully boss at Myriad .

"Good morning, Marsha," I said, passing my coworker's cubicle.

"Hi, Rory. Good morning and happy Friday," Marsha Wilson said cheerfully over her shoulder.

"Happy Friday," I responded.

Sitting on my chair, I fitted my electronic notebook into its docking station and turned the power on.

"Too bad you didn't join our happy hour yesterday," Marsha said, sliding her chair to peek inside my cubicle while I logged into my computer.

"Why? Did something happen?" I glanced at her before turning my attention back to the computer.

Still sitting on her chair, Marsha slid into my cubicle.

I should tell her to stop doing that because she looks silly with her bulging, six-months-pregnant stomach.

"Last night, Kelly was drunk and confessed her love to Ryan," she whispered.

I covered my mouth with my hand. "Really?"

She nodded. "Yup. Crazy, huh? I don't understand her. Did she think it was okay to get drunk during happy hour with her coworkers? If she'd wanted to get drunk, she should've just gone with her regular friends. We don't want to go out with people who can't control themselves. Besides, our happy hour is for relaxing and bonding, not for drinking excessively. That stupid girl doesn't know how to limit herself, and she confessed love to her senior while Leslie joined us for the happy hour." Marsha rolled her eyes when she mentioned Sally's assistant manager. "It's a good thing Leslie doesn't care what people do outside the office. If she did, Kelly would be doomed."

"What did Ryan say?" I asked.

Marsha shrugged, tossing her bronze, shoulder-length hair behind her. "As you know, Ryan loves joking around. It surprised me how maturely he handled Kelly. Obviously, he isn't interested in her. Kelly knows he prefers you over her that's why she's always bitching about you."

It didn't take a genius to know that Ryan Harris had been crushing on me since I'd joined the company. He'd also been my classmate in university back in California.

I hadn't recognized him right away. Ryan had changed a lot, and the only things that had stayed the same were his sweet smile and his dimples. He was no longer a quiet, pale, lanky boy with long, dark brown hair, who wore black every single day. His lean and muscled body, along with his messy, medium-length hair made him look adorable. He'd also become a pleasant person to talk to, easy-going, and a reliable coworker. No wonder people, especially females, loved talking to him.

Meeting him again after years brought back the sweet memories in me. In college, we'd done everything together, starting from orientation, and some people mistook us for a couple. I didn't know what he'd felt toward me because he never said it. If he'd ever asked, I wouldn't have minded, because I liked him. Unfortunately, we'd grown apart after choosing our majors.

Since meeting again, Ryan had openly showed his attention toward me and looked unhappy upon learning that I had a boyfriend. I felt a familiar light flutter in my belly every time he looked at me, and I wished he had had the courage when we were in college.

I opened my mouth to respond when the general manager's office door opened. Sally emerged, her expression one of grave concern. She walked by us as though in a trance.

We exchanged glances, and Marsha slid her chair back to her cubicle while I focused on my monitor. We almost forgot to greet Ryan as he arrived and sat in his cubicle. When his head popped over the partition, he raised an eyebrow. I shrugged and jerked my head toward Sally's office. Without another word, he sat down and started working.

Twenty minutes passed, and Sally's urgent voice called out, "Rory, Marsha, Ryan, come to my office."

Right away, we all stood and hurried to join her.

"Please take a seat," she said, sitting in her chair.

I sat next to Marsha, and Ryan dragged an empty chair next to me.

Sally let out a heavy sigh before she laced her fingers together and gazed at us.

"Stone Dealership," she said, "our new automotive client in the California office, is in trouble. From their financial statements, I can tell they used the loan for personal expenses, because the million dollars we approved six months ago has quickly dwindled. This dealership is a subsidiary of Stone Transportation Services, one of our biggest clients. We can't share assumptions like that with them. Mr. Stone would be upset if we accused his younger brother of being incompetent." Sally stopped, taking another breath before continuing. "So, this project needs to be handled delicately, or Mr. Stone will move his businesses to another loan company."

My first day on the job, I'd been told that Stone Transportation Services had been one of the biggest clients at Veles Capital since its establishment two decades ago. The mutual relationship between the companies had been solid for years.

"And you know that, recently, Martin lost three of his field auditors and an accountant." She closed her eyes briefly before opening them again.

Martin Travers was the risk manager for the California office and Sally's counterpart. His team was smaller than Sally's, but I'd heard that he was losing some of his staff again this year because of his tough personality.

"I don't want to tell you why they quit simultaneously, but Martin needs our help. Also, the office doesn't have many clients in the automobile industry yet, and they don't have a person familiar with the business. So..." She turned to Ryan. "I want you to help the office."

The dimples in Ryan's cheeks became pronounced. I knew the business trip was a wonderful opportunity for him to expand his skill and experience, both of which would help him work toward a promotion. A willingness to go on business trips definitely improved the career outlook as well.

"And you, Rory," Sally turned to me, "your background in accounting would help Martin's team tremendously. You can give the dealership's employees basic accounting training. Martin also informed me that they've recorded everything incorrectly since the dealer joined us. The risk analysts are having a hard time analyzing Stone's financial report."

My heart leaped. California! I'd been thinking of it that whole morning, and suddenly, I'd been assigned there. What a coincidence. I couldn't wait to tell Peter. He would be dancing around like a crazy person.

I couldn't daydream about it for too long, though, because Sally's voice brought me back to the current conversation.

"And Marsha, I can't let you fly with them because of your condition, but I need your expertise to perform a deep analysis based on Rory and Ryan's findings. Leslie will take care of one of your clients, if necessary."

"How about you?" Marsha asked. "Are you going there too?"

She nodded. "I'll be there in two days, but I don't think you two will fly this week. You should be in California in a week's time. Belinda is already arranging our plane tickets and hotel."

Sally's eyes shifted to the picture on her desk of her husband hugging their daughter and son. Her finger trailed over it. Everybody in the office knew how much she loved her family. She didn't like to go on business trips, but she did what was needed. Her eyes remained on the picture another moment before she turned back to us.

"I know all of you have your own projects to do, but I need you to push them aside and focus on this one," she said solemnly. "And you two," her eyes shifted to Ryan and me, "I'm not your mom, but

I do take care of my staff. Please act maturely and professionally, especially you, Ryan."

Ryan chuckled and spread his arms to each side. "Why me? How about her?" He pointed at me. "Her boyfriend is in California."

Sally rolled her eyes. "I was young once too."

"You're still young," Ryan said smoothly. "How old are you? Thirty-five?"

Sally chuckled. At fifty-three, she looked much younger than her age.

"Stop kissing my butt, Ryan," she said in her Boston accent, and laughed, waving her hand toward the door. "Get outta here!"

Grinning, Ryan walked out of the office, followed by Marsha and me.

We all loved Sally. She could be serious, but she could also be an easy-going person who loved to joke around.

When we returned to our cubicles, I checked the distance from the California office, which was located in a city called Irvine, to Peter's apartment and almost yelped. It was only twelve miles. Not far. My heart burst in anticipation of seeing his face in person, and I couldn't wait to tell him about my business trip to California.

Chapter 2

"**I**'M COMING TO CALIFORNIA!" I almost shrieked during our video call that evening.

Peter's face broke into a wide smile. "Wow, that's awesome," he said in his British accent. "After that, can you take a week off?"

"I wish," I said, taking my phone to the kitchen so I could grab a glass of water. "This project will keep me busy starting next week until it's completed. I can't take any vacation until next year."

Aunt Amy, who was cutting fruit on the countertop, raised her eyes to me as I entered the kitchen and mouthed, "Peter? Say hi from me."

I nodded. "By the way, Aunt Amy says hi to you." I turned my phone toward her and let them wave before turning it back to me.

Peter rubbed at the back of his neck, and an expression of disappointment showed clearly on his face. "When will you fly here?"

"My boss said we're scheduled to fly next Sunday morning. I guess I could be there by Sunday midnight and rest before going to the office. Then I should fly back on Friday night," I said, taking a sip of my water.

"Could you fly out on Friday and stay at my house for the whole weekend?" he asked.

"Stay at what?" I asked, nearly choking on my drink.

"My house."

Across from me, Aunt Amy raised her eyebrows.

I shrugged. It was news to me, too.

"Don't you mean your apartment?" I asked.

Peter shook his head. "No, my house. I bought it two weeks ago."

What?

"You hadn't said anything." I glanced at my aunt before walking back to my room.

"Well…" Peter scratched his temple. "I wanted to surprise you, but since you mentioned you were going to fly here, I just blurted it out."

"Ouch, what a bummer," I teased, trying to imagine the kind of house he'd bought.

He grinned. "The house is small," he said as if he could read my mind. "Let me send you the link so you can see what it looks like."

I opened the link on my notebook and immediately thought the term "small" meant something far different for Peter than it meant for me. The 3,200-square-foot, two-story house on a 7,000-square-foot plot of land was huge compared to my aunt's 1,500-square-foot townhouse. My eyes nearly fell from their sockets to see the price of the place, but Peter's family could afford to pay that much.

Located in a beach town, Peter's new house was a combined design of modern and tropical, consisting of two-and-a-half bathrooms, four bedrooms, and a loft space. The backyard led to a sandy, white beach. The master bedroom included an en suite bathroom with a skylight above the bathtub, and its interior featured a palette of white, gray, and beige colors, giving it an elegant and cozy appeal.

"Have you checked the link? Do you like the house?" Peter asked when I'd gone quiet. "The picture doesn't do it justice. You need to come and see it for yourself."

"Yes, I'm looking at it now. It's awesome," I nodded. "I like the kitchen. It looks modern and roomy."

"Yes, I can imagine you sitting in there while I make pancakes for you." His smile broadened. "I *do* hope you can fly earlier on Friday."

I held my breath, imagining the possibility of spending time with him on the weekend. Besides, I was curious to see the house in person.

Chewing my lower lip, I said, "I hope so too. We'll see if my boss approves my flying on Friday morning."

Leaning forward, Peter looked at me. His light brown eyes widened and shone. "It would be fun to have you over for the weekend. I miss you, Rory. It took me a while to get used to living here without you. I miss living with you like we lived in your old apartment."

I smiled, remembering the good times we'd had as roommates.

"Yeah, I miss that time too," I admitted. "By the way, let's say I'm allowed to fly there earlier. I still can't stay at your house for the whole business trip. I may be needed for a late meeting or overtime."

"Yeah, I understand," Peter said. His shoulders drooped as he rubbed his eyebrows.

"At least we could have each other for the weekend. So, keep your hopes high and I'll let you know what happens tomorrow," I said, smiling.

He nodded.

"Hey, tell me about Tom. How's he doing?" I asked, curious about what his half brother had been doing.

Peter met my gaze and nodded, understanding that I didn't want to continue talking about staying in his house. "He's doing fine. But we haven't seen each other in ages because we've both been so busy. Just so you know, I think he still feels guilty about what Phil did to us last time, because he's avoiding me." He sighed. "I know my brother, so I'm giving him some space until he's ready to open up again. I hope he doesn't mind seeing you while you're here."

Phil, Tom's ex-boyfriend, worked as a finance manager for White Water, Incorporated, a prestigious wine distributor for US and Canada, where Peter was working as president of the company.

Born into the Sandridge family, Peter and Tom were part of Britain's old entrepreneurship families called Sandridge Group that had run many businesses in several countries for decades.

Their last name wasn't Sandridge but Ryder. It was from their grandpa's last name, the current chairman, who was born from the youngest daughter of Sandridge. Although their last name was different, Peter and Tom were in line to take over the businesses when the time was right.

Four months ago, when Peter had been assigned to replace his sister as president of White Water, Inc., Phil didn't like it. He didn't think Peter deserved to take the position, considering his wild youth of partying, drinking, causing trouble, and using drugs. Phil sabotaged the selection and spread rumors, fabricating photos of Peter. He hoped the elders of the Sandridge family would revoke the decision and choose Tom instead. However, Phil didn't know that Tom had zero interest in the family business, which was why he lived in California rather than London. Tom found out about the dirty trick his boyfriend had played and broke up with him after asking Peter to fire him immediately.

"Tom shouldn't feel that way," I said, feeling sad for the man. I liked him, and we'd been friends for a while. "This hasn't been easy for you either, has it?"

"No, it hasn't." Peter shook his head. "I already lost Jane, and I don't want to lose my brother too. I love him. He barely talks to me now, and of course I can't talk to Jane. I feel especially lonely when I want to share a burden that relates to our family."

He let out another sigh and stared into the distance, his face reflective.

I didn't have siblings, but I could understand his loneliness. "Let's hope he shakes those feelings of guilt sooner rather than later," I comforted him. "I miss him too."

A slight smile appeared on his lips. "Yes, let's hope so. Don't forget to let me know if you can fly in earlier, because I want to let him know you're coming."

I nodded. "Okay."

ALTHOUGH TIRED, PETER SMILED. NOTHING made him happier than seeing his girlfriend's smiling face, and she would be there next week. If he hadn't remembered he was in his office, he would have hollered with joy.

Since that morning, he'd been in back-to-back meetings. He wanted to rest on the couch in his office for at least an hour before teleconferencing with London, but he didn't want to miss a video call with Rory. Since he had another meeting soon, their call had been cut short, but it had been enough to make him happy.

"Rory," Peter whispered, caressing the picture sitting on his desk. She looked lovely in her pale-yellow dress. The light freckles on the bridge of her nose, that she always complained about, made her look adorable. He chuckled as he looked at her photograph, remembering how chaotic their first meeting had been.

He'd never wanted to work in his family's businesses. When Jane had asked him to help her with her project in California, he couldn't refuse. However, a week before Jane flew to the States with him, she'd had emergency surgery that forced her to stay in the hospital. Later, Jane instructed Peter to fly alone and stop at a rental place to cancel her stay, where she'd already signed a six-month lease.

Knowing her eccentric personality, Peter hadn't bothered to ask further. He'd assumed Rory was Jane's ex-boyfriend or male friend. Everyone in the Sandridge family, including his grandpa, let Jane do whatever she wanted because she was a brilliant businesswoman. If Jane didn't want to stay in a hotel, they would rent her a house. If she decided to rent a room in someone's home, they wouldn't argue with her.

When he'd stopped by to tell Jane's roommate about the cancelation, it had surprised him that Rory was a female name. In Britain, it was a male's name.

Jane's new roommate had seemed shocked about the cancelation, and Peter detected that Rory had some financial troubles. Seeing her distress, he'd offered to continue his sister's rental agreement.

To his surprise, she'd accepted.

It had never crossed his mind that living with Rory would change his life forever.

She taught him everything, including valuing money, something he'd never concerned himself with. He also learned to appreciate the money he earned.

Rory also taught him about honesty and acceptance. She wasn't shy to admit that she'd been born out of wedlock and raised by her old-fashioned aunt after her mom passed away. She told him the truth about not knowing her father. He also knew her aunt didn't approve of Rory having a male roommate, afraid Rory would make the same ill-timed decisions her mom had made.

Something had slowly changed inside him. Peter learned to be a good man, different from the spoiled and selfish person he'd been in his youth. He wanted to be better for Rory.

If Jane were alive, she would have been happy to see his transformation.

Thinking of Jane made his heart thud dully in his chest. She'd been gone for more than three months, but he couldn't seem to shake his sadness. Jane had been more than his sister, especially after his mom abandoned him as a child. Peter had attached himself to

Jane. She'd been his confidant, his protector, and his "little mom." Whenever he had an issue, he'd always asked for his sister's advice.

Now, she was gone forever, and his brother wasn't talking to him. No one had been around for him through his anxiety over the new position as president of White Water.

Their father, Archibald "Archie" Ryder, had flown from London to California to give him some management training. Peter didn't have a close relationship with him. His presence didn't help because Archie was known for having an iron fist, and he never let Peter slack off. Nights, mornings, weekends, and weekdays, his father forced Peter to work better, harder, and faster. As a result, his body and mind were tired, and he wanted to take a break.

When people in the States were celebrating Thanksgiving, Peter had to fight to take some time off and spend his first American Thanksgiving with Rory and her aunt.

For the first time in a while, Peter felt brighter and happier, knowing Rory would be there soon.

Chapter 3

I COULDN'T CONTAIN MY SMILE WHEN Sally allowed me to fly on Friday instead of Sunday morning. She knew my boyfriend lived in California and that I wanted to spend time with him.

Sally was an amazing boss who knew how to deal with the staff. Although harsh at times, she also knew when to loosen up. When someone made a mistake, she would call them in privately and speak calmly with them, making her one of Veles Capital's favorite managers.

Guess who else was excited about my upcoming visit with Peter?

Aunt Amy.

Once she knew I was flying to California in a few days, she bought ingredients to bake marble cakes, chocolate chip cookies, and brownies, because Peter loved them so much. When I first met Peter, he didn't like those things. Then, when he visited for Thanksgiving, he found he really liked my aunt's cookies and cakes.

That made her happy, but it made me nervous. I knew my aunt, and I was afraid she would go overboard.

When I came home from work, the countertop was covered with two marble cakes, two nine-inch square pans of brownies, and three dozen chocolate chip cookies sitting on cooling racks. A few plastic containers sat nearby, ready to be filled with all the goodies.

"Wow!" My jaw dropped. "That...those cookies and cakes are enough for twenty people."

"I don't think so," said my aunt, glancing at the sweets.

"Now, how am I going to bring them with me?"

"I already found extra luggage," she said, slapping my hand when I reached out to steal one of the cookies. "That's for Peter," she scolded me.

I snatched one anyway. "I'm your niece. Shouldn't I get priority? You haven't baked me anything, and now, you're feeding him like he's starving. Well, if you want to make him fat, keep feeding him with your sugar and carb-filled snacks."

She chuckled. "Rory, sweetheart, these are healthier than the store-bought ones because I use organic ingredients and not too much sugar." Aunt Amy glanced at me as she cut into a tray of brownies. "And I smell some jealousy from you."

"Nope, not jealous."

"Yes, you are," sang my aunt.

"No, I am not," I sang back, taking a seat on a stool as I watched her. "All right, fine, maybe I am."

My aunt gave a cheery smile.

I didn't like it. "That's because you never bake me anything. Not even for my birthday," I added.

My aunt stopped and stared at me. "I always baked birthday cakes for you."

"Nope." I shook my head. "You always bought those cakes from France Bakery."

She laughed, her shoulders shaking. "My dear Rory, that's because you always complained that you wanted to be the same as your classmates, whose parents always bought a birthday cake from some famous bakery. I...we didn't have money at the time. I had to trick you. On the day before your birthday, I asked my friend who worked at the bakery to give me a box and a ribbon with the store name printed on it. I put my cake in the box and gave it to you, so you'd think I bought the cake from the bakery."

I almost choked on the cookie in my mouth as her eyes twinkled.

"So…" I cleared my throat, and guilt rose into my chest. "You always baked it for me?"

"Yes, sweetheart. I always did on your birthday. Once you were twelve, I stopped baking because you said you wanted to control your weight. I baked a few times for different events at the church or for my friends. Now, I have Peter to spoil with my baking."

"Sorry for being selfish," I said.

She chuckled as she finished packing and looked down with pride at the containers. "That's okay. It was my fault too. I should admit that I wasn't patient enough with you, anyway, and caused you to misunderstand me. If I'd been kinder and more open, we wouldn't have had so many arguments, and maybe you would've been more open with me. I could've given you different advice about many things."

Her words touched my heart. I stood and walked around the counter and threw my arms around her.

"Oh!" she exclaimed.

I heard the smile in her voice as her arms tightened around my shoulders.

"Well, enough of this sentimental stuff." My aunt gently pushed me away, a smile still lingering on her lips. "Now, bring me the blue luggage so I can pack this."

I retrieved the luggage, and she loaded the containers inside.

"So, are you going to stay at Peter's house?" she asked, fastening the zipper on the luggage.

Her question didn't really surprise me, and I'd expected it, anyway. It might have sounded odd for most people that my aunt asked a twenty-four-year-old woman whether she was going to stay at her boyfriend's house.

I'd never known my father. My mom had always been upset whenever I asked about him, so I stopped. I understood, because her pregnancy had brought too much stress to her family and strained her relationship with her parents. My Japanese grandpa, Grandpa Kenji Ishida, couldn't accept the fact that his daughter would have a baby without a husband. His extended family shunned us, but my Grandma Audrey Arrington Ishida, who was German-Australian, was more open-minded about her daughter's pregnancy. As she couldn't hold her upset feeling any longer, my grandma brought my mom to America, a country where she immigrated with her family when she was ten years old.

After my mom passed away, my aunt took me under her wing and vowed to try and prevent me from making the same mistake her sister had made. She watched me like a hawk, only becoming more lenient after I graduated from college. I eventually understood her strictness, especially after seeing a few of my friends and coworkers around the same age who had a tough life because they were raising babies without husbands.

Some regretted their decisions and wished they could turn back the clock. Witnessing their struggles, I felt sorry for them and didn't wish to be part of the group. I didn't want to burden my aunt with my fatherless child, as she'd had enough problems raising me.

I cleared my throat and said, "Well, I'm planning to stay at his house over the weekend, and then move to the hotel on Monday because I want to show Sally that I'm professional and don't take this business trip lightly." I looked at her solemnly. "And I won't break the promise I made to you on the day you allowed me to live alone a few years ago."

Aunt Amy looked at me and tapped me on the shoulder. "You're an adult now, and honestly, I'm more concerned about your professionalism. This is your first business trip for this company, and if you've been chosen for this job, it means your boss trusts your skills. However, I'm relieved that you understand the importance of this project for your career."

I smiled at her.

"Now," she added, glancing at my suitcases, "let's weigh your luggage. I hope it isn't too heavy."

"If I ate some, they wouldn't be overweight," I offered.

My aunt glared at me and shook her head when I gave her an innocent grin.

THAT NIGHT, I TOSSED AND turned in bed. My eyes refused to shut, and my mind was racing. The thought of seeing Peter again thrilled me to bits. The last time we'd been together was on Thanksgiving Day. I wished we could meet more often, maybe once or twice a month. However, our working situation didn't allow us to have such a privilege. Peter was busy with his management training, and I was busy in my new office. We'd acknowledged the issues at the beginning of our relationship and promised to endure the challenges.

However, I dreaded to think about being alone with Peter.

It was nothing to do with the promise I'd made to my aunt. It was my traumatic experience that no one knew about because my lips were sealed tight.

I was sixteen when it happened. Behind my aunt's back, I'd had a boyfriend. My aunt watched me like a hawk, but she couldn't be with me twenty-four hours a day. I'd learned to wiggle free from her watch.

My first boyfriend was a classmate and one of the cutest boys at school. I'd never imagined that he would ask me to go out because I wasn't an attractive girl, and I was too skinny for my age. After that, we went out a few times.

One day, when we kissed, his hand slipped into my shirt and

touched my bosom. I cringed and told him to stop. He looked at me as if I were from another planet. "It's normal to show your boyfriend how you care about him," he argued. I knew it wasn't right, but I didn't want to be seen as immature. It wasn't a secret that a few of my female classmates, including my best friend, had had the experience. Everybody was doing it, as they said. Besides, we didn't do anything more than touching above the waist underneath our clothes. After debating with myself, I let him have his way.

The next day at school, he avoided me, and a few of his close friends giggled when they saw me. Feeling confused, I asked him what was going on. His answer surprised me. He said he wasn't interested in me anymore because I was too flat and too rigid. A cold sweat dripped down my back as I felt an invisible hand slap hard across my face, again and again. It wasn't my fault if my body hadn't developed in time.

Feeling dirty and sick to my stomach, I left school that day and sat under the cold, running shower at home for hours, hoping I could forget my foolishness for letting him touch me. When my aunt came back from work, she didn't understand why a girl who was healthy in the morning had come down with a fever in the afternoon in summer.

Then, six months later, we moved to a different state because of my aunt's work. By then, my body had filled out in all the right directions, and I always looked good and sexy in any dress. Still, I became self-conscious and careful about choosing close male friends. My relationships consisted of no more than kissing and hugging.

My final year in college, I met Ben, my ex-roommate, Lizzy's, coworker. We met when Lizzy and I were in a mini-golf amusement park. Somehow, we felt a connection and saw each other often after that.

Everything went smoothly for a while. Ben was six years older than me, mature, and independent. He wasn't a man who would drag his girlfriend into bed after just ten dates. I'd thought Ben was "the one." Even my aunt had the same thought.

When our relationship became serious, Ben said that I was too chubby. Stupidly, I accepted it and forced myself to diet hard until I collapsed and was rushed to the ER, while Ben was cheating on me with some pretty, skinny woman. For almost two years, I avoided having a romantic relationship with a man until I met Peter.

Peter was interesting. He wasn't as sexy and handsome as Chris Hemsworth or Chris Evans, but he was the type of man who could make girls whirl their heads and gawk at him in awe. He stood out with his six-foot height, chiseled face, fine bone structure, and trim body. His nonchalant gaze and aloof smile drove girls crazy. Still, every time we were together in public, Peter kept his eyes on me as if I were the only girl on the planet, and that flattered me. He seemed to enjoy spending time with me, without sending any signal to go further than kisses and hugs. Even when he kissed me, he always did it gently and lightly, as if making sure I was comfortable before his kiss became firmer and more certain.

I wasn't naïve or afraid of going to the next step in a relationship. I dreaded it because it had taken me years to glue the shards of my self-esteem back together, and I couldn't imagine someone breaking it again. If things went the way I thought they were going at Peter's house, this trip would change me forever.

Chapter 4

*L*IGHTS FROM BUILDINGS AND MOVING vehicles sparkled from above, like scattered sparkling pieces of jewelry, as my plane descended toward John Wayne Airport.

When the plane landed, joy at being back in California consumed me. The last time I'd seen this state was at the end of summer, and now, only a few months later, I'd returned. I'd thought I wouldn't be here again for at least a year or two.

While waiting for the seat belt sign to go to "off," I turned on my phone and saw a few text messages from Peter. I grinned as I read his texts.

> *Miss you, and it is 2 p.m. here.*
>
> *Miss you at 2:15 p.m. Oh, why does it feel like it's been two hours already?*
>
> *Are you here yet? Maybe not.*
>
> *On my way to the airport.*
>
> *I'm waiting in the arrival area.*
>
> *Are you here yet?*
>
> *Please tell me you're here.*

Rory...

Rory...

His last message said, *Now I'm turning into your possessive boy-friend.* He followed it with a grinning emoji.

I smiled but refrained from responding because people were getting their luggage out of the overhead compartments. Once I got mine, I waited patiently to get off the plane.

The baggage claim area wasn't very crowded. After waiting ten minutes, I found my luggage, piled them on the airport cart, and pushed it toward the arrival gate. I paused to fish out my phone and send a text to Peter.

My flight got rerouted back to Boston.

My phone rang.

"Hi, Pet—"

"Really? Seriously, your flight got rerouted back to Boston? Are you at the Boston airport now?" Peter asked without saying hello. "But why does the flight status say your plane is on time?"

"Maybe they haven't changed it yet because we turned around halfway into the flight," I said, biting my lip to keep from laughing.

"Are you already at the Boston airport now?" he asked again after some silence. His tone sounded disheartened. "When will you be coming, then?"

"Um, I'm not sure when," I said, pushing my cart toward the waiting area. "Too bad. You can't eat Auntie's cookies and marble cake—"

"I'd prefer you to be here," Peter interrupted me sharply. "Now I'm upset."

"Sorry," I said, scanning the crowd until I spotted a familiar figure in a light orange sweater over his untucked gray shirt. He stood with his back to me, holding a phone against his ear.

"What happened? I don't understand." Sounding upset, Peter scratched his head with his other hand.

He didn't hear me behind him and shrieked when I poked his back. As he spun on his heel, his eyes bulged, and his mouth dropped open.

"Ta-da! Miracles can happen if you believe," I said, grinning widely.

"Oh my God, you…" His voice trailed off.

In one movement, I was in his arms.

"Hi, Peter," I said, my voice muffled against his sweater.

"You…" He didn't finish voicing his thoughts, but he tightened his arms around my shoulders. "That's not funny, you know. That's…not…funny. Don't joke like that. Promise me you won't do it again."

"Sorry, I just wanted to tease you," I said, hugging him. A warm feeling spread through my chest, and I inhaled his familiar scent. I made a note to tell him not to change his cologne because it smelled good. Tightening my arms around his waist, I pressed my forehead against his chest. "If my flight was canceled, of course I would've told you earlier."

"Still not funny," he grumbled. "I'm almost crying."

"I don't believe you," I said, looking up at him and grinning.

Peter rolled his eyes but smiled back at me. "So." He tilted his head. "As much as I love holding you, if we don't leave soon, people will eventually start to suggest that we get a room."

"Ha ha ha. Funny," I said, releasing him.

"Come on." He took my cart, offering his arm. "I parked nearby." He smiled when I looped my hand around his arm.

My heart squeezed in my chest as I noticed his gentle gaze. I'd missed that.

Once we'd loaded everything into the trunk of his Tesla, I slid into the passenger seat.

"Rory," Peter called as I reached for my seat belt.

"Hmm?" I turned toward him, attempting to click the seat belt into place.

Leaning over the center console, Peter cupped my face with his hands and kissed me. His lips were soft against mine. The seat belt recoiled as I shifted closer to kiss him back.

"I'm happy to see you again," he said, brushing my cheek with his thumb.

"Me too," I said.

"Are you hungry?" he asked after pulling back. He put the car in gear and headed toward the exit. "I already bought some food for you, unless you want to stop somewhere else."

I glanced at the clock on the dashboard. It showed 7:30 p.m., which was 10:30 Boston time. I was alert enough to eat, but I wouldn't mind going straight to his house and hitting the sack right away.

"Nah, let's eat at your place," I suggested.

"Okay."

The I-405 North traffic was crowded as we hit the freeway. Cars moved slowly, and one or two vehicles tried to cut off the cars merging onto the interstate. I didn't really care because I was excited to be back with Peter again.

"Auntie baked and forced me to bring your favorite cakes and cookies," I said. "Believe me, those cakes and cookies are more than enough to feed an army. Next time, don't tell her what you like."

Peter chuckled. "I love her food and cakes. Why can't I tell her the snacks I like?"

"Because she'd find a way to feed you until you became fat and couldn't move, lying on the floor like a starfish." I stretched out my arms and feet, pretending to be a starfish.

"Do I detect some jealousy?" Peter looked upward as though searching for something in the sky. He laughed when I reached out and poked his cheek.

"I'm not jealous."

"Yes, you are," he sang in the same tone of voice my aunt had used. He grinned widely as his hand stroked the back of my head.

31

It was good to be with him. I'd missed even the simple things like his big smile and riding around town with him. Long-distance definitely sucked.

Chapter 5

ETER'S CAR SLOWED AT THE curb and stopped in front of a house with a white picket fence. "Welcome to my house," he said, his eyes gleaming with pride.

I got out of the car and stood there, gazing wide-eyed at his new home.

The two-story house looked even better than it had in the pictures Peter sent me the week before. Although we arrived at night, the sky was clear, and the moon was visible. Illumination from the garden lights and the streetlight gave me a clear view of the house. I caught the subtle fragrance of roses and jasmine as I stepped onto the stone path leading to the front porch.

"Come in. I'll show you around," Peter said, my luggage in hand. He opened the door and waited.

I nodded and followed him inside. As I stood in the hallway, I instantly fell in love with the house.

The interior was mostly white, and the flooring was a sandy color. The gray furniture gave the spacious room a cozy, contemporary feeling.

Peter took me through the first floor, giving me a tour of the sunroom, living room, and dining room, which had a tall glass window with a beautiful view of the beach. French doors topped by trapezoid-shaped windows led from the sunroom outside to the backyard.

The kitchen, spacious and modern with a beautiful marble countertop and backsplash, was also on the first floor. If Aunt Amy were here, she would have been thrilled to cook and bake in that kitchen.

Like in my aunt's townhome, all the bedrooms and bathrooms were upstairs, and the powder room was on the first floor. As we stepped onto the landing, Peter sat my luggage near the first door.

"My room," he said, as though he could read my mind. "I'll show you the other rooms later. This is the loft." He gestured at the open space above the living room and then took my hand. "I'm going to convert it into a library. I've already ordered books and bookshelves. Also, I'll add a coffee table, chairs, and big pillows to make this room comfortable for reading."

"That's gonna be nice."

"I think so too. Now, let me show you the guest room." He pushed open the door of the first room. It had two nightstands, a dresser, a queen-size bed, and a long closet on the other end, with tall windows opposite the bed. The room had far more space than my bedroom in Boston.

The other two rooms were the same size. Peter used one of them as his home office.

"Now, let's go to my room." He gently pulled my wrist, leading me as he walked back to the room next to the loft.

I held in a gasp when he opened the door. His bedroom was even more spacious than the other three rooms and had the same tall window, but it covered half of the room. A blackout privacy curtain hung to the side. His king-size bed faced the window that overlooked a beautiful view of the beach.

"Wow, look at that!" I moved closer to the window. "This breathtaking view sprawls in front of you every time you wake up or go to bed."

"Yup." He nodded.

"You know what?" I looked at him over my shoulder. "If you moved your bed closer here, Peter, you could stargaze before going to sleep."

"Good idea," he agreed, placing his hand on my shoulder. "And it would be nice if I could enjoy the view with you by my side. Besides," he turned me to face him, "this room and the bed are spacious enough for two."

I felt my breath catch in my throat and noticed his light brown eyes narrowing on me.

Our first night together in his beautiful house would have been an unforgettable, steamy, heart-pounding night, if only I could respond to him by wrapping my arms around his neck, kissing him hard, and pushing him onto the bed.

But I couldn't. I didn't.

My throat tightened as I reached up to brush his brown hair and touch his cheek. With his eyes still on me, he leaned against my palm after giving it a quick kiss.

Then I felt a nervous, squirming sensation in my stomach. Unaware, I chuckled.

Peter looked at me with a question in his eyes.

Taking a deep breath, I looked at him and said quietly, "I love you, Peter, and I'm so excited to finally be alone with you again, but"—I searched into his eyes—"I don't think I'm ready, because it's gonna be a huge leap for me to slee—"

My word stopped midway because Peter leaned in and gave me a quick kiss. The corners of his eyes wrinkled as he straightened his back.

I was stunned. Frowning, I continued. "As I said, it's gonna be—"

Peter stopped me again with a quick kiss.

"You keep stopping me," I said.

His smile widened as he tilted his head. "What was your assumption when I said this room and the bed are spacious enough for two?"

"Uh…" I blinked. "Do you want me to…?" My voice trailed off.

His eyes widened, prompting me to go on, but I clamped my mouth shut.

Peter tsked and put his finger on my chin. "Stop overthinking. Didn't I only say, 'This room and the bed are spacious enough for two'?"

I detected no joke in his eyes. He was sincere.

My lips parted, and then I frowned. Now, I wondered if I wasn't attractive enough for him.

"So?" Peter made his way out of his bedroom. "Which room would you choose?"

"Um, the second one," I answered, following him.

His eyes sparkled as he turned to me. "Are you sure you want to sleep in the room next to mine?" he teased me.

I chuckled and whacked him on the arm.

Peter touched my cheek and said solemnly, "You must be hungry and tired. Go unpack your clothes, and I'll heat up our dinner."

"Let's prepare it together," I offered.

The corners of his lips drooped. "Are you afraid I'll burn the food?"

I snickered. "Okay, but don't forget to take the suitcase with your cakes." I pointed at the other suitcase in front of his bedroom.

"Got it."

After I was done unpacking, I went down to the kitchen as Peter was putting the cakes and cookies in the fridge.

"Aunt Amy really worked hard on these," he said. "I'll call her tomorrow morning to thank her."

"She'll be happy to get your phone call. You're her favorite person, you know."

"Am I your favorite person, too?" he asked, closing the refrigerator door.

I moved toward him and rose on my tiptoes to kiss him on the nose. "You're my special one, how about that?"

"That sounds better."

I smiled.

"Hey, why don't you go check the backyard while I'm preparing dinner? The sky is clear, and you'll get a good view of the oil platforms," he suggested as he reached out to turn on the stove dial to light it.

I looked at him for a few beats before nodding. "Okay." I walked toward the sunroom and opened the French doors leading to the backyard.

A gentle breeze swept my hair to the side as I stepped onto the crushed gravel path. I stopped in the middle of the path and looked up at the sky, where thousands of stars were twinkling against the black background. I had a clear view of the moon too, shining like a spotlight in the air.

Peter was right. I could see the light from the oil platforms on the horizon under the starry sky. They'd been strung with LED lights and turned into a sort of offshore decoration.

"One...two...three...four...five...," I counted. I could see five platforms clearly from where I stood.

Curious, I walked closer to the chest-high fence and turned to watch Peter cooking through the window. It was hard to imagine that he used to be so clumsy in the kitchen. But now, he appeared confident and...so handsome too. I chuckled and took a few minutes just to stare at him.

Continuing to explore, I realized that his house was in a secluded area with only two other houses farther down the beach, one on the right and one on the left. There was a hill near the left house.

It was peaceful and quiet here, which gave me a brilliant idea.

Maybe I would ask Peter to sleep outside tomorrow with sleeping bags. It might be nice to sleep under the stars without neighbors snooping around. I felt giddy at the thought and hoped Peter would agree.

"Rory, the food is ready," Peter called from inside.

"Okay."

On the countertop, he'd set out a few plates with all the foods I liked: a variety of onigiri—Japanese rice balls wrapped with seaweed—a spicy salt pork chop, and a big bowl of Taiwanese beef soup.

My stomach growled instantly at the delicious smell coming from the pork chop.

"Someone is complaining," Peter teased me, pulling out a high barstool for me.

I sat, and Peter sat next to me.

"Thanks for buying the food for me," I said, pouring the soup into a small bowl for myself. I didn't pour any for Peter because I knew he didn't like it.

"Don't mention it. I know you miss the food here." He reached for the onigiri.

"You like it now," I commented, watching as he ate it.

"Yup. Initially, I didn't like it because of the seaweed. It tastes like paper, don't you think? I'm used to it now, though."

"I'm happy you like it," I said.

Peter's eyes sparkled as he gazed at me.

After dinner, he cleared the table and washed the dishes, and I went to the guest room and took a shower. It was wonderful to have a warm shower after my long flight. It helped my tense muscles relax and alleviated the cramps in my right thigh from sitting too long.

Part of me wanted to sleep right away, but I also wanted to see Peter before going to bed. I went to the living room, where he sat watching TV. He'd already taken a shower, and he'd changed into a long-sleeved shirt and sweatpants. Smiling, he patted the empty spot next to him.

"What are you watching?" I asked, sitting next to him and looking at the TV.

"Just a series that I recorded because I don't have much time to watch. Oh, I have something for you. Give me your hand."

As I held my hand out to him, Peter slid something onto my wrist. I took a closer look at it and smiled. A bracelet of gold-filled glass beads on an adjustable black nylon cord was tied around my wrist.

"Aww…so cute! Thank you."

"Could you tie this one for me?" He slid a similar bracelet, but with black beads, onto his wrist.

"Oh, is it a couple's bracelet?" I asked, tying it for him.

"Yup." He nodded and then admired the bracelet he'd bought. His eyes caught mine as I gazed at him.

"Why are you looking at me like that?" he asked.

"Do you know the meaning of these bracelets?"

He nodded.

"It means a commitment, and people would see us as a couple," I said, as if I didn't see him nodding.

He nodded again.

"Are you sure?" I looked directly into his eyes.

Peter's hand brushed against my bangs. "Why not? I want people to know we're a couple. How about you? Are you sure?" he asked back.

I smiled and gave him a peck on the lips.

"That's it? Man, I expected long, hot, sexy kisses," he teased me.

I laughed and punched his arm playfully. Little wrinkles showed on the bridge of his nose when Peter laughed and pulled me closer. I looped my hand under his arm and leaned my head on his shoulder.

"Oh, you should feel the beads' surface," he suggested.

I rubbed my fingers on the beads and felt the dots there. "What is this? Braille?"

He nodded. "On yours, it says 'love,' and mine says 'forever,' with number four before 'ever.' And this part"—he pointed at the charms dangling on our bracelets—"is a magnet. If we hold our hands like this…" He positioned his hand next to mine, and the charms clung together. "The charms attach automatically."

For a moment, we admired the bracelets. His looked good on him too. Then Peter turned his eyes to the TV again, and we sat quietly together. My eyelids grew heavier, and my vision became blurry. I smiled sleepily when I felt Peter drop a soft kiss on the top of my head.

Chapter 6

"RORY, IF YOU FEEL SLEEPY, let's go upstairs," whispered Peter, reaching for the remote to turn off the TV. His eyebrows rose when he didn't hear a response.

Tilting his head down, he chuckled because Rory was already sleeping on his shoulder. Her breathing was deep and even.

Peter was mesmerized by her face and couldn't take his eyes off her. He'd seen her sleeping once on the patio in her old apartment when they were roommates, but not this close up. She looked beautiful in her sleep.

Almost without realizing it, he lowered his head to study her more closely. Her hair cascaded around her face. He brushed back the long locks, revealing her flawless face that bore no makeup. Her soft, angled eyebrows looked as though someone had painted them on. Her eyelashes were long and thick, but they looked as soft as a feather. He wanted to run his fingers over them, but he didn't dare.

Lowering his eyes, he gazed at her nose before glancing down to her slightly parted, pinkish lips. Peter's heart drummed in his chest, and his eyes fixed on those soft lips. He'd kissed them many times, but his heart beat at an erratic pace every time he looked at them.

His heart wrenched, then leaped as he leaned in closer to steal a kiss from her lips, but he stopped a couple inches away, close enough to feel her breath on his face.

"No." He shook his head. "If I do, she'll wake, and I don't want that. I want her to feel secure around me. Maybe one day, when she's my wife, I'll wake her up with a feverish kiss that will make her beg for more." Grinning sheepishly at the thought, he pulled away.

In his early twenties, he would never have given that thought any consideration. If he'd wanted to give his girlfriend a kiss, he would have done it no matter how sleepy she was.

But with Rory, everything was different. His heart had softened, and what he wanted most was to protect and cherish her. He was worried about her being hurt. Maybe he'd finally become the mature man Jane and his mom had always wanted him to be.

Whatever it was, Peter wanted Rory to feel secure around him no matter what. In silence, he continued looking at her innocent, sleeping face.

"Why do people look vulnerable when they're sleeping?" he couldn't help wondering. Soon after, his eyelids grew heavy, and he let out a big yawn. Glancing at his watch, his eyes widened at the time. It was almost twelve. With Rory leaning on his shoulder, he didn't know what to do.

"Maybe I should carry her up? She isn't that heavy, right?" Peter wondered under his breath.

That's a good idea. But wait…maybe not.

She might wake up and get scared, then they'd fall on the floor.

Nah, it wouldn't be a good weekend if that happened.

Peter sighed. "Let her sleep on the sofa, then."

Carefully, he rose from his seat while holding Rory's head. He lowered it after sliding a sofa pillow under it.

"Wow, she didn't even budge." He gave a soft chuckle. Lifting her feet up, he took her slippers off. "Uh…yeah…blanket."

Peter tiptoed to the stairs and climbed each step carefully. A few minutes later, he came back down with two blankets and two pillows. Rory didn't move when he covered her with a blanket and changed her pillow for the one he'd brought from upstairs.

"Good night, Rory," he whispered, kissing her hair.

Sighing, he lay down on the carpet, placed the pillow under his head, and pulled the other blanket over his shoulders. What a night he'd had! No one would believe that he was sleeping on the floor in his own house while his girlfriend slept on the sofa. Since he'd been born, he'd always received the attention he wanted and had gotten used to people striving to please him. People who knew how he'd acted in the past would wonder, "What happened to Wild Fred, and why doesn't he live up to his nickname anymore?"

Yup, he used to act however he wanted, which was why he'd chosen "Wild Fred" as his nickname. It was derived from his confirmation name, Frederick, because it sounded better than "Wild Peter."

Rory had changed him, and he would do anything to make her happy. No girls in his past had deserved to get this attention because most of them approached him with an ulterior motive, his money and his family's status in society. If he were a nobody, they wouldn't have given him the time of day.

Peter looked up at Rory and touched her hand, which was sticking out from under her blanket.

"Sleep well," he said, yawning again.

Although he wished they were in his bed, what he wanted more than that was to see her face when he woke in the morning.

Chapter 7

"**H**MM...SMELLS GOOD," I MUMBLED.
My aunt must have cooked breakfast.

"One more minute." I turned, and my shoulder bumped into something soft but firm. Through sleepy eyes, I saw a pale gray wall in front of me.

What is this?

My groggy mind became confused at hearing the relaxing and comforting sound of waves crashing on the shore. I turned onto my back and noticed a white ceiling with a modern, flush-mount light. Slowly, the night before came back to me.

I sat bolt upright.

I'm in Peter's house, in the living room, and I slept on the sofa!

"Ahh!" I jumped off it, causing the blanket to fall on the floor. Shoving my feet into my slippers, I glanced at the bed pillow that I'd used. Peter must have brought them down for me. Then I heard a soft *clunk* coming from the kitchen.

After hurriedly folding the blanket and fluffing the pillow, I noticed another bed pillow and blanket on the armchair.

"Wait, did he sleep here too?" I wondered aloud.

But I pushed away that thought. It couldn't be.

My heart pounded. I couldn't believe that my first night in his house, I'd fallen asleep on the sofa. How embarrassing!

Straightening my clothes, I brushed my hair with my fingers and walked toward the kitchen.

Peter, concentrating on the food he was preparing in a small frying pan, looked up as I came into the room. "Good morning. Did you sleep well?"

"Morning. Yes, I did." I nodded. "Let me go upstairs to wash my face and brush my teeth."

"I already put a clean towel in your bathroom," he said, breaking an egg into a bowl.

"Thanks," I said, climbing the stairs.

In the bathroom, I splashed water on my face and wondered what Peter would think about me sleeping on the sofa. He must have been surprised.

"You really *are* something, Rory," I mumbled, scolding myself while brushing my teeth. "You should be ashamed of yourself."

After changing my clothes with a light blouse and khaki pants, I went down to the kitchen again. The clock on the wall showed 7:50.

"Do you need help?" I asked Peter, who was taking a butter plate out of the fridge.

"Nope, I'm done. Just take a seat," he said, jerking his head toward the barstools.

I took a seat and smiled at the light brown apron tied around his neck and waist. It featured the words, "A man who can cook." I'd bought it last month when he stayed with us in Boston. It had an adjustable neck strap, so it fitted his tall body perfectly.

"I'm sorry about sleeping on the sofa." My cheeks warmed, and I was sure they were crimson. "You should've awakened me so I could go upstairs."

"You were sound asleep, and I didn't have the heart to wake you up and tell you to go upstairs, so I let you sleep downstairs," he answered, putting a fork next to a plate in front of me.

"And…did you sleep in the living room too?" I asked carefully. "I saw an extra pillow and blanket on the chair."

"Yup. I couldn't let my girlfriend sleep alone in the living room, so I slept there too."

"But…there's only one sofa there," I said. "Did you sleep on the floor?"

"On the carpet," he corrected, taking off the apron and hanging it on the tiny wall hook.

"Oh.…"

"Why?" Peter shrugged. "Haven't you seen someone sleep on the floor before?"

"B—but you could have slept in your r—room, right?" I stuttered. It surprised me that he'd decided to sleep on the floor, on the carpet, and in his own home, while I was asleep on the sofa.

His eyes twinkled gently as he turned my chair to face him. "Would you have preferred I bring you upstairs? Did you know which room I would've entered if that had happened?" He leaned his face close to mine, grinning widely.

"That's not what I meant." I pushed him away. "Just…why did you sleep on the floor when you could've gone upstairs and slept in your own room?"

Still looking at me, Peter placed his fingers under my chin. "You don't know me well enough, then, Aurorette Arrington," he said, touching his nose to mine before lowering his mouth to kiss me. His lips were light but warm, increasing the adrenaline in my body and making sparks fly.

Closing my eyes, I wrapped my arms around his neck and parted my lips to kiss him back.

"If every morning were like this, I'd be the happiest man on earth," Peter said, his lips brushing mine.

"Hmm."

"And," he said, his lips still on mine, "if we keep kissing like this, we'll never eat our breakfast, and my cooking effort to impress you would be in vain."

Peter smiled widely as I opened my eyes, pulling myself away. I grinned back at him.

"Let's eat," he said, turning my chair back and taking a seat next to me.

Peter had become a good cook. The scrambled eggs with mushrooms were soft and tasty. The bacon was perfectly crisp, and he hadn't burned the toast. The best part was that he'd brewed my favorite coffee, Big Bang, from Peet's Coffee. Although he didn't like coffee, Peter had bought a coffee machine to use whenever I stayed at his house.

A sudden wave of nostalgia hit me as I glanced at Peter, who was chewing his breakfast. *Here we are, just you and me, sitting side by side, eating our breakfast together like in the past.*

"Are you hiring someone to clean your house?" I asked, shaking off my sentimental feelings.

A smile tugged at the corners of his mouth. "I'm not good at cleaning," he said. "Besides—"

"They can clean the house better than you," I intercepted his words. "Yup, I remember those words." I raised my mug to him.

"You got it." He chuckled. Laughing, we clinked our mugs.

"Hey, after we finish our breakfast, I'm going to show you something," he said.

"What's that?"

"It's a secret." He winked.

I snickered and continued eating my breakfast.

After we ate, as promised, Peter took me to the house next door, the one on the left. Standing in front of the door, he gave me a mischievous smile.

In less than a minute, a silver-haired man of medium height, wearing glasses, answered the door. He smiled at me. The last time

I'd seen him was in my old apartment a couple of days before Peter returned to London for his sister's funeral.

"Marcus!" I exclaimed.

"Miss Rory! Long time, no see." Marcus reached out to hug me.

"Just call me Rory, Marcus." I hugged him back.

He chuckled, and his hand gently tapped my back before releasing me. Marcus had worked with Peter's family for a long time. He'd taught Peter to ride a bike, swim, and play soccer because his parents were barely at home, busy with work and social gatherings. They weren't around for birthdays, school performances, or Christmas holidays. Peter grew up with Marcus and a bunch of domestic helpers. Marcus was Peter's special person.

"Why don't you come in?" Marcus invited us. "Too bad my wife, Rosa, won't be here until next week. She would've been happy to see you, Peter, and Miss Rory."

"Maybe not today, Marcus," Peter said. "I'm going to drive Rory around. She misses California."

"I understand." He smiled, turning to me. "Yes, you should enjoy everything you don't normally see in Boston."

"That's the plan." I smiled back.

After visiting Marcus, Peter and I walked barefoot along the sandy shoreline. The morning sun kissed my skin as I inhaled the fresh, salty ocean air. My body relaxed and my mind quieted as I picked up the sound of ocean waves washing up against the beach and the seagulls squawking as they soared in the air above us. The waves crawled to the shore, wetting the sand beneath my feet. When the waves became stronger, I moved to the dry sand because I didn't like the water washing over my feet. Peter chuckled to see me, and, in a sudden movement, he lifted me by my waist and marched farther down into the ocean. He stood behind me and then let the waves crash against his back. I shrieked with laughter as I felt the cold waves hitting my thighs. Breaking away, Peter laughed and danced a jig around me every time I wanted to smack him.

Around noon, we met Tom for lunch. Peter's half brother hadn't changed much, still skinny and laid-back. His red hair had changed a bit, and his tousled hairstyle made him look younger than his twenty-six years.

"Hi!" I waved to him.

"Good to see you again, Rory. It's been so long since we've seen each other." He hugged me tightly.

"I missed you too, Tom, and…your squeezing hug," I teased, trying to breathe.

Chuckling, he eased away, gazing at me for a moment before shifting his eyes to Peter, who watched us.

"I don't miss *you*," he said, stepping forward and jabbing Peter playfully in the stomach before giving him a quick hug.

"Me neither," Peter responded. "Theo isn't here yet?" he asked, glancing at his watch.

"He'll be here soon," Tom said. "He needed to pick up Emma on the way here."

Peter raised one of his eyebrows. "Oh? I thought Emma couldn't join us."

"I'm not sure, but that's good. Rory can meet her. Let's wait inside. I already reserved a table for five," Tom urged us.

"Okay," Peter and I agreed.

As we entered the restaurant, Peter explained to me that Theo Adams and Emma Hathaway were his and Tom's childhood friends, who happened to live in the same neighborhood in Richmond, London. Theo's father used to be a US consular general in London, and Emma's dad was a scientist. Ten years ago, they moved back to the States.

"I'm sure you'll like them," Peter assured me before excusing himself to go to the restroom.

While waiting for him to return, Tom and I caught up with each other, mostly talking about work.

Peter had been right when he said that Tom felt guilty for what his ex-boyfriend had done to us. I didn't want to say anything, as I wanted to let him heal and forgive himself. There was no need to rush things.

Theo and Emma arrived, meeting Peter as he returned from the restroom. Theo was a head shorter than Peter. He wore glasses and had wavy, light brown hair, which was cut short and swept behind his ears. Emma was as tall as Theo and also wore glasses. Her copper hair was tied loosely to the side.

I liked them instantly.

Despite seeming quiet and reserved, Theo bantered with Tom and Peter. Emma and I talked as well, and, once in a while, we listened to the guys' conversation and joined in their laughter.

Nothing felt better than having a good conversation with good people. Theo and Emma were down-to-earth people, regardless of their family backgrounds. They could have followed in their parents' footsteps, but they chose different career paths in education as professors for an undergraduate school.

After a fantastic afternoon with his half brother and their childhood friends, followed by light shopping in Fashion Island, Peter and I drove back to his house. It was almost four when we arrived and decided to relax at home before going out again for our Cruise of Light dinner in Newport Beach.

As we entered the house, Peter asked, "How do you like my friends?"

"I like them. They're very down-to-earth."

He nodded. "Yup. That's why I like them. I've been friends with Theo since we were young. I learned a lot about being humble from him."

I chuckled. "Did he beat you up when you acted snobbishly?"

"Not really, but he would definitely give me a piece of his mind."

"I can see that."

While Peter dug into his freezer for some ice cream, I asked casually, "Do you think they like me?"

"Of course. I thought that was obvious. Why do you ask?" he answered as he continued to rummage through the freezer. "Ah, there you are." He put the pint of rocky road ice cream on the kitchen counter and looked for an ice cream scooper.

I shrugged, tapping my fingers on the counter. "Um…just curious."

"You don't seem to be convinced."

"No, I believe it."

"Really?" He stopped searching for the scooper and turned to me.

I nodded, but Peter cocked his head, raising one of his eyebrows. Solemnly, he walked around the counter with his eyes fixed on me. I bit my lower lip and looked away.

"Something's bothering you. What is it?" He stood in front of me.

I studied his face and nodded. "Okay." Stepping closer, I placed my hands on his waist and looked at him, and Peter clasped my hands in his. "Why do you like me?"

Peter blinked. "What kind of question is that?"

My stomach tightened, and I felt stupid. I clenched my jaw. "You're a good-looking guy with a good education and a good family. It wouldn't be difficult for you to find a girl with a good background, like Emma. Why have you continued dating me after knowing who I am?"

His eyelashes fluttered. A crease appeared between his eyebrows. "Does it matter?"

I nodded slowly, and I saw his jaw clench.

51

"Why does that suddenly matter to you?" he asked, his voice rising.

My throat became dry. I drew in a shaky breath and forced myself to look in his eyes. "Because I'd never thought about it until I met your friends today," I said. "Since meeting them, I've been wondering what your family would think of me."

I noticed a flicker of surprise in his eyes as his jaw tightened further, and he only gave me a hard stare.

I frowned. "Just…forget what I said." I tried to pull my hands away, but Peter held them tightly.

"Rory, tell me what's wrong," he asked again. His voice took an authoritative tone that I'd never heard before.

From the way he looked at me, there was no way to dodge the question. Raising my chin, I said, "I feel inferior in front of your friends. It wasn't easy to answer their questions about my parents. If I said I'd grown up with my aunt, it would lead to them asking what happened to my parents. And that would lead to another awkward answer about my mom passing away and never knowing my father because I was born out of wedlock. I used to be okay with all the questions because I'm not the only one born without knowing their father. But somehow, today, answering the question became tiresome, and that's…tough." I shrugged a shoulder. "Compared to them, I'm nobody."

I felt his fingers around my wrists became cold and sweaty. "You—what?"

"I'm nobody," I repeated quietly.

Lightning fast, Peter released my hands, grabbing my shoulders roughly and backing me into the kitchen cabinet. His face became purple, and he breathed heavily in and out. My heart sank as he leaned toward me, watching me as his eyes glittered.

"You're hurting me," I protested and pushed against him, but Peter was stronger and didn't seem to hear me. His eyes were fixed on me, but his mind was somewhere else. I was baffled by the hurt and sorrow in his eyes. My mind couldn't process it further as the pain in my shoulders increased, as if they were clenched by iron fists.

A groan of pain escaped my lips, and, as if snapping out of his trance, Peter released me. The purple color drained from his face as he took a few steps backward. Inhaling deeply, he closed his eyes briefly before opening them again. "Don't you ever say you're nobody. I hate that word. Don't you understand how special you are to me?" His voice broke.

"Why did you act like that?"

He shook his head, his fingers curled into a fist. "Just...don't say that word again. It hurts me to hear you say it."

Giving me another look, he turned and went upstairs, leaving me dumbfounded with my back leaning against the cabinet.

I SPENT THE NEXT HOUR alone in the garden. The gentle afternoon breeze and the subtle fragrance from the flowers calmed me down. Gazing at the orange and yellow daisy-like flowers, I reached out to touch the petals of the closest one. My knowledge of flowers' names was zilch. If my aunt were here, she would know what they were by heart. I wasn't interested in googling their name because my mind was preoccupied with Peter's peculiar behavior. Why did he look so upset when I said, "I'm nobody"?

I sighed and caressed the flower. I'd never seen Peter act like that because, most of the time, he was an easy-going person. I wasn't sure how long I'd been staring at the flowers when I began to feel someone was watching me. Glancing up, I saw Peter standing on the veranda with one arm holding his other at the elbow. He blushed and shifted his weight from one foot to the other as I stood from where I'd been sitting beside the flowers.

"They're called calendula," he said.

I blinked. "Uh—what?"

"Calendula," he repeated, striding toward me. "That's the name of the flowers you were admiring. I've known because that's my grandma's favorite flower. "

Peter came to a halt a few feet from me. A crease on his forehead deepened as I walked around the bench and stood behind it, as if I were ready for another surprise. His head hung low as he took a deep breath. "What I did to you earlier was very improper," he whispered, raising his head, dejection brimming in his eyes. "I shouldn't have, but I…" He stopped, swallowing hard before offering his hand to me.

"Why did you do that?" I demanded, ignoring his hand.

Peter heaved and dropped his hand to his side. For a few moments, we faced each other without saying a word.

Finally, Peter broke the silence. "If I don't tell you in detail, will you forgive me?"

"Try me."

Lowering his gaze, he scratched his foot on the ground before looking up. "My mom left home when I was five years old and never returned. Her last words were, 'I'm nobody.' Once I understood her meaning, I hated those words. It never crossed my mind that today, in this house, someone I love would say the same words." His voice trembled as he forced a smile when our eyes met. "I was afraid you'd leave me just like she did."

That explained the hurt in his eyes.

The massive stone that had been hanging in my heart rolled away. Exhaling, I stepped forward and hugged him. Peter pressed me against his chest as he buried his face on my shoulder, breathing out hard against my neck. "I'm sorry for hurting you. Your words and your expression brought back something I wanted to forget. Promise me, don't say those words ever again," he whispered. "Please."

I nodded. "I promise."

It was almost five-thirty, but the sun went down early in winter.

It was sinking sluggishly beyond the horizon, leaving the blue sky with brilliant orange and red colors. At the same time, we heard something screeching over our heads, too loud to be ignored. Still in each other's arms, we looked up to see a group of tiny black birds flying over us, followed by some ravens. Our eyes followed them until they disappeared into a thicket of trees at the park nearby. As we couldn't see them anymore, almost in unison, we turned to each other and smiled as our eyes met. Letting out a sigh, Peter broke gently away and took my hand, and we entered the house with the afternoon's awkward feeling behind us.

LATER IN THE EVENING, PETER paced in his bedroom, feeling restless. After thirty minutes, he stopped and sat on the edge of his bed with his elbows on his knees and clasped his hands tightly. His heart hurt as if thousands of needles pierced it. He'd never wanted to hurt Rory, but her words had been like a knife thrust into his heart.

"Oh God." Groaning, he covered his face with his palms. His mind went back to that night when he was five years old. His mom had come to his bedroom, tears flooding down her cheeks.

"Don't cry, Mommy," he had said wearily. "I'll be a good boy."

His mom had hugged him. "You are a good boy," she reassured him.

"Then why are you crying?"

"Because I'm nobody, Peter. I'm nobody," his mom said softly. "If I were somebody, he wouldn't dare humiliate me this way."

"Daddy hurts you?" he asked.

His mom didn't answer. "You'll understand when you grow up." She leaned forward to kiss his forehead and told him to sleep.

It had never crossed his mind that that kiss would be the last she would ever give him. A month later, Jane came to live with them.

Peter didn't understand why he suddenly had a twelve-year-old sister. Where had she been hiding the whole time? Maybe the stork that was supposed to bring her to his house got lost and had just found it years later?

His dad said she was his sister, but other adults said she was his half sister.

No one would explain to him what a half sister was.

"What's a half sister, Marcus? People say Jane is my half sister," he asked one day when Marcus was driving him to his preschool.

Marcus was his parents' assistant who had been working in the house since Peter was young. As far back as Peter could remember, Marcus had always been near him and treated him with love and patience.

Through the rearview mirror, Marcus glanced at Peter. "It means you and Jane have the same father but different mothers," he answered after carefully choosing his words. "She used to live with her mom far away from here. Now, she's staying in your house because your dad wants her to get a good education."

Peter looked at his feet. They hung down without touching the car floor. "My mom is my dad's wife, right? Why did you say that Jane was born from a different mom? Does it mean my dad has two wives? I don't get it," he whispered.

But Marcus heard him. "It's okay to feel confused," he soothed him. "When you grow up, you'll understand more about everything."

Marcus was right. His mom was right. Once Peter grew up, he understood more.

He understood why Jane had come to the house when she was twelve years old.

He understood why Tom had come to the house when he was nine years old and only three months younger than him.

He also understood when Eliza, his younger half sister, showed up at ten years old.

He had a reason to hate his half siblings, especially Jane, who had caused his mom to leave. But he couldn't. He loved Jane because, on the day he realized that his mom had left, he had a tantrum, and only Jane could soothe him. Since then, Jane had become his little mom, the one who kissed his boo-boos, read him stories at night, or scolded him when he didn't do his homework.

Peter rubbed his face to shake the memory off. He didn't have any recollection of his mom's face without a picture. However, he never forgot her words—the painful memory that he wanted to forget but that had been triggered by Rory's words.

Furthermore, her remarks about "what your family would think of me" cracked another matter that he'd sealed carefully away.

In his family, only Jane, Tom and Marcus knew about his relationship with Rory.

Since he'd fallen in love with her, Peter believed his family would love Rory too. She was sweet, kind, and smart. No one would bother to dig deeper about who she was, as he hadn't been holding a position in any of the Sandridge businesses.

Alas, everything had changed since Jane's passing, and he had agreed to replace her working in the family businesses. Starting that day, all the elders in the Sandridge family began to scrutinize his work and daily life, including his love life. They set a high standard for his future wife because she was expected to aid him in expanding the family business.

In a tiny corner of his heart, Peter knew what his family's reaction would be if they found out about Rory. He coughed, releasing the tightness in his chest, as he understood that the path ahead of him wouldn't be smooth. It wouldn't be an issue if only he'd refused Jane's request. For the first time in his life, he had no idea what to do or how to move forward.

Chapter 8

THE NEXT MORNING, WE HAD a quiet breakfast, and Peter's mood was much better than it had been last night. Although his smile didn't reach his light brown eyes, he began to tease me again. I wished he would tell me more, but I gave him space to sort out his issues. Once he was ready, he would tell me anyway. I supposed it wasn't easy for him to share, but I appreciated him trusting me with his secret.

After breakfast, we decided to spend our time outdoors visiting the Butterfly House in Newport Beach and going to Downtown Disney. I felt relief to see Peter's eyes sparkled after getting our caricature drawn at that outdoor shopping center.

Around 4:50 in the afternoon, carrying a blanket, I walked toward the pier for the family beach movie night event that had been coordinated by the city. Peter had already left earlier to save a good seat for us, since the event was the last one this year and the place would be packed. We were going to watch the animated movie, *The Secret Life of Pets*. It wasn't a new movie. I'd seen it twice, but I thought it would be fun to see it outside with the ocean waves crashing against the shore. Initially, Peter wasn't interested, but he'd changed his mind after I said I'd never experienced watching a movie on the beach.

The sun was almost kissing the horizon by the time I arrived, but the sky was bright enough to find him seated amongst the crowd. He sat cross-legged on the blanket, conversing with several young women who looked like they were in their early twenties. I frowned as I watched one of them, a thin girl with blonde hair braided down her back, sit next to him and lean her chest close to his upper arm.

"Hmm." I felt heat swirling up in my chest at the sight.

Peter wore a nervous smile as he answered one of the girls' questions. The blonde inched closer every time he attempted to crawl away from her.

I maneuvered around blankets, kids, parents, and some outdoor chairs before I reached Peter.

"Hi, there!" I called in a high-pitched voice, waving my hand at Peter and the girls.

Peter let out a visible sigh of relief when he saw me.

"Can I join you guys? It's gonna be boring watching the movie by myself. Besides, that guy"—I pointed toward Peter—"is super cute!"

Peter looked puzzled but didn't say a word.

The blonde pouted. "It's too cramped. Find another spot. There are lots of empty spots there." She pointed a fair distance away from them. She must have brushed her bosom against Peter's upper arm because, at that moment, he moved it away.

"Please?" Widening my eyes, I looked at Peter with a sweet smile on my face.

Peter didn't get it, and before he said anything, a girl in a cute Minnie Mouse sweater motioned with her hand and invited me to join them.

"Aw, thank you," I said coquettishly before stepping into the circle and sitting next to her. Peter stared at me but dropped his eyes when one of the girls offered him a cookie.

"What are you guys talking about?" I asked the girl in the Minnie Mouse sweater. I glanced at Peter, who looked like he was being fed a spoonful of chili.

She giggled. "Nothing much. Since this guy has a British accent, we've talked about London, Prince William, and Prince Harry. Isn't he adorable?" she whispered, gazing at Peter.

I gave an exaggerated nod. "He is." Fluttering my eyelashes, I clasped my hands on my chest.

I didn't find the situation funny anymore when the blonde looped her hands on his arm. I clenched my jaw. *This has to be stopped!*

"What's his name?" I asked the girl in the Minnie Mouse shirt.

"Peter."

"Does he have a girlfriend?"

"Well, we haven't asked him yet." She tilted her head. "But since he was sitting alone, we assumed he was single."

"Really? What a coincidence! I'm single too," I said in my high-pitched voice. I stood up and walked toward Peter.

"Hey!" the girls complained in unison.

I ignored them as I sat in front of him. "Your name's Peter?" I asked, placing my hands on his muscled arms. The blonde, surprised at my bold behavior, dropped her hands and moved away, looking at me curiously.

"Yup." He nodded without hiding his smile. "What's yours?"

"Rory." I tipped my head and smiled sweetly. "Do you have a bae?"

"Do you have one?" he asked back.

Turning the corners of my lips down, I shook my head.

"Me neither," he said.

Screeching happily, I knelt and took his hands, placing them around my waist.

"What's she doing?" I heard one of the girls murmur.

"Be my bae!" I said loudly, leaning my face toward him.

"Hmm." Peter slanted his head toward mine as though he expected to be kissed. "Why?"

"Because you're handsome and—" I stopped.

"Handsome and…?" Peter repeated.

"I love your eyes."

"Just my eyes?"

"Your nose."

"That's it?"

I chuckled. "I love your lips too." Slowly, I leaned in and kissed him.

Peter did something that surprised the girls and me as well. He pulled at my waist and lay me down on the blanket, using his arm to support my neck. A mischievous twinkle appeared in his eyes as he looked at me before leaning down to kiss me. Intentionally, I slipped my hand under his sweater.

"Eww…," I heard one of the girls say.

"Sheesh, I've never met anyone this bold!"

"He let her do that and even kissed her back."

"Disgusting! I thought he was a gentleman. Ugh!"

"Let's go. I don't want to see this."

As their footsteps faded, Peter raised his head and glanced over his shoulder at the retreating girls. When our eyes met, we giggled and gave each other a high five, and then he helped me sit up.

"Oh my God, you *are* a bad girl, Rory," he said.

I smoothed my sweater and smiled widely at him.

"But I like it," he continued.

"That's because you were too comfortable with those girls," I pouted.

Peter cackled. "Really? I'm glad you're jealous. Yeah, that blonde girl kept leaning on me. It was annoying."

I squinted at him. "I thought guys *loved* that kind of attention." I raised my eyebrows as high as I could.

"Maybe other men, but not me." He shuddered. "Honestly, I'm

scared of aggressive girls like that. It would've been a different story if she were you, and I wouldn't have let you go away."

Before I reacted to his comment, Peter grinned and shifted closer to me. "I'm surprised by your attack, Rory. I never imagined you could pull a trick like that." He nudged my arm.

I smiled, then showed my teeth while hissing at him. "You'll find me even more interesting if you stick around for a long, long time," I teased him.

"That's my intention," Peter said, tilting his head to kiss me.

I smiled and kissed him back.

Our kiss was interrupted when the movie began.

Chapter 9

ETER DROVE ME TO THE office on Monday morning. I'd thought of taking an Uber, because the cost would have been reimbursed anyway, but he insisted.

"I'm sad that, after tonight, we can't see each other again until Friday," Peter said.

"Let's meet for dinner tonight," I said, giving his hand a light squeeze.

"No. When you're on a business trip, having a social dinner with your boss and people involved in the project is important. You also have the opportunity to mingle with other employees from different departments."

"Yeah, Aunt Amy said the same thing. Well, if I don't have a dinner gathering, I'll let you know."

He nodded, gazing at me.

"What?" I asked.

"Can I ask you a question?"

"Sure."

"Why don't you go back to work with Myriad again? That bitchy boss is no longer there. If you worked with Myriad, you'd live here, and it'd be easier for us to be together."

I looked across the car. "You aren't joking, are you?"

"Do I look like I'm joking?" he replied.

I shrugged. "I'm not interested in working in accounting anymore."

"But you can work in a different department, right?" he asked. "I checked last night. There are many positions open right now. Maybe you should check and see if there are any you'd be interested in."

I almost said, "If I worked there, I'd feel that I owe you."

But I didn't say it. Instead, I gave his words some thought and said, "Well, I like working with Veles. I feel useful when I'm helping clients maintain their financial records. Sometimes, it can be boring, but I'm happy there. I also like my boss and my coworkers. If I worked for Myriad, most of the accounting and finance people would know we're dating. It would be hard for me because they'd assume I'm getting special treatment. After all, I'm dating their partner's president. Honestly, I want to have a good career because of my hard work. If I wanted to live comfortably, I'd have returned to Myriad once the bully manager left."

"I kind of expected you to say that," Peter said.

"Am I disappointing you?"

"Of course not. You're an independent woman, Rory, and you aren't a person who depends on someone's status. That's what I like about you." He looked at me for a moment before his gaze shifted to the windshield. "I asked you the question because I want to see you often. Looking at you in person is better than looking at you through a video call."

I gave a light chuckle, resting my hand on his strong lower arm. "I want to see you more often too, but the timing isn't in our favor. You started your training with your dad, and I got this job before we decided to date. Then we agreed to the long-distance relationship. Did I remember that wrong?"

Peter didn't say a word. His face was gloomy when he looked the opposite way and mumbled, "If she were alive, I wouldn't have to take that position, and I'd find a job near you."

"What did you say?" I turned to him.

"Nothing," he said without looking at me.

"Why do you look so sad? Is it because of what I said?"

Peter turned to me and smiled, but it didn't quite reach his eyes. "No, it's not because of what you said."

I raised an eyebrow but didn't press on. Too bad I hadn't quite caught everything he'd said.

Peter didn't say anything more about it, and I didn't want to ask. For the rest of the drive, he remained quiet. Every once in a while, he would let out a heavy sigh.

The parking lot was packed with cars when Peter stopped at the curb in front of the building. His hand pressed a button to open the trunk. "What time do you leave today?" he asked before I opened the door.

"At five, maybe. But I'm not sure about today's schedule," I said. "And today I'll have a rental car, so wherever we meet after work, we can both drive there."

"Ah, yeah, you'd have a rental car today," Peter said. "Yeah, that sounds good. Let me know your schedule tomorrow and if we can have dinner together. Don't forget to tell me what hotel you're staying at."

"Okay," I said, pushing the door open.

Peter held my elbow to stop me. As my head whipped toward him, his lips landed on mine.

"I'll miss you," he said.

"I'll miss you too."

When I pressed my lips against his, Peter looked over my shoulder. "Is that guy your coworker? He's waving at me."

Following the direction of his stare, I saw Ryan standing on the curb, smiling and waving at us. He looked professional with black trousers and a lightweight black pullover over a lighter shirt.

Heat rushed to my face.

"Yes, he is," I said quickly, giving Peter a final, quick kiss before slipping out of the car. "I'll take the luggage myself," I said when he was about to open his door. I pulled my luggage from the trunk and leaned in the window. "I'll call you later. Bye, Peter!"

I waved at Peter, who looked puzzled but waved back at me. As Peter's car slowly left the curb, Ryan sent me a meaningful smile.

"Shut it," I hissed when our eyes met.

He smiled, nudging my shoulder. "Did you feel embarrassed because I caught you kissing your boyfriend before going to work? If I were a girl and had a handsome boyfriend like Peter, I'd let people see me kissing him."

I shot him a dark look, but it didn't work because his grin widened.

"Now, after you've seen your boyfriend again, can you see my point about the difficulty of having a long-distance relationship? Communicating in person is better than through video calls or text. Besides, cuddling and kissing are important parts of dating, you know. If you live in Boston while he's in California, how can you do that?" His big smile faded as his eyes fixed on the bracelet around my wrist before he looked away.

"Okay, Dr. Phil. Should I break up with him and find a new boyfriend in Boston?" I challenged him, stuffing my hand in my blazer pocket to hide the bracelet. Somehow, I didn't like the look in his eyes.

Ryan turned to me and leaned in. "Yes, and the new boyfriend should be me."

I scoffed and pushed him back hard, nearly causing him to bump into a woman walking in the opposite direction. She glared, but when she saw Ryan's handsome face, she turned her angry face toward me.

Ryan grinned when I gave her a signal of apology.

"Stop grinning," I mumbled, and walked faster, entering the building.

Chapter 10

MY FIRST DAY IN THE California office was busy and tiresome.

After meeting the owner of the dealership and being introduced to those who worked with the Boston team, Sally and our legal team began working closely with the owner, and Ryan and I spent time with the accounting employees.

I couldn't believe how messy the company was. There was no teamwork between the employees, but there were plenty of pointing fingers. A white-blonde-haired woman from accounts receivable drove Ryan crazy and dared to pick a fight with a short, plump woman from another department right in front of us, saying, "Since she started working here, everything has been falling apart."

Noticeably frustrated, Ryan continuously bit his lower lip to control himself and not say something stupid when the talkative controller monopolized the meeting by going on and on about issues we didn't need to hear.

No wonder their financial report was messy and they needed us to clean it up.

AFTER A LONG, TOUGH DAY, we had an early dinner with our legal team—Randy Smith and Sam Williams, the attorneys from

Williams and Partners. They didn't work for Veles but, rather, sub-contractors, hired as legal representatives against our clients. Any legal advice or litigation in court would be done by their law firm.

In the restaurant, I glanced at our team, who were laughing, smiling, telling jokes, or talking over one another. The excitement made me feel part of them. I was glad I'd been chosen for this project because it would be the best chance for me to get to know people in the California office. For all I knew, I could be transferred to that office in the future.

Just as we were about to leave the restaurant, Sally asked me to go with her since we were staying in the same hotel.

"I need to get a rental car first," I said. "You look tired. You'd better get to sleep soon, Sally. I can ask Ryan to drive me there. Besides, my luggage is in his car."

Ryan nodded. "Yes, get some rest, Sally. I can take Rory to the rental car place." Then, suddenly, he slapped his forehead. "Oh no. I can't. I left my cell phone in the office earlier. No wonder I felt like something was missing." He turned to me. "Sorry, Rory, I can't drop you off, but since I'll arrive first at the hotel, I'll drop your luggage off at the front desk, so you don't have to take it with you."

"I can drive her to the rental place," Sam offered suddenly. "I'm going in the same direction anyway."

Sally looked at him before nodding. "Okay. Thanks, Sam, and see you tomorrow, everyone."

We walked toward the parking lot, and I followed Sam to his car.

Sam was pleasant to be around. On our way to get the rental car, we talked like old friends, which made it hard to believe that we'd only met that morning. Of the two lawyers, Sam was the one who displayed curiosity about my full name.

"Yes, it was derived from Aurora, the ancient Greek goddess of the dawn. Since my mom liked everything about the French, she changed it to Aurorette," I chuckled.

Sam whipped his head toward me. His eyebrows flew up and his eyes broadened for a brief second before his face became calm again.

"It's interesting to know that someone else loves reading ancient mythology stories. My uncle liked them too," he said. "Hey, Rory, can I ask you a question?"

"Sure."

"Have we met before this?"

I tipped my head and thought about it. "I wondered that too, when Sally introduced us earlier."

Sam chuckled. "Really? How funny."

"It is, but I can't pinpoint where."

"I wonder where and when we could possibly have met." He looked at me before turning back to the road.

"I have no clue." I shrugged and tugged my hair behind my ears.

Sam's eyes widened and he pointed at me. "Oh, those earrings!"

Automatically, I touched the earrings that I'd received from my aunt.

"They have a unique R shape. Now I remember where we met!" he said.

"Where?"

"At the café in Boston," Sam answered. "I was standing behind you when someone bumped your drink and—"

"Most of my mocha fell on you," I finished, nodding. "Ah yes. Now I remember you. The ugly pink sweater guy." My hand flew over my mouth after saying that.

Sam laughed. "Yeah, the sweater was ugly. Bright pink. Who wants to buy a sweater that color? I'm not against a guy wearing a pink shirt, but the color of that sweater was unbelievable! I bought a new sweater once I was at the airport. No offense to your friend's taste of color."

"No worries. I won't tell him," I said.

"Hey, is that the place?" He pointed to the Advance Rent-A-Car neon sign.

"Yup, that's the one." I nodded. "Thanks for the ride, Sam. See you tomorrow."

"Sure, see you tomorrow."

I waited until Sam's car left the curb before entering the building.

Chapter 11

THE WEEK IN CALIFORNIA FLEW by. In the blink of an eye, it was already Friday, and the next night, I would be flying back to Boston. I booked a red-eye flight for Saturday night in order to spend most of the day with Peter before heading home.

My project hadn't run smoothly. There were many hurdles, mostly because of the Christmas holiday. The project would continue the second week after the New Year when everybody returned to the office. In the meantime, we would analyze the data we had collected. Despite everything, I was happy because in two more weeks, I could come back to California.

"What time is your flight tomorrow?" Peter asked on our way back to his house. He'd picked me up at the rental car dealership earlier after I'd driven Sally and Ryan to the airport.

"Two in the morning. I didn't go through John Wayne because I wanted to spend more time with you, so I chose to fly from LAX. You can drop me off at LAX before midnight tomorrow," I said.

"Okay," he said, taking my hand and holding it while driving.

"Where do you want to go for dinner?" I asked.

"What do *you* want to eat?" he asked without looking at me.

"Um, how about the sashimi rice bowl?"

As I expected, he wrinkled his nose. He'd tried a few of the

Japanese foods I liked, but the sashimi was still beyond his taste. He didn't understand why I craved raw fish. When I debated about how he liked his steak rare, he always argued that the meat was at least grilled, and the fish was raw.

"See?" I huffed. "Don't ask me if you don't agree with what I choose."

He rolled his eyes. "Okay, fine. Since this is your last day here, I'll go to the place. But don't order me that sashimi bowl. I'm gonna order something cooked."

"Something cooked is for little kids," I teased.

"I'll order you a rare steak next time."

"Don't you dare!"

"I dare," he said, poking my side, which was my ticklish spot.

I shrieked and pushed his hand away. "Stop tickling me," I protested and shrieked again as he pretended to poke me.

Laughing, he stopped teasing me and focused on driving.

I loved the sushi restaurant. To our surprise, we bumped into Sam, who was having dinner with his coworkers. He called out to me first because I didn't see him as I passed his table. Sam gazed at Peter with rather intense focus when I introduced them. They exchanged business cards before saying goodbye.

"Does your office only employ handsome guys?" Peter whispered as we settled at our table.

"What do you mean?" I glanced up at him.

"Your coworker I saw in front of the office last time is a good-looking guy, and so is this attorney. Now I don't feel comfortable letting you work there." He pressed his lips tight, his eyes focused on the menu list.

"You're an attractive man too." I grinned, tilting my head toward him. "Are you jealous?" I whispered.

He raised the list so I couldn't see his face.

Snickering, I reached up and pressed the menu down with my

hand to see his sullen face. "I'm glad you feel jealous, but don't worry. I'm not easily swayed."

"I should've given you a ring, not a couple's bracelet," he said, rereading the menu.

"What?" My breath caught in my throat. A sudden tightening in my chest loosened as I spotted a mischievous twinkle in his eyes. *Thank God, he was joking.*

After we finished our dinner and were about to leave the restaurant, we met an acquaintance of Peter.

Peter didn't seem to like him and didn't bother introducing me. Noticing my curiosity about him, he filled me in briefly on the way back to his place. His acquaintance's name was Isaac Fournier, and Isaac's father had a business that was important for the Sandridge Group, with the possibility of a partnership.

"We've known each other since we were young, but he's too sneaky and narrow-minded for me," Peter said, peering through the windshield. He didn't say anything more about it until we reached his home.

After showering, I went to the backyard, hoping to enjoy the view of the beach on my last night here. Leaning against the chest-high fence, I saw lights from the oil rigs sparkling in the dark. The crescent moon hid behind a thin cloud, and gentle waves hit the shore.

"What a beautiful night," I said, inhaling slowly as the calm breeze touched my face. The temperature had dropped a bit, but to me, the weather was still bearable.

Something soft fell over my shoulders, and I whipped my head around to see Peter standing behind me. He'd placed a thin blanket over me.

"I'm not cold," I said.

Peter smiled and put his arms around me. "I know, but the longer you stay outside, the colder the weather becomes. Besides, I want to make sure Aunt Amy knows I'm taking good care of you."

He pressed a light kiss to my cheek and placed his chin on my shoulder as he looked into the distance.

"I'll tell her that you're treating me well," I said, squeezing his arm gently.

He didn't say anything but tightened his arms around me. I rested my head against him, feeling his warmth on my back while breathing in his fresh, minty smell. I wanted to soak in the time with him since it would be a while before I saw him again. For a time, we didn't say anything, just gazed silently at the glistening winter sky.

"When Sunday comes, I'll be alone." Peter sighed, straightening his back. "I'm sad."

"Why?" I asked, glancing at him over my shoulder.

He scoffed, and his arms dropped to his sides. "Ugh, you're so cold!"

Grinning, I turned around and held his hands. "Are you going to miss me?" I teased.

"I'm not." He pouted.

I grinned from ear to ear. Cupping my hands against his face, I forced him to look at me. "You're so grumpy." I chuckled lightly. "I'm gonna miss you too. But I'll be happier if you miss me more than I miss you."

I pulled his face to me to give him a light kiss on the tip of his nose and then on his mouth. As I broke away, my heart leaped to find how intently he was looking at me.

In one smooth movement, Peter pulled me closer, turned us around, and leaned his back against the fence. The blanket fell off my shoulders, but we didn't bother to pick it up. I leaned against his muscular body as Peter tightened his hand on my waist. Our eyes met, and I was mesmerized by the way he looked at me. So warm, so sincere, and so tender. There was something else. My heart hammered in my chest as I realized what it was—desire.

I swallowed hard.

By the time I thought of dodging it, Peter had already slid his fingers behind my neck and kissed me gently. His lips were warmer than usual, and his body radiated palpable heat. I felt his heart galloping through my palms as they pressed against his chest.

I gasped and felt a thrill rip through my body as his lips reached the soft skin below my ears.

"Peter," I called, my voice strained.

"Yeah," he whispered in my ear, giving me goosebumps. He raised his head before leaning in and kissing me harder than earlier, pushing my lips apart

Sighing, I closed my eyes and wrapped my arms around his neck.

The waves rolled and crashed into the shore over and over again. The air was growing colder, and the wind was picking up. The fallen blanket remained wrapped around our ankles, but we barely noticed it as our kisses became more fevered.

The logical part of my brain flashed warning signs, but my hands had their own agenda. One had crept into his hair, and the other reached under his sweater to feel his taut back muscles.

I shivered when Peter slid his hands under my sweater, drifting around my waist to the small of my back. I wanted his warm hands to stay there.

My insides felt like someone had injected my veins with wine. Peter's hands traveled up and down the curve of my waist. I felt his heavy breath against my skin as his lips traveled down my jaw, over my neck, across my collarbone, and returned to my lips again.

When I kissed his neck, I heard him calling my name. "Rory."

I ignored him.

"Ror—" He swallowed as I kissed the hollow beneath his throat, and he let out a heavy sigh as his fingers moved to my waist. "Rory."

Something in his voice snapped me awake.

"I'm sorry, we should stop," he said, pushing me gently away.

He was panting slightly. His eyes showed no desire now. They only seemed to hold disgust and regret.

I stiffened and raised my brows. The warmth of his hands lingered on my lower back as I pulled my sweater down.

Why did he ask me to stop?

Then a sudden wave of shame hit me like someone had poured a bucket of ice water over my head. What I'd always feared came back to me.

Sniffling, I shuddered and looked at the disgust in his eyes before taking a step back and rubbing my hands over my arms to search for comfort. "Yeah, we should stop, and…" I sighed, feeling hollow in my heart. "I know I'm not skinny, but please don't stare at me like you're disgusted, Peter." Spinning on my heels, I darted toward his house.

"Hey!"

I ignored him and quickened my pace, but he followed me.

"Hey!" He grabbed my elbow to pull me to a stop and turned me around. "What's the matter? I just said we should stop."

"And I agreed to stop." I brushed his hand away.

His eyebrows rose. "Yeah, I heard that. But what did you mean by the last thing you said? I don't understand."

I scoffed. "You don't?"

Peter's thick eyebrows furrowed. "No."

"Did you stop because…you feel I'm fat?" I asked, almost choking on the words.

Tears welled in my eyes, forcing me to bite my lower lip. I would have hated it if he saw me crying. I stepped toward the house, but Peter blocked me.

"No. You aren't fat. Even if you were, so what? You're perfect to me anyway. Where did you get that assumption from?"

"Then why did you say, 'We should stop'?" I raised my voice.

"I have a reason…" His voice trailed off as he raised his eyebrow. "Wait…do you *really* want what we were doing?"

Tongue-tied, I frowned at him for a few beats before shifting my eyes away. "You were the one…" The wind gusted and tossed a strand of my hair over my face before I could finish my sentence. I pushed my hair back, tucked the stray lock behind my ears, and opened my mouth, but the wind blew the hair back into my face again.

Amusement flicked in Peter's eyes as he watched my battle against the wind.

Letting out a huff, I shifted slightly to let the wind toss my hair back.

"Don't *you* want what we were doing?" I asked him.

His expression became solemn, then he swallowed. Under the bright moonlight, his face reddened, and he avoided my eyes. For a few moments, we stood in silence.

"I'm sorry. I should've controlled myself and not given you the wrong idea," he finally said, closing the space between us. "I was… captivated by you because you're so lovely."

"But why…did you look at me like you were disgusted?"

"Huh?"

"Don't deny it. It's written all over your face, Peter." I glared at him. "Is it because I'm not as thin as you expected?"

Peter's mouth dropped open. "What? Oh my God…no." He waved his hands in front of me. "Why do you think that about yourself?"

"Why did you want us to stop and then look at me like that?" I raised my voice.

His eyes softened as he looked at me. "I have a reason. Let's go inside, and I'll tell you why."

Stiffly, I walked toward the house, and Peter followed me inside. The blanket was still lying somewhere in the backyard, and no one remembered to pick it up.

Chapter 12

"I CAN'T BELIEVE THIS IS HAPPENING again," I groaned as I slammed my butt down on the sofa. I crossed my arms in front of my chest as Peter took a seat across from me. Under the golden light from the chandelier, his cheeks brightened as he gazed at me. After a short moment, he cast his eyes down. I felt an ache in my chest as I realized he must have lied when he said I wasn't fat. Blinking my tears away, I gave a huff and looked straight at him.

"What do you want to tell me?" I asked coldly.

Peter's eyes shifted back to me, and he gave me a slow nod. His finger rubbed the side of his nose briefly before he cleared his throat and asked, "Can you guess how many wives my dad has had?"

I felt my eyes widen at his question. It wasn't exactly perfect timing for a joke. But I answered it anyway. "Umm...two, because Tom's your half brother."

"Not two. Four."

I scowled and looked into his eyes. There was no joke there. "You must be kidding," I said.

"Nope." Peter leaned his back on the sofa, smiling. "He isn't as handsome as George Clooney or Tom Cruise, but he is charming, and women easily fall in love with him."

Without thinking, I chuckled at his comment. "You must've inherited his charm, because I think you're pretty charming too."

His brown eyes widened for a moment before he frowned, creating a deep crease between his eyebrows. He shifted on his seat and said stiffly, "Well, I'm different. Shall I continue?"

I shrugged.

"My dad's charming behavior didn't stop even after he married my mom. I was too young to understand why my mom cried a lot, and I assumed it was because I'd done something naughty." Peter paused, pressed his lips tightly together, then continued. "When I was five, my dad brought Jane into the house and said she was my sister. He told me she would stay in the house and go to school. She was twelve at the time."

He'd told me this before, but something didn't add up.

"Wait…" I raised my hand to stop him. "If she was twelve and you were five, that means your dad…" My voice trailed off because I didn't have the heart to continue.

His lips twitched before he raised a shoulder. "That was my question too," he said. "Tom is only three months younger than me, and Eliza is five years younger."

Unbelievable! I brushed a hand through my hair and let it stay on my neck. I stared at him. His family affairs were just as bizarre as those in the soap operas my aunt loved to watch.

Lowering his eyes, Peter heaved a sigh and clasped his hands in his lap.

"Jane's mom," I asked, letting my hand drop back onto my lap. "She was still in a relationship with your dad after he married your mom? Why?"

He nodded slowly. "I don't know for sure, but Marcus said it was because my grandpa disapproved of his kids dating someone who wasn't from his social circle. My dad rebelled and secretly continued their relationship."

"Oh." I was speechless.

"Yeah, my grandpa is snobbish. He even tried to bribe my mom into not divorcing my dad because it would hurt his reputation, but she didn't care and divorced him anyway." Peter's laugh was full of sarcasm. "Everyone in the Sandridge family was shocked. A woman everyone thought was a perfect wife, a sweet daughter-in-law, and a gentle mom turned out to be a tigress after marrying my dad. A year after that, my dad married Jane's mom."

"B—but," I stuttered, "why did your grandpa allow them that time?"

"Because of Jane," Peter answered. "My sister was a brilliant woman. She had a sharp sense of business and could learn things quickly. My grandpa loved her and wanted her to be his ally, so he let her mom marry my dad."

My jaw dropped open. "And Tom's mom?"

"Tom's mom married my dad three years ago, after Jane's mom passed away. I'd say that's decent of her."

"I see." I gave a nod. "Now, your dad is with Tom's mom, but what about Eliza's mom?" I asked again.

Pursing his lips, Peter fiddled his sweater sleeve with one hand and didn't answer right away.

"Well…" He cleared his throat. "Her mom isn't interested in being with my dad. She just wanted to have a baby from a good man with good genes and a good family background. Once she became busy with her career, she gave Eliza to my dad to be raised. I was fifteen when Eliza was brought into the house." His shoulder dropped as he gazed at me. "See, you aren't the only one who's had a broken family. Mine is the worst!" he said bitterly.

"So," I licked my lower lip after digesting his story, "is that what you wanted to tell me?"

"No, that's the introduction." Peter's cheeks turned pink as he took my hand and cradled it in his.

Exhaling, he said, "I can't deny that I wanted you. It's hard to control myself whenever we're alone because you're so beautiful and sexy. But then…I realized that my family is messy because my dad couldn't control himself. He slept with numerous women and had kids with three of them. I don't want to be like him. I don't want to repeat my father's mistakes. I don't want my future children to face the same issues I've had.

"I'm not an innocent man either. I've made many of my own mistakes. I've been caught a few times for DUIs, speeding, and drinking. And…" He stopped for a second before continuing. "In my early twenties, I made a mistake that I've regretted for a long time, and I don't want it to happen again. Feeling ashamed, I swore on my mom's death bed that I would be a man who treated his woman with love and respect. I want to have a strong relationship with a woman I love based on trust, respect, and not based on sex." He laced his fingers with mine. "Earlier, if we'd continued, we might've had a few seconds of pleasure, but if one of us felt regret, it would affect our relationship in the long run. I don't want that."

I felt a gentle flutter in my chest while listening to his blunt confession and his wish for a loving relationship based on trust and respect, something I wanted to have too. I lowered my eyes. I couldn't meet his light brown eyes and the way they looked at me so tenderly. I murmured, "What a gentleman you are, Peter."

Peter leaned forward and placed his finger under my chin. "Now, you've heard my explanation and my confession. It's your turn to give me your explanation."

The flutter in my chest stopped, and I felt the tips of my fingers suddenly grow cold. Swallowing, I blinked and looked away.

"If you don't want to say it, that's okay. We can do it in some other time," he suggested.

"No." I shook my head, squeezing his hand. "I want to share it with you."

His eyes studied my face for a few beats, and he nodded, resting his elbows on his knees.

The air in the room was pleasant, but a cold sweat dripped

along my spine as I recognized the anger, self-loathing, and disgust spreading in my chest as if the sixteen-year-old me had taken over my body. Somehow, I even felt the cold shower hit my body.

After pondering, I decided not to tell him about how my first boyfriend had hurt me. I only told him the trauma I'd had because my last boyfriend kept mocking me for not having a thin body and then cheated on me while I was in the ER because of the strict diet I'd been following.

Peter's eyes were cold and stern while listening to me. Somehow, he sensed that I was hiding something, but he didn't ask for more. Sighing, he took my hands that had curled tightly into fists and smoothed them down before bringing them to his lips.

"I'm sorry for what he did to you," he said quietly. "I don't know how to comfort you. I can only promise that I won't do such things to you."

"Thanks." I bit my lower lip hard, and we fell silent.

"About earlier..." I broke the silence, gazing at him as he stared at my hands. "You were irresistible." My cheeks grew warm. "Although I was afraid of the possibility...and the warning kept flashing in my mind."

A smile crept onto his lips as Peter moved from his seat and sat next to me. With a sigh, he pulled my shoulder to lean on his chest. Against my ear, his heartbeat was thumping as hard as mine.

"Thank you for trusting me with your story," he whispered.

"Thanks for trusting me, too, with your reason." I glanced up.

He smiled as I leaned back.

The clock on the wall was ticking loudly as we fell into silence and listened to each other's breathing and heartbeat.

"Rory," Peter broke the silence, "I have a request."

"What's that?"

"Would you mind sleeping in my room tonight?" He looked deep into my eyes. "Not that kind of sleep," he corrected quickly, as he must have noticed a surprise in my eyes. "What I mean is that I want you to sleep next to me, by my side, so I can see you before I go to sleep and after I wake up in the morning."

I sat straight on my seat, pondering his words, and nodded. "With one condition."

"Huh?"

"Let's move your bed near the window, because it has a perfect view for indoor stargazing."

He widened his eyes and then chuckled. "Okay, let's do it."

With our hands intertwined, we went upstairs to his room and pushed the bed near the window to see the starry sky. The night was clear, and we could see the face of the man in the moon. I even swore that I could see the Milky Way.

Peter seemed to have a hard time opening his eyes once we were in bed. We'd been gazing up for some time, but there hadn't been any of the shooting stars I'd hoped to see.

"Don't sleep yet," I begged, shaking his shoulder. "Wait for a shooting star."

Nodding, he yawned, and his eyes closed again. I scoffed and turned to the sky. Then I saw something. "Peter, look!" I squealed.

Two incredible streaks of light sliced across the dark sky, leaving behind a short trail of light. The sky turned dark again, and stars twinkled shyly.

"Peter, did you…" My voice trailed off as I found he was deep in slumber.

"You missed it." I tsked. "Oh well."

Lying on my back next to him, I gazed up at the sky. An old song that my mom used to sing for me during our stargazing floated in my mind. Inadvertently, I hummed the melody while waiting for another shooting star.

Chapter 13

$\mathcal{A}$ FEW DAYS HAD PASSED SINCE I'd flown back to Boston, and in two more days, we would celebrate Christmas. I couldn't wait because Christmas had always been my favorite holiday.

It would have been nice if Peter could join my aunt and me for Christmas. Unfortunately, Peter had an annual Christmas dinner with his family in London. Otherwise, we would have celebrated the holiday together.

Veles Capital's office had been beautifully decorated, and that day, we had our annual Christmas luncheon followed by the exchanging of gifts in the lunchroom.

"Rory, come on. It's time for our gift exchange," Marsha called to me.

I stopped typing and looked at her. "It's time for that already? Wow, time flies." I opened a drawer and took out a gift: a sweater from Downtown Disney, purchased when Peter and I had visited there. I'd bought it in a neutral color so anybody could wear it.

"Oh, that's so cute!" Marsha took it from my hand. "Can I have it?"

I laughed. "Wait until you can steal it from someone."

She wrinkled her nose. "Yeah, that's what I don't like about the white elephant gift exchange's rules. Someone will steal it from me if I take it first."

"I'll buy you another one when we go to California next month," I promised.

Her eyes widened. "Really?"

I nodded, pointing at her belly. "If not, your baby will blame me for making her mom miserable."

Marsha grinned, caressing her baby bump.

"Ladies, aren't you joining us for the gift exchange?" someone yelled from the corridor.

"We're coming!" I yelled back.

The lunchroom was packed when we arrived. Piles of unwrapped gifts sat on the portable stage next to a ten-foot Christmas tree, so everybody could see and choose what they wanted. During the gift exchange, exclamations were heard from people who received an item they liked but had it stolen by someone else. It was a fun day for everyone in the office, and I was enjoying it until Kelly stumbled near me, and her cheesecake, which we had for dessert, fell on my sweater. I cleaned it with water, but the cheese smell lingered, and my sweater was wet.

In the cubicle, I rubbed my arms, feeling cold without my sweater. Wearing my heavy outer coat wouldn't be comfortable, but it was better than nothing.

"Shouldn't you look happy with my stolen gift, Arrington?"

I looked up to see Ryan standing at my cubicle entrance with a gift bag in hand. He looked handsome in his white sweater. At our luncheon, women had whispered about how his sweater made him stand out from everyone else wearing Christmas-themed clothes. I'd agreed with them and found myself taking him in as if I hadn't remembered what he looked like—his blue eyes, his short, messy hair, his sweet smile, his dimples. Then, when I realized what I'd done, it ticked me off.

"Of course, I'm happy," I said casually. "My old speaker stopped working, and when I had a chance to get a new one, I snagged it."

"Meany Rory." He chuckled, sitting in the empty chair next in my cubicle and putting the bag on my desk. "As the person who switched my speaker with a jigsaw puzzle, you should take responsibility and help me finish it."

"Didn't you say that you were still jet-lagged? Puzzles are good for killing time, right?" I laughed, eyeing the bag. "Kelly likes playing puzzles. Ask her to help you."

Ryan pouted. "Do you think I came here to hear your suggestion to ask Kelly to help me? If I wanted her help, I would've asked her directly." His eyes remained locked on mine. "You know who I like the most."

I closed my eyes, avoiding his stare. "Ryan, you know that I can't retu—"

Before I could finish my sentence, Ryan leaned forward and placed his forefinger on my lips. I opened my eyes and widened them as I felt something buzz gently in the pit of my stomach in response to his touch.

"I don't want to hear that," he said, his voice strained. He pulled his finger away. His eyes fixed briefly on my lips before he shifted them away and pushed to his feet. "Merry Christmas, Rory. I hope you like the present I gave you, and wear the sweater if you don't want to catch a cold in winter." Then he left without waiting for my response.

My heart pounded as the warmth of his finger lingered on my lips. I slapped my forehead. "Stop that!"

After collecting my thoughts, I reached into the bag and pulled out a cranberry-colored sweater with a note that said, "It's mine, and it's clean," pinned on it, and a gift neatly wrapped in red and green paper. I looked hesitantly at the sweater but decided to wear it since I was freezing. The scent of detergent wafted into my nose when I put it on.

I noticed a little note underneath the ribbon. It said, "From R to R. You make this season very special and magical for me. Merry Christmas."

Ryan's handwriting was usually hard to read. You generally couldn't tell the difference between his *L*s and his *I*s, but he'd written this message neatly. For a few seconds, I let my fingers run over the note. Then, I ripped the note off the box before tearing it into pieces and tossing it into the trash can.

Chapter 14

MY AUNT AND I HAD just finished our dinner and were doing the dishes when the doorbell rang.

"Are you expecting someone?" I glanced at my aunt.

"No."

"Who's here at this hour on Christmas Eve? Our party's tomorrow. Let me check."

"Just ignore it, Rory," my aunt said. "Maybe it's a solicitor selling things in the neighborhood."

Following my aunt's suggestion, I returned to the dishes. But the bell rang again, followed by two knocks on the door.

"Okay, I have to check," I said, taking my washing gloves off and setting them on the edge of the sink.

The wind was blowing hard as I opened the front door. Peter, with his black-and-white plaid topcoat and tartan wool scarf around his neck, stood under the porch light, grinning and slinging a backpack on his shoulders.

"Wha—" I didn't finish my sentence because he leaned in and gave me a quick kiss. His lips were cold from the wind.

"Who is it, Rory?" my aunt asked from inside.

"It's me, Auntie," Peter answered loudly before I could.

I heard a stifled shriek followed by scurrying footsteps. My aunt pulled the door open wide when she reached my side.

"Peter, you're here!" She smiled, stretching her arms out to hug him.

Taking a step back, I raised my eyebrows. She seemed happier to see Peter than she'd been to see me, her niece. I'd received no excitement from her when I arrived home from my business trip.

While hugging my aunt, Peter caught my expression. Grinning widely, he mouthed, "I love you."

I wrinkled my nose in return but then mouthed, "I love you too."

"Come on in, come on in," Aunt Amy said after releasing Peter. "It's cold outside. Are you hungry?"

"Don't worry, Auntie, I'm—"

"Oh, look!" I interrupted his words, raising my hand, palm up. "It's snowing."

A soft, fluffy snowflake floated down from the dark sky and landed on my palm. In unison, Peter and I stepped outside and looked skyward.

Oblivious to the cold, I reached for his hand. "Beautiful, isn't it?"

"Yes." He nodded, stretching out his other hand to catch a flake.

"If it's snowing hard tonight, I could get my white Christmas," I said wistfully.

Peter looked at me. "Next year, come with me to England. I'll give you a white Christmas."

Before I said anything, my aunt urged from inside, "Come on, kiddos, it's cold outside. "You must be hungry," she said as Peter and I stepped inside.

"A little bit," he said, taking off his topcoat and his scarf and hanging them on the coatrack.

"Let me heat up some food," my aunt said before she turned to me. "Get some hot tea for Peter, dear. He must be cold." Then she went to the kitchen.

I turned to Peter and asked, "Who's her family—you or me?"

Peter snickered, but he cupped my face and kissed me. "I'm her favorite one," he said.

Before I responded, my aunt called from the kitchen and asked me for help.

"Just wait here for a second, favorite one," I told him. "I'll humbly bring food and tea for you." I gave an exaggerated bow.

An hour later, Peter sat on the sofa in the living room with me. Aunt Amy had remained with him while he ate. Then she went upstairs to find an extra pillow and blanket so that he could sleep comfortably on the couch that night.

"I thought you couldn't come," I said when we were alone.

Peter raised a shoulder. "To be honest, I don't really know what happened. After you left, I worked hard, sometimes until midnight. Then, two days ago, my dad said I didn't have to attend the annual Christmas dinner, but he wants me in London for the New Year, so here I am. And," he pulled out a camcorder from his backpack, "I brought this again so I can record my first Christmas with you like I did our first Thanksgiving."

"Speaking of which, you haven't given us the Thanksgiving video yet," I said.

He nodded. "Sorry, I promise I'll give it to you together with the Christmas video."

"Peter, why did your dad change his mind?" I asked, leaning back in my seat and watching him put his camera away. "From what you said about him, he sounds like a strict person. He might be stricter than my aunt. The fact that he let you go so easily seems odd, don't you think?"

"I don't care why he did it." He smiled. "The important thing is that I'm here now."

"Yup." I was leaning forward to kiss him when my aunt called me to bring Peter's bedding down.

"I'm coming," I responded, almost rolling my eyes.

I stole a quick kiss from Peter before heading up. When I came back down with the items, I handed them to him.

"Here's your blanket and pillow," I said, "and your towel is the blue one in the guest bathroom."

"Thank you," he said, putting the bedding on the couch.

It made me smile to see his glowing face, as though sleeping on our old couch thrilled him. Although my aunt didn't mind him staying here, he could have slept on a bed in any expensive hotel he wished. I wondered if it would have been better for him to stay at the hotel than here, at my aunt's house.

Peter was one of the most unique men I'd ever encountered, which was one of the main reasons I fell in love with him. The most important thing was I loved having him there at Christmas.

Chapter 15

ON CHRISTMAS DAY, OUR GUESTS enjoyed my aunt's food and cakes and continually praised her. Her cheeks were pink and her eyes twinkled, making her appear ten years younger. I thought she should smile like that more often, rather than looking stoic every day.

I looked around at my aunt's friends: Aunt and Uncle Tanaka; Sonia Warren, her husband, John Warren, and their twelve-year-old daughter, Keira; Luther Owen and his wife. I used to feel guilty when my aunt got sick and I wasn't there for her. Now, I felt better knowing that she had good friends around her who could help right away when she needed.

Other than my aunt, Peter was the happiest person at the party.

Although Peter's birthday was in the first week of January, my aunt decided to advance it and give him a surprise party. She probably remembered the story I'd told her about how Peter, when he was a child, had always had his birthday alone without his parents. When she entered the room holding the cake, everyone except Peter and I sang "Happy Birthday."

A big smile split his face, and he blew out his candles while receiving birthday wishes from people he'd just met. He looked like a happy little boy when he opened his presents.

His favorite present was a navy blue sweater with an intricate cable pattern, knitted by my aunt. It came with a matching scarf and beanie. The sweater fit perfectly, as though my aunt could measure with her eyes. Her cheeks reddened when Peter threw his arms around her in thanks for the gift.

He didn't seem excited when he opened my Christmas gift: Montblanc cufflinks with silver and black onyx. Didn't he know that they cost me more than two hundred bucks before shipping?

I was sitting on the porch swing when Peter came outside, holding a cup in each hand. From the smell, I knew it was apple cider.

"There you are! I was looking for you," he said, handing me a cup and sitting next to me. "Aunt Amy told me to bring you this because you love it so much."

"Hey, there." I took the cup from him, looking with envy at my aunt's sweater that he wore. "Thank you."

"'Hey, *there*'?" he asked, repeating my words.

"Hey, babe, love, handsome," I teased him.

He chuckled. "What are you doing out here? Why don't you join us?"

"I'll come in later," I answered casually. "It's a bit stuffy inside."

"Are you okay?" he asked, studying my face. "It doesn't sound like you're in a good mood."

"I'm fine."

"You don't sound fine." He took the apple cider cup from my hand despite my protests. Putting our cups on the bench, he crouched in front of me and stopped the swing with his hands. "Tell me what happened."

"I told you, I'm fine," I said stubbornly.

He studied my face. "Are you upset about something?"

"Nope," I said, shaking my head.

"Hmm." Peter sat next to me.

The swing swung gently as he used his feet to push it. For a few minutes, we rocked in silence.

"Are you going to wear the gift I gave you?" I asked suddenly.

He nodded. "Only if I'm wearing a long-sleeved shirt. Why do you ask?"

I pouted. "Because you didn't look happy when you opened my present."

"I *am* happy."

"No, you aren't."

He chuckled and turned me to face him. "Why do you think I'm not happy?" His gaze made my heart flutter.

"You didn't seem as excited as you were when you opened the present from Auntie Amy," I said. "Don't you know I had to rack my brain to come up with that gift?" I mumbled under my breath.

"Why did you rack your brain to get me a gift?" His eyebrows drew together.

I sighed. "Peter, you're a man who has everything. I wanted to buy something special, something memorable. It took me a long time to find the cufflinks that I felt matched your personality, hoping you'd remember me each time you wore them."

Peter looked at me, and then I saw a tear drop as he looked down.

"Peter?" I jerked my head back. "Are you crying?"

He sniffed, wrapping an arm around my waist to hug me close. "No one has ever taken such time and effort to buy me something. Or to knit a sweater like your aunt did," he said softly. "I feel loved." Pulling back, he smiled as our eyes met. "Thank you, Rory. You and your Aunt Amy make me feel like I'm worthy and appreciated."

"Even though, sometimes, my aunt scolds you or asks you to vacuum the carpet or do the dishes?"

"Yes, even then. You don't know how happy it made me every time she asked me to do something or scolded me. It meant she was treating me like a regular person. You don't know how many parents of girls I've dated treated me special because of my money or my family's status. They hoped their daughter would marry me. Many times, when they invited me to go on vacation with them, they gave me the green light to sleep in their daughter's room. Well, they didn't say it directly, but I knew what they wanted." His cheeks flushed suddenly. "Their acts disgusted me, and I refused to be part of their schemes. That's why I respect Auntie Amy's strictness, because she doesn't use you to get to me, and that makes me want to protect you even more. Now you know why I prefer to stay in her house over a hotel, because I feel like I'm at home here."

I stared at him in disbelief. I'd never thought I would meet someone who admired my aunt's strictness and didn't mind being scolded by her.

Peter leaned forward, putting his lips next to my ear. "Next time, don't rack your brain trying to buy me something. You're the best gift I could ever have," he whispered.

I closed my eyes as the tingling sensation from his breath spread from my neck down to my arms and chest. When I opened my eyes, Peter grinned mischievously. I knew he'd done it on purpose. Laughing, he jumped from the swing and ran toward the house when I wanted to get my revenge.

As I caught him, Keira, Sonia's daughter, shrieked and pointed at us. "Kissing time!"

Peter and I stopped and looked around.

Luther laughed. "You guys should kiss," he said, pointing at the mistletoe hanging above us.

"Kiss! Kiss! Kiss!" people chanted.

"Yeah, a looooong and passionate one," sang Uncle Tanaka, turning Peter's camera to us. He'd volunteered to record our Christmas party so Peter could be in the video, too.

"Yes!" shouted the others.

My aunt chuckled, shaking her head.

With a big smile on his face, Peter turned me to face him and proceeded to kiss me long and passionately. It would have been better if we were alone. I heard cheers and whistles. They grew even louder when Peter bowed and waved at everyone after kissing me.

"You enjoyed that, didn't you?" I hissed, forcing a smile.

People continued to gaze at us until we sat on the sofa.

"Very much," he whispered cheerfully. "Too bad no one took a picture, because I'd love to have a picture of your lobster face."

"Shut it." I pinched his arm.

"Ouch!" he shouted, rubbing the pinched spot. "That hurt."

I made a face and, leaving him alone, I went upstairs to the second floor.

Chapter 16

I WAS IN MY AUNT'S BATHROOM, looking for a new toothbrush in the cabinet under the sink, when I heard voices. At first, I thought it was my aunt.

"Amy said she has piles of garments for our Sunday school class in her room. I can't see them," Sonia's voice rang out.

"Maybe they're inside her closet?" Aunt Tanaka replied. Footsteps shuffled and a closet door slid open.

"By the way," said Sonia, "do you think they'll marry soon?"

Aunt Tanaka chuckled. "That's a good question. We should ask Amy later."

"I bet it'll be sooner," said Sonia confidently. "They look good together. Have you seen the way Peter looks at Rory? Oh my God, my heart is pounding now."

"He can't take his eyes off her. It's hard to find a refined young man like him. Young men nowadays are less polite and respectful of others, even their girlfriends," said Aunt Tanaka. "Too bad my only daughter's already married. If not, I'd ask Peter if he had a single friend."

The women chuckled.

"Yes, I agree. I hope when Keira grows up she'll meet someone nice like Peter," said Sonia. "Oh, hey, I think I found the stuff Amy was talking about. It's behind the door."

"Good, I can take them with me and give them to the church's drama club tomorrow."

"Okay, let's go back downstairs. We can tell Amy that we found them."

The shuffling sounds of their footsteps departed, echoing on the narrow hallway before going down the stairs.

My cheeks burned at having eavesdropped on their conversation. Before going out, I peeked behind the door to make sure no one had stayed behind.

"Is it true that Peter always follows me with his eyes?" I wondered aloud, feeling giddy at the thought.

As I went downstairs, I noticed Peter in the living room with the men. They were watching TV while discussing football, which Peter had developed a liking for since moving to California.

I didn't join them but passed in front of them so I could see if Sonia's words were true. My heart jumped when Peter gave me a quick glance in the middle of the men's heated discussion.

Later, when I was speaking to my aunt, he turned his head just to see where I was. He gave me a small smile when our eyes met before he turned to Luther, who had asked him something.

Warmth expanded in my chest, and I smiled. I tried to wipe the grin from my face, but it kept returning.

"Rory, did you hear what I said?" My aunt's voice brought me back to the room and our conversation.

"Uh…yes." I turned my attention to her. "The garments."

"Garments?" She raised her eyebrows. "I asked you to bring the chicken pot pie to Ruth, our next-door neighbor, after the party."

"Yes, the chicken pot pie. Yes, absolutely," I said with an exaggerated nod.

Aunt Amy shook her head and mumbled, "Girls nowadays."

Chapter 17

THE PLANE WAS HALF FULL, and only seven passengers, including Peter, were in business class. He didn't know how many people sat in the economic class, but the line had been shorter than usual.

Christmas had only been two days before, but many people would still be on vacation until after New Year's Day. It made sense, as there were only six days between Christmas and the New Year. Not many people, including him, were lucky enough to take a week-long vacation. The offices in California and Vancouver were both open.

Whoever said it was easy working for family was wrong. They should have worked for the Sandridge family just once, then they would have revised their comments. Among other private companies in Britain, the Sandridge Group was known as a company that valued hard work and dedication, which meant working long hours. In their opinion, twenty-four hours a day wasn't long enough.

Peter wasn't looking forward to the annual New Year's dinner. He'd dodged it in the past, but he couldn't anymore, especially after accepting his current position. The people he cared for the most wouldn't be at the party. Granny Philippa was too sick and weak to attend. Jane had already passed away. Tom, ever the rebellious one, wouldn't be at the party, but no one really cared about him—including his mom—since he'd come out of the closet. Perhaps Aunt Helen would be happy to see him again. Maybe even his sister, Eliza, if she wasn't still upset with him.

Eliza was a talented fashion designer. Before she had reached the age of twenty, her collection had become known amongst high-profile people in London. Last year, he'd been invited to attend her fashion show, and his presence had stolen the spotlight at the event. That was an insult for Eliza, who was overly competitive with her siblings. He mentally cringed at the events leading to her agitation.

Absently, he pulled out his phone to make a call.

"Hi, Peter!" a cheerful voice said on the other end of the line.

Peter broke into a smile. "Hi, Rory."

"Do you miss me already?" she teased him.

He chuckled. "I always miss you."

"I like it," she said. "By the way, Auntie said you forgot your T-shirt. I can mail it to you, or bring it with me when I go to California next month?"

"Yeah, bring it with you so you'll have another reason to see me."

She laughed.

"How's the office?" he asked. He loved hearing her talk in her crisp, melodic voice.

"It's quiet now—only a few people here," Rory responded. "Sally, Marsha, and Tony are off until the beginning of January. Ryan said it'll be slow like this until around January fifth. I like it, actually. No phone calls from clients either. It'll be nice to relax until then. I'm a lazy person, huh?"

"No, you're not."

"Are you saying that because I'm your girlfriend?" Rory laughed.

"I guess so." He laughed too. "By the way, who's Ryan?"

"Oh, he works in the same department as me. I haven't mentioned his name yet?"

"Not so far. You've mentioned Sally and Marsha. Was he also on the last business trip?"

"Yes, he was. Oh, you met him briefly when you dropped me off that Monday, remember?"

A deep crease appeared between his thick eyebrows, and then, a second later, he nodded. "Oh, that one, yes—the good-looking guy. Now I can put a name to his face."

"Ryan was my classmate during my first two years of college," Rory said. "Then we barely saw each other because we had different majors. Isn't it funny that we met years later at the office?"

"Yup, that's unusual. I hope he treats you well since you're new. He's a senior there, right?"

"Don't worry. Ryan's a nice person."

"I see." He nodded as though she sat in front of him. "Anyway, what's your plan for the New Year?"

"Um, we won't have a gathering, that's for sure. On New Year's Eve, Auntie usually goes to the midnight service at her church after dinner. The next day, we'll have a simple lunch together," she said. "I wish you were here with us."

"I wish the same," Peter said, sighing silently. "When will you fly back to California? I won't be back until mid-January. My grandpa has something to discuss with me, and that kind of thing usually takes a while." He chewed on his lower lip, stopping himself from saying more than he should. "Oh, Rory, I forgot to give you my house key. I want you to stay in my house even when I'm not there."

"That's okay. I'll stay in the hotel," she said.

Peter frowned. He was happy that his girlfriend was independent and didn't take advantage of his wealth, but he wasn't happy when she refused his offers. As her boyfriend, he wanted to spoil her, but she never accepted it. Maybe this was a normal feeling when a man dated an independent woman.

"Peter, are you there?" Rory asked, bringing him back to the conversation.

"Yes, yes, I'm here." He cleared his throat. "Sorry, my mind started wandering for a moment. I'll let you get back to work, and I'll text you when I arrive."

"Yes, please," she begged. "I'll be worried if you don't."

"Don't worry, I will," he promised. "I miss you."

"I miss you too," she said, and hung up.

Peter gazed at his phone before putting it in the small compartment. After reclining his seat, he looked at the ceiling until he found himself drifting off to sleep.

Chapter 18

As planned, Sally, Ryan, and I returned to California after the New Year. We'd arrived three days before, working like crazy to catch up on the things that we'd left before the holiday.

I glanced at my phone as I waited for a printout of the financial report. I hadn't seen a text from Peter since we'd spoken on New Year's Eve, almost a week before. I frowned. I'd sent him a few texts, but he'd never responded. I felt uneasy.

Is he sick? Did he have an accident?

If something had happened, Tom would have informed me. No news from Tom meant everything was okay.

"Maybe I should text Tom," I decided, taking the printout from the tray. While holding the paper to my chest, I typed a message.

> *Hi, Tom. How are you? I hope you had a good time in London with your family.*

I pressed the send button.

I was walking down the narrow hallway to Martin's office when my phone buzzed with a text.

> *Hi, Rory. I'm great. Actually, I didn't go there this year. Didn't Peter tell you?*

I raised an eyebrow. Peter had told me that the New Year's gathering was a must for the whole family, but Tom hadn't gone?

> *No, Peter didn't mention it. He hasn't returned from London yet.*

A second later, he replied.

> *Maybe he had an urgent thing to do there. Well, don't worry, your bae will return sooner than the blink of an eye. If I have any updates, I'll let you know.*

I chuckled after reading his text. I was typing my response when I sensed someone walking toward me, but I was too late. We collided. I dropped my phone and my papers, and they all fell to the carpet.

"Oh, I'm sorry," I said in unison with the person who had collided with me. I glanced up and saw Sam, the attorney, who also happened to be working on the same project as me.

"Rory," he said in surprise. His finger adjusted his glasses that had gone a little lopsided. "Sorry, I was checking my phone. Did I hurt you?"

"I'm okay," I said. "I was looking at my phone too."

Sam crouched and helped me gather my papers. He picked up my cell phone, glancing at it before handing it to me. "This is yours."

"And this is yours," I said, giving him his phone.

Our eyes met, and we laughed together.

"We were too busy with our phones to look where we were going," he said.

I nodded. "True. Maybe HR should put out a 'No texting in the hallway' warning."

"Ha ha ha. That's a good idea. Are you sure you're okay?"

"Yes, no worries. Hey, I gotta go. Sally's waiting for this report. See you"—I glanced at my watch—"at the two o'clock meeting?"

"Yes, see you there."

Chapter 19

"**Y**OU MADE ME LIE TO her." Tom placed his phone on the coffee table next to a few empty beer bottles.

Peter groaned and rubbed his hands across his unshaven face. His clothes were rumpled, and his hair was unkempt.

It was unusual for Peter to drink alcohol at this hour. He'd been sober for years. But something had upset him. He'd seemed furious and agitated since his return from London. He hadn't even contacted Rory.

Tom sighed and tented his hands in front of his mouth, looking at his brother's miserable face. For years, he'd always thought that he was the unlucky one. His mom was a smart and pretty American model. She'd quit modeling because she'd fallen in love with a wealthy married man before becoming his mistress for a decade. Tom didn't understand why she'd done it, because it had always been easy for her to find a good man. But somehow, she'd fallen in love with the wrong man, Archie Ryder.

When he was twelve, his mom had brought him to Archie's house, where he'd met his half siblings, Jane and Peter. He'd hated them instantly and wanted to run away.

Jane had helped him in the transition. Her gentle words made it easier to stay in the house, and she'd been a bridge between him and Peter. Since his mom was not always at home, and Peter's mom had left, they decided to call Jane their "little mom."

When Jane passed away, Tom became depressed and swore never to return to London. Like Peter, he'd never had a close relationship with his mother. Losing Jane was like losing his own mom.

When he'd discovered that the ignorant, wild, and unruly Peter had unexpectedly agreed to become the president of White Water, entangling himself in the Sandridge businesses, he'd been surprised. Any time Tom had asked about it, Peter had remained tight-lipped.

"Didn't you say that Grandpa only asked you to take Mr. Fournier's daughter out on weekends while she worked on her master's degree here? Why has this caused you to start drinking again? And why are you ignoring Rory? She's innocent."

Peter scoffed. "You're talking like you've never met the old man. He's interfered in Jane's life, my mom's life, and now he's doing it to me."

"Well, you shouldn't immediately assume that Grandpa wants to pair you up with Sophie. Maybe that's not his intent." Tom leaned back in his seat.

Another scoff came from his half brother. "You must've forgotten his attempt to match you up before you came out last year. That's how he is, Tom—always trying to throw us together with his business connections' children."

"Yeah, I remember," Tom said, nodding. "But you shouldn't throw such a tantrum. I don't mind seeing your anger, but don't do that to Rory. She doesn't know anything about this. And maybe, if you hadn't taken the job, this wouldn't have happened," he added.

Peter slouched. "I promised her."

Tom's ears pricked up. "Her? Do you mean Jane?" he asked curiously. "Come on, tell me the truth. Was it Jane who asked you to take the position? I know Grandpa let her manage White Water."

A flush rose in Peter's cheeks, and he shifted awkwardly. "Stop asking about that," he said. "About Sophie. I can't tell Rory that I'm babysitting a girl who's been forced on me by my grandpa."

Tom sighed. "I suggest focusing on maintaining your schedule while Rory's here. I can help you take Sophie out while you're with her. She knows me, Theo, and Emma as well. We can help."

"You don't know Sophie." Peter shook his head. "She's stubborn, and she expects to get what she wants. If she wants me to entertain her, it has to be me."

"Sure, but you can take me with you. No one ever said that you have to accompany her alone, right?"

Peter blinked and nodded slowly. "That's right."

"See, if you share your burden, I can help you." Tom shoved him playfully. "You owe me this time."

Refusing to retaliate or budge from where he sat, Peter gave him a thin smile.

"By the way, I don't understand. You're usually confident around women. Why do you seem intimidated by Sophie?" Tom raised his eyebrows.

Peter looked away, seeming to deeply consider the question, then turned to Tom. "It's complicated."

"I'm listening." Tom leaned forward and nodded encouragement.

Peter sighed. "Do you remember how she looked when she was young?"

Tom nodded. "She was chubby, like her dad, with thick glasses and braces. Kids teased her when they came to our family parties."

"Yup," Peter confirmed. "And one time, I found her crying. Feeling sorry for her, I attempted to comfort her. Since then, she's followed me around whenever we would get together. When she turned ten, she stopped coming. Years later, on Jane's birthday, she showed up again looking totally different. Her glasses and braces were gone, and now she's thin and pretty."

"Yeah, she was the prettiest girl at the birthday party." Tom nodded. "How could an ugly duckling turn into such a beautiful swan?"

"Plastic surgery, for sure."

Tom's eyes widened. "Wow…that must've been painful surgery. Looking at her perfect nose, I'll bet that was two procedures alone. And I couldn't even tell you about the rest."

"Her family can afford it," Peter said indifferently.

"Did she really do that for *you*? You aren't a handsome guy." He received a pillow in his face a split second after the words were out of his mouth.

"I was handsome, even back then."

Laughing, Tom threw the pillow back at Peter. "She must be blind." His laughter faded when he noticed a deep crease across his brother's forehead. "What happened?"

"On my twenty-second birthday, I was hanging out at the bar with my close friends. You were already in America at that time. Sophie and her friends showed up. My friends and I were tipsy. She offered to drive me back to my apartment. I didn't want to, but it was better than getting a DUI. Mom was sick at the time and I didn't want to upset her by being arrested. So, I let Sophie drive me to my apartment, but she drove me to *her* apartment instead."

"Oh!" Tom exclaimed.

"And…" Peter paused, swallowing. "I don't know what happened. Vaguely, I remember her dropping me on her sofa. Then, she…" He shook his head. "I don't remember any details. I just know that when I woke up, I was on her bed, she was next to me, and we were naked. I got scared, grabbed my clothes, and left."

"Is that the reason you've been reluctant to see her after that night?" Tom's eyes widened when he noticed Peter's ashen face. "Was she…?" His voice trailed off while his hand rubbed his own belly.

Peter looked down at his hands and nodded. "One night, she called me and said that she hadn't had her period in two months.

I felt panicked and hopeless. I didn't want to be like Archie, so I offered to marry her, but she refused because she didn't want her daddy to cut her from the family's will and living trust if he knew that she was pregnant out of marriage."

Tom sat quietly, giving his brother time to talk.

"When I asked her if the baby was mine, she said yes. She even had a picture of me naked and in her arms."

"What? That's crazy!"

Peter rubbed his face. "She claimed that she'd been happy to sleep with me and had taken a selfie. Then she told me that she planned to abort the baby in a week, but a couple of days later, she called me, crying."

Tom remained silent.

"She was in pain and urged me to come. When I got to her apartment, she was lying on the living room floor, and blood was everywhere. I panicked and brought her to the hospital. The doctor said she'd had a miscarriage, and that she'd been pregnant for nine or ten weeks. He suggested letting the miscarriage progress naturally, but Sophie forced him to perform a dilation and curettage to finish things off."

Tom stared at him, his mouth agape.

"I detested myself. Although she had a miscarriage, I felt guilty. If I hadn't gotten drunk, I wouldn't have slept with her."

"Did Jane know?"

"Yes. Marcus and Mom also knew. I asked for Mom's forgiveness on her death bed." Peter rubbed his eyes. "I swore to her that I'd only sleep with a woman I loved and was married to. I don't want to walk in Archie's footsteps, sleeping with women freely and ending up with multiple children."

Tom nodded. "I see. Now I understand why you'd stopped drinking until…last summer, when Rory kicked you out."

Peter sighed, but a small smile appeared when his girlfriend's name was mentioned. It lasted for only a moment before it disappeared. "Yeah, I was devastated because I'd never been in love like that before."

"How about you and Rory? Were you guys…?"

Peter's face twitched. "Rory's special. She isn't timid, but I have this urge to protect her from everyone, including myself. I'm always afraid I'll lose control whenever I'm around her. But I swear to you, I don't want to be like Archie. I want to honor her, build a trusting relationship, and avoid any possible regret in the future. I would never want us to be in a position where we're getting married just because she's already pregnant. That's something I want to avoid. I know I'm ready to marry her, but it's too soon for her, and I don't want to scare her off. So…" He sighed, wanting to pull his hair out. "With Sophie in town, I'm scared that my secret will come out. I'd be crushed if Rory left me, and you know how orthodox her aunt is."

"By not letting her know that you're already in town, you aren't treating her well, bro," said Tom. "Trust can't be built in a night, just so you know." He reached for Peter's phone and threw it to him. "Call her. Don't let her wait too long." He met his brother's eyes. "You've backed me up when I was in trouble, so it's my turn to have your back. Now, call Rory. She's waiting for you."

Chapter 20

OUR TWO O'CLOCK MEETING THAT should have only been an hour long had dragged into three hours. As we left the conference, my eyes felt heavy. Sally and Ryan looked tired, too, with dark circles under their eyes.

I ate my dinner alone in a kebab restaurant. We usually ate together, but Ryan had dinner plans with his high school friend who lived near our hotel, and Sally had a video call scheduled with her husband and kids. After dinner, I went to a boba tea place in the same shopping center.

I was waiting for my drink when my phone buzzed. My heart skipped a beat as I saw Peter's name on the caller ID.

"Hey!" A few people inside the store looked up from their phones and toward me at hearing my loud, excited voice. "How are you, stranger?"

"Hi, Rory." I heard a smile in his voice. "Do you consider me a stranger now?"

"Yup, since you went MIA," I said, emphasizing the letters. "Has all the Wi-Fi in London been disconnected for nearly three weeks? Or did your dog run away with your phone?"

"Missing in action? Really?" Peter laughed.

"Yeah, yeah, yeah, keep laughing now," I said.

"You sound upset. Did you miss me that much?"

"No. Who said I missed you?" I gave a huff as I heard the store call my order number. "Hey, could you wait for a second?" Without waiting for his answer, I picked up my order and took it with me.

"Are you in your favorite boba place?" asked Peter when I brought my phone back to my ear. "Can you wait for me there?"

I shook my head as if he could see me. "Nope."

"You're mad at me," he said, and I detected remorse in his voice.

"I'm not. I'm just waiting for someone to say sorry for not calling or texting me," I said, walking to my rental car.

"Who did that to you?" Peter teased.

I rolled my eyes and started the car after putting my phone in its holder. "I have to hang up because I'm going to drive now. Bye, Peter."

"Hey!" I heard Peter shout.

"What?" I asked impatiently.

"I'll meet you at your hotel."

"I'm not going back to my hotel."

Peter chuckled. "It's almost eight in the evening. Where are you going if not to your hotel? Not to my house, for sure, since you're upset with me."

"Peter Ryder, you underestimate me. I have other friends here."

"I believe you and I'll see you at your hotel."

"You don't know where I'm staying."

"Of course, I know," he said stubbornly. "You texted me, remember?"

"You got my text, so why didn't you text me back?" I grunted silently. "Bye, Peter." I turned the phone off and headed toward the street.

When I stepped into the hotel lobby, Peter was already there. His hair was a bit longer and messier than usual, but it didn't hide his handsome face. If I hadn't been upset, I would have jumped and hugged him. As our eyes met, he smiled, but it didn't quite reach his eyes.

I didn't say anything but continued walking to the elevator. Peter followed in silence until we got to my floor and left the elevator. Once the door closed, he held my elbow. "Rory, please don't be mad. I'm sorry for not contacting you."

I pouted and turned to leave, but Peter blocked the way and hugged me.

"Sorry. I'm so sorry," he whispered.

Sighing, I hugged him with one arm since I was holding my drink in the other hand. We didn't move for a few moments, feeling each other's heartbeat, until I heard a soft ding from the elevator and pulled away.

"Let's go to my room, so we won't bother people," I said.

Peter nodded and walked behind me down the long, dull corridor covered by a leafy-patterned beige carpet. We stopped in front of my room. I unlocked the door and held it open for Peter to step inside.

"You can sit there if you want to." I pointed at a chair with my chin while putting the drink on the TV stand.

"Nice room," he commented, looking around. It must have been different from any hotel he'd ever stayed in. I had a standard hotel room with two queen-size beds, a table, an arm sofa near the big windows, a desk with a chair, a television, a telephone, and a coffee maker.

"Yeah, not bad for a budget hotel. As long as it's clean, I'm okay. And housekeeping has responded promptly every time I've needed something." I took off my jacket and hung it on one of the hangers. "Compared to the last hotel, this room is—"

Before I could finish, Peter hugged me from behind. His breath was hot on the tip of my ear. "Sorry for making you wait for me," he said, his voice low. "A lot of things happened while I was in London, and most of them upset me. I know that's a lame excuse, but..." His arms tightened around me. "I'm sorry. And I don't blame you for being upset."

"Well..." I cleared my throat. "Maybe you already forgot what we promised before we started dating. Didn't we agree to be honest with each other?" I sighed as his head rested on my shoulder. "I'd understand if you did that and we'd only been dating a month, but we've been dating for a few months now. Shouldn't we be a bit more comfortable about sharing things? I thought after sharing our sensitive issues last month, we should feel more comfortable with each other. Obviously, I was wrong. Am I not worthy enough to share your burden?"

"No," Peter said quickly. He turned me to face him. "I always want to share it with you because I want you to know me better. I want you to trust me and feel comfortable around me. I just... uh, this time is different, but..." He looked into my eyes. "Rory, I've always felt comfortable around you. Still, there are many things that I have a hard time sharing with other people, including you. And this is one of them. So, could you please be patient with me?"

I saw his face clouding over as he spoke. His eyebrows drew together, and the corners of his lips turned down. Soft lines appeared across his forehead. Most of the time, Peter was a happy person. If he was upset or sad or angry, it usually wasn't for too long. But this time, I knew something wasn't right. Something had happened that was causing him to act this way.

"Hey," I murmured softly, brushing his hair with my fingers.

Peter closed his eyes as I touched his cheek.

"It's okay," I said. "I'm upset because I was worried about you. I just felt uneasy when you suddenly stopped texting me, and then, out of the blue, you showed up like this. It isn't right to treat people, especially your girlfriend, like this. You can call me silly, but I'm afraid of you meeting another girl and deciding to break up with me." I choked on the last word, and a deep sadness overcame me at the thought.

"Silly girl." Peter gave me a quick kiss on the lips. "Why do you think that way?"

"Why shouldn't I? We aren't married. You aren't my fiancé. Anything's possible. Besides, after the New Year, I didn't receive a single text from you. Do you think I'm exaggerating?"

He shook his head.

"Next time, if you're too busy, just send a short message. That way at least I'll know you're okay."

"Yeah, I will." His voice croaked, and he forced a small smile.

"Promise?"

He nodded.

I smiled and gave him a playful punch on the chest. "I missed you, you know."

Peter caught my hand. "I missed you more." He sighed and leaned forward, kissing me. I stepped back until my back hit the wall. Leaning against it, I wrapped my arms around his neck to pull him closer. Maybe I drew him in too suddenly because he lost his balance. It was a good thing he was quick enough and reached forward, bracing his arms against the wall behind me.

"Are you tempting me, Rory?" He grinned.

Giggling, I leaned my forehead on his shoulder.

Peter regained his balance and caressed my hair.

"I've had a hard time controlling myself around you when we're alone," he whispered. "I think we should be more careful."

I nodded. "Okay."

Then we kissed again in a civilized manner.

"Have you eaten yet?" I asked when we sat on the bed, leaning our backs on the headboard. It was a comfortable way to rest in the small room. We were too lazy to move the sofa around. "I can order you some food if you haven't."

"Something light would be nice."

"All right." I picked up the phone and called room service for fruit, finger sandwiches, and bruschetta.

While waiting for our order, I asked Peter to show me the family pictures he'd promised to take for me during his family's New Year's dinner. He seemed reluctant, but he showed me anyway.

His dad, Archibald Ryder, was tall and slightly stiff. He wasn't handsome, but something in his eyes and mouth made him attractive even in his middle age. From a certain angle, I saw his resemblance in Peter. Next to him was a willowy woman with red hair. She wore a beautiful, long, elegant dress. From her hair color and the shape of her face, I easily guessed that she was Tom's mom.

"Who's this girl? She's pretty." I pointed at a thin woman with medium-length, straight blonde hair and side bangs. She wore an off-the-shoulder dress and held her pointy nose in the air.

"That's Eliza, my half sister," Peter said, seeming slightly embarrassed. "She doesn't get along with other people well, including us."

"I see." I looked at the other people in the picture. Next to Eliza stood a slightly built, middle-aged man with a big, crooked nose and lips that sort of sucked inward. He wore an expensive-looking gray suit and a scowling expression.

"My Uncle Ethan," Peter said as I pointed at the man. "My grandparents." He pointed at an elderly couple who were sitting in the middle, surrounded by the families. The serious-looking man held the hand of the sweet, white-haired woman next to him, who reminded me of Betty White.

"Your grandma has a nice smile." I looked at him. "I wish I had a sweet grandma like her."

Peter's eyes softened as he nodded. "I love my grandma, but not so much my grandpa. The only thing he talks about is business. Everything is transactional for him. He was often in charge of my aunts and uncles' marriages, making sure they were married to families who could benefit his businesses, well, our family businesses."

My heart sank a little. "Does that mean he's going to find you a wife, then?" I asked.

Peter's face turned slightly red. "Are you crazy? Do you think we're living in the nineteenth century?" His voice rose somewhat.

"Well, who kno—"

I was interrupted by a knock at the door. "Room service!"

Peter exhaled, his face lighting up at the interruption. "Great. I'm hungry." He jumped from the bed and walked to the door.

"I thought you said you weren't hungry." I crossed my arms as he brought the tray inside and placed it on the bed.

He took a piece of bruschetta and popped it into his mouth. "Looking at my family's picture always makes me hungry," he said with a full mouth.

Shaking my head, I took some fruit and ate them.

After our light dinner, we turned on the TV but didn't bother watching it. We spent our time catching up, kissing, laughing, kissing again, teasing each other, and talking until Peter dozed off on my lap. I let him. I was tired too, but I wanted to look at his sleeping face.

I watched Peter's chest rise and fall as he slept. "Why does he seem miserable?" I wondered, brushing his hair with my fingers.

Maybe his family was stricter and had higher expectations than my aunt. Something bad had happened in London. Maybe one of his family members had been killed to prevent them gaining an inheritance, like in the drama series I'd watched.

Well, that was impossible considering how sweet Jane, Tom, and Marcus were. Whatever the reason, something was bothering him.

I let him sleep for a while before waking him.

He rubbed his eyes. "What time is it?" he asked sleepily.

"Eleven," I answered.

When he was fully awake, I walked him downstairs after making sure the corridors were clear. I didn't want to run into someone from work. I knew I shouldn't have felt that way because we were adults. Sally knew my boyfriend lived in California, but professionalism was important to me. I'd already proven to her that I was serious about my job and wouldn't neglect my projects, and I wanted to keep it that way.

Chapter 21

FROM THAT POINT ON, PETER did everything he could think of to make me happy. When he knew I wasn't having dinner with people from work, he picked me up.

"Do you still feel guilty?" I asked as we strolled, holding hands, through an open-air shopping center after dinner. The LED lights adorning the giant Ferris wheel behind us reflected beautifully on the store windows.

"Not anymore," he said.

"Hmm." I watched him carefully.

He glanced at me and shrugged. "Maybe a little bit."

"You shouldn't. I'm not a petty person, you know."

"I know," he said, covering my eyes with his hand. "But why are you looking at me like you're suspicious? Stop looking at me like that."

I shut my eyes beneath his hand. "Like what? I can't even see you now."

Peter laughed and took his hand away, then tickled my waist. I yelped and pulled away, avoiding his long fingers, but he continued to tickle me. He leaned forward as I crouched on the ground, protecting my waist from his fingers.

"All right, I won't look at you like that." I laughed, falling on my side. "Stop it."

Laughing, he stopped tickling me and took my hand to pull me up. My forehead hit his collarbone as I stood.

"Too bad you aren't ticklish. If you were, I'd tickle you back," I protested. "Now, promise me you're not feeling guilty anymore."

"I still feel a little guilty. I picked you up today because I want to spend time with you while you're here. Is that okay?" he challenged, tilting his head.

"Okay, if that's your reason." I placed my hands on his waist and looked up at him. "I like spending time with you too, Peter Ryder."

He smiled, lowering his head to kiss my nose. "Promise me that you'll be sweet like this to me forever."

"That's a selfish request. What about you?"

"I think I've always treated you sweetly."

"Hmm."

"You don't believe me?"

"Okay, yes, I believe you," I said quickly as his fingers hovered over my waist, ready to tickle me again.

"But *I* don't believe *you*."

"What?" I asked.

Peter smirked and raised his pinky up in front of my face. "Pinky swear."

Chuckling, I pushed his finger away. "That's for kids. People will laugh at you if they know you made a child's promise."

"Are you scared of making a promise?"

I scoffed and hooked my little finger around his. "Happy?"

With our pinkies locked, Peter looked at me, his expression solemn. "This is serious and can't be broken."

"Don't worry. I've made many pinky promises." I shrugged, looking at him. I almost burst into laughter when I saw the astonishment on his face. "I'm kidding." I snickered. "Why are you so serious tonight?"

"You scare me sometimes." He pouted, looking at our locked fingers.

"Peter Ryder," I said, touching his face with my other hand, "I promise you."

His eyes shone. He gave me a small smile and curved a hand around my waist as a man called his name. We turned.

A blonde man wearing a black jacket with a blue checker-patterned scarf stood behind us. I recognized him as the person we'd met earlier in the Japanese restaurant, and I knew Peter didn't like him. If I wasn't mistaken, his name was Isaac.

The man looked at me curiously.

Oddly, Peter dropped his hand from my waist.

"Isaac! I didn't know you were in town," he said, extending his hand. "When did you arrive?"

"A few days ago," he said, shifting his gaze to Peter. "With Sophie."

"Ah." Peter's eyebrows wrinkled. He bit his lower lip and nodded. "I see. I thought she'd be here next week."

"Apparently, she couldn't wait any longer." Isaac chuckled and turned to me. "And we met last month but didn't have time for an introduction. I'm Isaac. Nice to meet you."

"Rory," I said before Peter spoke. I extended my hand to Isaac, who shook it gently. "Nice to meet you, Isaac."

"And you are...?" His eyes trailed from me to Peter.

Peter firmed his jaw. His arm returned around my waist, and he pulled me closer to his side. "My girlfriend." His voice was strained as he turned to me. "Rory, Isaac's family is friends with my family, and their family does business with my grandfather. Isaac's here with his sister, who's working on her master's degree at Pepperdine University."

"Wow, that's great. And where's your sister now?" I looked around.

"Oh, she's in one of the clothing shops over there." He pointed toward stores behind us. "When she's in shopping mode, it's best not to bother her." Then he leaned toward me. "She's buying pretty dresses to impress someone." He glanced at Peter.

I chuckled. Deep down, I felt weird about how he looked at Peter, who suddenly became quiet and avoided Isaac's eyes.

Isaac glanced at Peter's hand, which was wrapped around my waist, then he gave a slight nod.

"Well, I have to go now. My sister will be happy to know that I bumped into you both." Isaac extended his hand to me, and I shook it. "Nice to meet you, Rory, and I believe we could meet again…soon. Bye now, Peter." He nodded and left to find his sister.

"Are you okay?" I asked Peter, whose eyes followed Isaac as he walked away.

Clearing his throat, his voice was clipped as he said, "Yeah, I'm fine."

Sensing his mood had changed, I took his hand. "Let's go home. I have to be in the office early tomorrow morning."

Peter let out a heavy sigh and pulled me into his arms, a strange expression in his eyes. He leaned down to kiss me, something he didn't usually do in public.

"I love you," he whispered, and his lips brushed mine.

"Love you more," I said.

He pulled away from me then. "Let's go back."

Lacing his fingers through mine, Peter held my hand tightly as we walked in silence through the parking lot. It seemed as though Isaac's presence had bothered him. His sudden silence was unusual. Other than helping me into the car and getting into the driver's seat, he didn't let go of my hand, even as he drove.

His behavior made me uneasy too.

Chapter 22

TWO DAYS LATER, IN HIS home office, Peter clamped his lips tightly shut. His head throbbed, and his heart pounded hard in his chest. Fixing his eyes on the monitors in front of him, he breathed steadily through his nose. Sucking air in and pushing it back out, he tried to calm his heart.

The Sandridge elders stared at him from the triple monitors, disappointment on their faces. The only people not upset were Aunt Helen—his favorite aunt, who looked at him warmly—and his dad, who regarded him curiously. The rest of his family, including his grandpa, uncles, aunts, and granduncles, had furrowed their eyebrows and crossed their arms over their chests.

It was what Tom called a "come-to-Jesus meeting," where the Sandridge elders gathered and asked questions on issues like the one Tom had had last year when he came out of the closet.

"Peter," called his grandpa, "can you explain these pictures?"

One of the monitors showed a picture of Peter smiling at Rory, his hands on her waist. Rory had covered her mouth with her hand, and her eyes were on him. Although the picture was a bit blurry, as if it had been snapped quickly, Peter clearly saw the adoration in Rory's eyes. His heart swelled, and he missed her badly. If she'd been living nearby, he would have rushed to her place and kissed her until she begged for him to stop.

But now wasn't the time to be thinking about her. He was currently in trouble because Isaac had secretly taken pictures of Rory and him, hugging and kissing near the Ferris wheel, and then he'd sent them to the Sandridge family.

Peter didn't like Isaac, but he'd never dreamed that the man would stoop so far as to spy on him.

"Who is she?" asked one of his aunts.

"My girlfriend," he said shortly.

In the past, he would have yelled at them to stop interfering with his personal life before storming out of the room. Now, he managed one of their businesses. Acting like a kid would do him no good. Short answers were the best way to deal with them. If Jane were alive, she would have been proud of him.

"How did you meet her?"

"How long have you been in a relationship with her?"

"Is she working or studying?"

Peter felt his head throb again at the onslaught of questions.

"What do her parents do for a living?"

"She grew up with her aunt after her mom passed away. I don't know about her dad. She doesn't know him either," he answered.

"What do you mean?" one of his uncles asked.

Peter sighed. "He doesn't know she exists."

There was a solid silence on the other side of the monitors.

"Why didn't you tell us you had a girlfriend?" his grandpa asked after a few seconds.

Peter pressed his lips together. "Why would I? My relationship with her has nothing to do with the Sandridge businesses."

Wham!

His grandpa slammed his hand down on the table. His face turned red, and he pointed at Peter.

"Since you agreed to accept the position, it *is* now. Remember, we sent you to California for business, not for love."

Peter frowned and opened his mouth to speak, but Aunt Helen interrupted.

"Peter," she said.

Her warm blue eyes took him in under long eyelashes. The petite sixty-year-old was a daughter-in-law, who shouldn't have been part of the Sandridge board of directors. Still, his grandpa respected her intelligence, charisma, and loyalty. After her husband passed away, she was chosen to take his place on the board.

"We care about the love lives of the young generation within the Sandridge family. Their happiness is our utmost priority, because we want to build something that will last for generations—"

"The apple doesn't fall far from the tree," someone said aloud.

Helen and the rest of the family turned to the source.

The comment had been made by Peter's loser uncle, Ethan, who was lazy and only liked spending money or complaining about everything, including when Jane was chosen to be the CEO of White Water before she passed away and was replaced by Peter.

"Shut up, Ethan." Archie scowled.

Ethan gave a hard look and opened his mouth to speak.

"Shut up, both of you," barked Peter's grandpa. "Continue, Helen."

She nodded and turned back to Peter. "As I said earlier, our utmost priority is our youngsters' happiness. But after decades, we've found that not all people fit into our family. Our family's businesses become stronger through the right partnerships and the right spouses. Hence, we expect to be informed."

"If I'd informed you about her, and if you felt that her background wasn't adequate, would you have forced me to break up with her?" Peter asked.

No one spoke.

"There are many good girls from good families back home," one of his granduncles finally said. "If you don't like British girls, I have connections in Italy, or Spain, or the Netherlands. Why have you fallen in love with a girl who has an unknown family background?"

Peter felt heat rush into his cheeks. He clenched his fingers, his palms hurting as his nails cut into them. He remained silent.

The room fell awkwardly quiet as everyone waited for Peter to say something.

"See?" Uncle Ethan said again. "I never agreed to let him replace Jane, but Jane vouched that he could do the job. Now look at what's happened. Suddenly, he has a girlfriend with an obscure family background."

"Stop belittling her!" Peter snapped. "Her family isn't obscure. Rory is a good girl and loves me for who I am, not for my money, unlike the girls you've approved."

His grandpa looked at him coldly. "Fine," he said, waving his hand dismissively. "Date her. Do whatever you want. But *Sophie* is your priority. If she's upset because you haven't treated her well and it affects our partnership with her father's business, be prepared to break up with this girl and marry someone we approve."

Peter's stomach twisted. He couldn't breathe. Before he could say anything, his grandpa disconnected the call. One by one, everyone else disconnected, leaving Peter staring at the dark monitors, feeling more alone than he ever had before.

Chapter 23

*I*T HAD BEEN MORE THAN two weeks since Peter and I said goodbye at John Wayne Airport. Peter had stopped calling me. The texts became fewer and fewer until they stopped too. Our video calls got rescheduled. A few times, I found myself staring at my computer screen, waiting for him to be online.

I'd known he was busy, and sometimes he had to work on weekends. I wanted to call him or send more texts, but I refused to be seen as a clingy girlfriend. Was he really *too* busy on the weekend to send me a short text?

The clock on my phone showed one o'clock on the East Coast, which meant it was ten in the morning on the West Coast. I considered calling Peter rather than waiting for him to text or call me.

I dialed his phone. It rang.

"Hello?"

I froze when I heard a woman's voice.

"Hey, what are you doing?" I heard Peter say in the background. "Give me back my phone."

"Gosh, you sound upset." The woman giggled, but she seemed to have given the phone back to Peter because I heard him grumble softly.

"Who's Rory anyway?" she asked.

Peter didn't answer.

"Rory, hi," Peter said, his breathing heavy as if he'd been jogging. "Sorry, I should find a quieter spot."

"Okay," I said, thinking of the woman. *Who is she?*

"Hey, you don't usually call this early," he said. His voice sounded calmer.

"Is ten o'clock too early for me to call? I thought you were an early bird."

"I just didn't expect you to call this early," he answered.

"Where are you now? Who's that woman?" I asked.

"Oh." Peter gave a chuckle. "That's Isaac's sister, Sophie. Remember Isaac, the guy we met at the outdoor mall?"

"Um…yeah," I answered.

"I just picked her up at her apartment. I'm having lunch with her, Isaac, and Tom later," he said. "Hey, can I call you back?"

I didn't answer for a few seconds.

"Do you realize how many times you've said those words? Don't you realize you haven't had time to talk for even a few minutes?" I knew my voice sounded strained as I clenched the phone in my hand.

Peter took a deep breath and slowly let it out. "I'm swamped. Ever since you left, I've had meetings on top of meetings. Since Sophie's here, I'm expected to accompany her during my free time."

"You have time for *her*, but not for a short text to your girlfriend?" I refused to back down.

Peter huffed, and silence fell upon us.

"I know it's hard for you to believe, but I'm not lying," he finally responded. "I've told you that their father's business is important to the Sandridge Group, and we want a partnership with them. My grandpa thought that, since Sophie's the apple of her dad's eye, I should make her happy by showing her around. Tom's helping too. On weekdays, I ensure the company runs well for my employees and their families because they depend on me. And, yes, I haven't had time lately. I even have to work during my lunch hour. I often wish I didn't have to work for my family's business so I could have more free time like you."

My stomach sank to hear that, and I stared out the window. The sky was bright and blue, with no clouds in sight. It was cold, but if you sat in the sun, it felt warm and comfortable. It was a perfect day to enjoy the outdoors and relax. But I didn't feel like going outside. My throat had gone dry after what Peter said to me.

"Wow, that sounds serious, like life and death," I said bitterly. "Well, then, since I've got so much time on my hands, I'm going to sleep again. Goodbye, Peter. Enjoy your day."

I hung up, turned off my phone, and threw it inside the drawer. I didn't want to accept any phone calls from anyone. My aunt never called me on the weekend, anyway. My Saturday was ruined by the one person I missed so much, and the main reason I'd called him was to remind him that tomorrow was Valentine's Day, and I'd wanted us to do a video call and celebrate it together. However, he'd annoyed me.

THE NEXT DAY, I CELEBRATED Valentine's Day with Aunt Amy. We spent the day baking braided bread together. I loved my aunt. Besides, the day wasn't only for lovers, right?

I knew my aunt sensed that Peter and I weren't on speaking terms. She didn't make a comment, and I preferred it that way. It was the first time since meeting him that I'd spent the weekend without his name being mentioned.

Chapter 24

O N MONDAY MORNING, AFTER BRUSHING my teeth, I turned on my phone and received texts and voicemails from Peter, apologizing for what he'd said on Saturday. I stared at my phone, a shadow of doubt creeping into my heart, and I began questioning myself about our relationship. It was undeniable that we lived far away from each other and had been busy at work. However, shouldn't we make an extra effort to keep our relationship going?

I didn't think Peter had the same perspective in this relationship. Every time I felt close to him, he pulled away. Every time I thought we were beginning to open up, he was the one who clammed up. He was also the one who kept breaking his promises and later asking for forgiveness.

Who am I for you, Peter?

I deleted his texts and voicemails without an urge to respond to him. When I was about to delete the last one, I frowned, reading a Happy Valentine's Day message from Ryan. Oddly, my heart brightened at seeing his text.

As my mind shifted to Ryan, his comment about how "the percentage of people who fail to maintain a long-distance relationship is higher than a successful one" rang loudly in my ears.

"Will our relationship be successful?" I rubbed my forehead

and let my hand cover my eyes for a moment, skeptical about the future of my relationship with Peter.

MY MOOD IN THE OFFICE wasn't good either, especially after Sally announced that our business trip to California was canceled because the dealer's owner had decided to continue his loan with Veles Capital. Martin didn't need extra manpower because we could help from afar. So much for my plan to use the upcoming trip to ask Peter directly about our relationship. I'd thought, if I were in California, I could push him to be honest about whether or not he put our relationship at the top of his priority list.

Sally stood near my cubicle as I returned from lunch.

"Hi, Sally. Do you need me?"

"Could you come over to my office?" she asked.

"Sure." I nodded.

Marsha, who was next to me, frowned. I could almost see the questions in her expression. I shrugged and strode into Sally's office.

"Please." She pointed to one of the chairs. "How was your lunch?"

"It was relaxing. The lunchroom wasn't too crowded today," I said, sitting down. "How about you?"

"I had a light lunch because I had a long phone call with Martin," she answered. "It was about you."

I looked at her and raised my eyebrows. "Did I make a mistake on the last report I sent to him?"

Sally shook her head. "On the contrary, Martin praised you about how diligent and smart you are and asked me to let him have you on his team. I told him I couldn't because I like you on *my* team. I also want you to learn about a few of Marsha's clients before she takes maternity leave."

She sighed. "I know it isn't easy for Martin right now. He has more new clients and no adequate staff. It would take longer to train a new employee in the business, even if they had accounting knowledge. Martin fought hard for you, so I negotiated a deal to lend you to him for two or three months. However, that depends on you. If you're interested, you can fly out there next week."

My heart thudded. What an excellent opportunity! I finally had a chance to have a serious discussion with Peter about our relationship.

Sally misunderstood my silence and hesitation. "Joining Martin's team would be good for you. I don't want to be a selfish supervisor by keeping you here. I want you to grow and embrace new opportunities. The good thing is that our business is stable right now, and I can rotate your clients to other senior analysts. Furthermore, the company will accommodate your lodging and loan you a car. But no food, internet, or electricity. You'll read the list of covered items from HR."

I looked at her. "Do you want me to answer today?"

"No, of course not. Think about it overnight and let me know tomorrow so I can arrange everything."

"Okay, I'll think it over," I said. "Thank you for the opportunity, Sally."

"You're welcome." Sally smiled. "You're a diligent employee and willing to learn. I'm happy for you."

My heart swelled with pride at her compliment. In my previous job, my supervisor had always pouted when someone complimented me. Under Sally's management, I was loved and taken care of.

"Thanks again, Sally."

She nodded, and I rose from my seat, heading to my cubicle.

At my desk, I stared at the monitor with mixed feelings. I was happy with the change in circumstances because I couldn't believe that Martin had asked for my help. On the other hand, I was anxious about whether my presence in California would lead my relationship with Peter in the right direction.

Maybe...

Or maybe not.

Chapter 25

ONE WEEK PASSED. PETER AND I had reconciled after he promised to change and give more time to our relationship. He also sounded happy when I told him about my two-month assignment in California. Unfortunately, on my arrival date, he couldn't pick me up because he had a quarterly meeting in his Canada office. My burst of happiness was depleted immediately.

I was writing something on a folder when Marsha rushed to my cubicle and gave me a bear hug. Tony stood behind her.

"Ooohhh nooo! Today is your last day here. This office will be so different without you, Rory," she said.

"And Cary will be transferred to me." The corners of Tony's lips drooped while he rubbed his eyes, pretending to cry.

I looked at him in sympathy because no one liked working for Cary from Stone Transportation. She treated everybody harshly.

"It's only for the short term," I reminded him.

A second later, Leslie and Kelly came to my cubicle.

"Rorrryyy…I'm gonna miss you, my friend," Leslie said, giving me a hug.

Since people knew that Martin had requested me to work on a special project, everybody looked at me in a different light whenever they bumped into me. Martin was a tough manager, but once he liked a person and begged for them to work with him, it was a different ball game. Even Kelly, who'd used to be bitchy to me, became nicer.

"Good luck there," she said, tapping my shoulder.

"Thanks," I said, smiling at her.

"Well, I hope Martin treats you well over there. If not, I'll ask Sally to pull you back here," Leslie said.

I chuckled at her comment.

"Hey, where's Ryan?" asked Marsha, realizing that Ryan wasn't with them. "Did he know that today is your last day here?"

"Well, maybe he went to the kitchen for some water," said Tony.

Kelly shrugged. "I saw him step out of his cubicle a moment before you and Tony came to Rory's cubicle. I didn't bother to ask since he's been so moody lately."

I stood stiffly. Ryan had been avoiding me since I'd agreed to help Martin's team. Maybe he was upset because Martin chose me instead of him.

Ryan went back to his cubicle long after Tony, Marsha, Kelly, and Leslie returned to theirs.

"Hey, Ryan," I heard Tony call. "Today is Rory's last day here."

"Yeah, I know," Ryan responded shortly.

"Make sure you say goodbye to her," said Tony.

Ryan didn't say anything.

A dull pain pricked me because I'd thought I could say goodbye properly. I hadn't known he would be jealous because Martin had chosen me instead of him. Ryan had more experience than me, but it wasn't my fault that Martin wanted me for my accounting experience.

I was waiting for an elevator at the end of the day when the automatic doors in the lobby slid open, and Ryan came out from inside. He gave a small smile as he stopped next to me.

"I thought I was the last one in the office." I didn't hide my surprise. "I couldn't see you in your cubicle."

He shrugged. "I had a lot of things to do and worked in an

empty room near the lunchroom. Sometimes I need to concentrate in a quiet place, and that room is perfect."

"I see." I nodded. It must have been hard for him to see me without feeling jealous.

Then we fell into silence, standing side by side as we waited for the elevator.

"So, are you flying tomorrow?" Ryan asked.

"Yes." I nodded.

"Good luck. Martin is tough, but, personally, he's nice," he said, facing me.

"Thank you." I smiled at him.

"I'm gonna miss you, Rory."

"Thanks. It's just for a short period, and it doesn't mean I'm going to stay there forever," I said. "He needs someone with an accounting background. He would've chosen you if he needed someone with an auditing background."

Ryan frowned. "Wait a second. Did you think I was jealous of you?"

"Aren't you?" I asked, returning the question.

Ryan didn't say a word but looked at me intensely.

"If you're jealous, I understand. I'd feel the same if I were you." I shifted my eyes back to the elevator.

To my surprise, Ryan took a big step toward me and cupped my face in his hands. I felt a palpable heat and ferocious intensity as his fingers brushed my cheeks. My eyes widened as he brought my face closer to his and kissed me. I wanted to break away, but my body froze as soft electricity ran through my veins when his lips touched mine.

Our eyes met as Ryan pulled away, a winning smile on his lips as he gazed warmly at me.

"You like me too, right? Don't deny that you felt something from that kiss, because I felt it too."

Those words pulled me back to my senses. I pushed him away

abruptly. At the same time, the elevator door opened. I rushed in and held my hand up to stop him from entering.

"Don't enter if you don't want me to hate you." My voice trembled, and my vision was blurry.

Nodding slowly, Ryan obeyed. He stepped back, but his eyes were on me until the doors closed.

Leaning on the wall, I covered my face with my palms. My cheeks were warm, but my fingers were cold as guilt and anger rose like a strong wave in my chest. Once the elevator reached the ground floor, I dashed to my car. The tires screeched loudly as I turned the corner toward the main street. From the side mirror, I saw Ryan standing on the concrete steps in front of the entrance, but I didn't dare look at him. I stared straight ahead and concentrated on getting through traffic.

Chapter 26

BY TEN O'CLOCK IN THE morning, I was already at the gate, ready to board. My aunt had teased me, saying I couldn't sleep well because I was anxious about seeing Peter again.

I didn't say anything because I knew why my sleep had been disturbed.

No matter what I did, I couldn't shake the memory of Ryan kissing me. The warmth of his lips on mine lingered, although I'd already put a bag of ice cubes on them.

I like him more than I'd realized.

I groaned and rubbed my hands over my face. I wanted to be true to Peter, so why had my heart shifted?

My thoughts were interrupted by my phone buzzing. I tapped my finger on the screen and saw two messages, one from Peter and the other from Ryan.

I read Peter's text. **Have a safe trip and see you soon.**

I smiled when I saw his message and replied to it. **Yes, see you soon.**

Without even reading it, I deleted Ryan's message. My heart felt shaken because I couldn't brush aside the fact that there had been sparks when he kissed me. It ticked me off. My relationship with

Peter was a bit shaky, but it didn't mean my heart had turned to Ryan.

I was relieved once all the passengers at my gate were allowed to board the plane. Standing, I gathered my backpack and light jacket, looking around to make sure I hadn't dropped anything.

I'm boarding now, I texted Peter.

He didn't send a text back, and I eventually had to turn off my phone when the warning sign for electronic devices flashed.

I sighed, put the phone in my backpack, and slid it underneath the seat in front of me.

IT HAD BEEN FIVE DAYS since my arrival. Peter was still in Canada and would be back in a few more days. My stomach pinched when I checked my cell phone and found no text from him. I sighed, put the phone back on the bedside table, and stood in front of the apartment window to stare at the city skyline.

"Have you been that busy? Don't you think I deserve to receive a piece of whatever time you have?" I whispered as the sadness of losing him buzzed in my chest.

By far, Peter was the best boyfriend I'd ever had. He always made me feel beautiful and appreciated who I was. He got along well with my aunt and gave me enough space to make me feel comfortable around him. He was an interesting man and fun to be with. I knew he'd been born with a silver spoon in his mouth, but he seemed to enjoy being with me, even though the places I took him weren't glamorous or famous. I'd never been loved the way he loved me.

Everything had changed since he'd returned from London on his last visit. I didn't know what had happened. Peter kept it hidden even though we'd promised to be open with each other. The worst part was that, somehow, his life now revolved around a woman named Sophie.

In the midst of feeling lonely and uncertain, a familiar face with a sweet smile flashed behind my eyes, and the sweet moments when we were in college flooded back into my mind. He was the one who had comforted me when I got an F on my mid-term, who fell asleep on the floor while waiting for me studying in the library, who shared his pizza for lunch because I hadn't received my pay from my part-time job, and who dropped me off at my apartment when I had a late class. Now, I remembered who had made me like mint mocha lattes. My fingers trembled as I touched my lips, remembering the kiss we'd shared before I flew to California. It was shocking but sweet.

A tear rolled from my eyes, and I quickly wiped it away.

"Stop that!" I chastised myself.

Letting out a heavy sigh, I took my laptop, brought it to my bed, and started working. Only work could take my mind off the battle going on inside me.

Chapter 27

IT WAS BARELY EIGHT-THIRTY, BUT I'd already had two cups of coffee and just returned from making another cup. I'd only slept four hours last night. The best part was that I'd finished most of my reports, but the worst part was, I was sleepy in the office and longing to be back in Boston.

Someone tapped on the wall of my cubicle. Startled, I looked up to see Martin just outside. Despite what people said about Martin, I liked him. He was a reasonable person who gave me reasonable tasks. I had to admit that his demand for perfection was unbelievable and drove me crazy. Like Sally, he didn't mind when people came to him with questions, and he detested when someone pretended to know how to do a job, but then didn't do it correctly.

"Hey, Martin! Sorry, I didn't hear you," I said.

Martin shook his head. "Don't apologize. I'm the one who should say sorry because I'm interrupting you from your work, Aurorette."

I heard a muffled giggle from either Sebastian or Zoe, whose cubicles were next to mine. Martin was French and said my name correctly with his French accent. He used my full name, Aurorette, and the *R* vibrated in his throat each time he said it. A chain reaction would then occur because, once he said my name, I'd hear a giggle from one of my coworkers. Martin didn't realize it. Or, if he did, he didn't care.

"Can I help you with anything?" I asked.

Martin nodded. "I want you to meet Sam this afternoon, instead of tomorrow as we planned, so he can brief you again from a legal standpoint. Are you open at two?"

I checked my office calendar and gave him a nod. "Yeah, I am."

"Great!" He smiled, walking back to his office. "Merrrci, Aurrrorrrette."

Two minutes later, I heard,

"Merrrci, Aurrorrette, for entertaining us." Giggling, Sebastian and Zoe popped their heads over the partitions between my cubicle and theirs.

"Shut it." I chuckled. "You need to gurgle your *R* deeper and longer like him."

Sebastian grinned. "Only Martin can pronounce your name perfectly."

"Our boss looks more relaxed since you've been here," Zoe commented, pointing with her head toward Martin's office. "That makes our office life bearable."

Sebastian nodded at me. "Yup, I wish you could join us for real."

I gave a light laugh in response to their comments. "Thanks. I'd like working here too," I lied.

At that moment, I didn't want to work here *or* in Boston because both places gave me a headache.

At two o'clock that afternoon, I went to the fifteenth floor and entered Sam's office. I'd been there before and loved the whole look of the place. The cozy reception area had several pots of white orchids in each corner, and a square coffee table sat between comfortable armchairs. The office was quite big, with more than enough room to fit the twenty lawyers and associates working there. What amazed me was the office's library and its tall bookshelves, which covered the walls from floor to ceiling. It must have been nice to work in such a quiet room.

When I arrived, I was greeted by a woman with bronze hair and a light blazer, who was sitting behind the curved, glass top receptionist's desk.

"Good afternoon. May I help you?" she asked.

"Hi, I'm Rory from Veles Capital, and I have an appointment with Sam Williams," I said.

"Oh yes." She nodded. "He told me this morning. Please take a seat, and I'll call him."

She picked up the phone and had a short conversation while I settled on a beautiful plush armchair. The soft instrumental music playing in the background calmed my nerves, and I felt relaxed in the big chair.

The peaceful atmosphere was interrupted when Sam stepped into the room and called my name. He wore a dark gray suit and light blue shirt without a tie. Behind his glasses, his eyes shone as our eyes met. Smiling, I stood and extended a hand.

"Hi, Rory, how are you?" He shook my hand. "Welcome back to Southern California."

"Thanks, Sam. It's nice to be back."

"I'll bet. The weather's nicer here than on the East Coast, right?" he asked.

"Totally," I agreed, laughing.

"Come on, let's go inside." He pointed toward the door from which he'd just emerged.

Holding it open, Sam let me inside before leading me to a room I'd never seen before. I noticed a big picture of a gray-haired man in a suit hanging on the wall behind the elegant desk. His brown eyes were warm and gentle. I moved closer and read the name engraved on the personalized acrylic desk plate: Jonathan P. Williams.

"The founder's son," Sam said next to me, "and my old man."

"Oh," I exclaimed, looking from him to the picture. "Oh yeah, your last name is Williams too. I thought it was just a coincidence."

He smiled. "Actually, he wasn't my real dad but my uncle. I grew up in his house after my dad passed away, and my mom left me in my grandma's house."

"Oh."

His eyebrows rose. "Oh?"

"Sorry for the odd response. I grew up with my aunt after my mom passed away. Kind of like your situation."

Sam's eyes focused on me. "I see." He nodded. "And your dad?"

I shrugged. "He doesn't know I exist."

"I'm sorry." He regarded me with sympathy.

I waved a hand dismissively. "I'm not the only child in the world who doesn't have a father, right?"

Sam's chuckle was light. "Yes, you're right, but aren't you interested…in finding him?" he asked carefully.

I shrugged. "Maybe when I was little, but not anymore. If a man leaves a woman after getting her pregnant, you can usually guess what kind of man he is. And, yeah, I'm afraid that I'd be disappointed if I found out the truth. I'd rather not know anything about him, and"—I shrugged again—"I'm happy not knowing him."

Sam opened his mouth to say something, but he seemed to change his mind because he closed it again.

"So, are you going to show me the standard briefing for the new case?" I asked.

He nodded. "Yes, it's similar to the one you signed last time, and you need to sign in front of me for validation. Shall we begin?"

"Sure."

Chapter 28

RIDAY AFTERNOON, PETER PICKED ME up at the office after work because, Thursday, on the way home from the airport, he'd called me for the first time since I'd arrived and asked if I could spend the weekend at his house. Holding onto a thread of hope for something good to happen, I'd said yes.

The next morning, as I was drinking coffee, Peter came into the kitchen to join me. He seemed tense. His shirt was half tucked and his hair was a bit messy.

"What happened?" I asked, placing my cup on the table.

"I just got a text that my dad wants to discuss something about the sales reports I sent yesterday." He frowned. "Unbelievable. Why can't the old man ever let me enjoy the weekend?" Letting out a huff, he looked at me. "I'm sorry, Rory."

"That's okay." I did my best to hide my disappointment. "Just go. I'm fine here," I comforted him.

Peter leaned down and hugged me tightly.

"Are we still doing the barbecue later?" I asked.

"Yes, of course. I'm looking forward to showing off my barbecue skills."

"Don't burn my steak."

He pushed me gently, hurt in his eyes. "Hey, I'm good at it now."

"Now?"

Color rose in his cheeks. "Marcus and Rosa were my guests when I experimented."

I clicked my tongue. "Poor them."

"I'm better now," he defended.

"Fine, I believe you." I winked. "Okay, go. I'll make some salad and a side dish. By the time you come back, we'll just have to grill the meat. Do we need to marinate it?"

"No. Just coarse salt before we start grilling."

"Got it."

"See you later, love." Peter kissed me.

I was in the middle of chopping fried bacon for a Cobb salad when the doorbell rang.

"Did he come back already?" I asked aloud. Frowning, I glanced at the kitchen clock and walked toward the entrance.

I opened the door to find two gray-haired men in suits standing on the front porch. One was tall and slender, and the other was short and chubby with a crooked nose. The tall one had a small smile on his lips, but the crooked-nosed man scowled at me. Worry hit me when I realized I recognized them from somewhere.

"Can I help you, sirs?" I asked, my voice unsteady.

"I'm Archie Ryder, Peter's dad," the slender man said. He pointed at the crooked-nosed man. "And this is Ethan, my elder brother and Peter's uncle."

"Oh." My face felt hot as I extended my hand to shake his. "I'm Rory, Peter's girlfriend." I pulled my hand back when his uncle didn't shake it. "I'm sorry if I seem surprised, but Peter didn't say anything about your visit."

Didn't Peter say earlier that his dad wanted to discuss something in the office? Why is he here?

Peter's dad smiled.

"Please come in." I pushed the door wider, allowing them to enter.

They walked into the living room, and I felt uneasy when Ethan gave me a sharp glance as he spoke to Archie. "I don't understand your son," he said with a shake of his head. "This house isn't elegant. Why did he buy a house in this city? Bel-Air or Beverly Hills is better, no? Or Manhattan Beach."

Archie didn't make a comment as he looked around.

"Please have a seat," I said politely, pointing to the sofas.

Ethan grunted. "We can sit anywhere we like."

Heat shot into my face again. "Yes…yes, of course." I stammered. "I'm just trying to be polite."

"Come on, Ethan. Watch your manners. This young lady is my son's girlfriend. Don't give her a hard time if you want Peter to behave himself," Archie said. Then he raised his nose and sniffed. "It smells like bacon. Are you cooking?" He turned to me.

"Oh, I'm preparing Cobb salad and side dishes for our barbecue lunch," I said. "I would've made more if I'd known you were both going to be here, sirs."

"Don't call me sir. Call me Archie," Peter's dad said calmly.

"Umm…all right, Archie," I replied.

Peter's uncle squinted at me. "Are you and Peter living together?"

I shook my head. "I don't live here. Actually, I live in Boston, but I'm here on business and I'm staying in a hotel."

He frowned. "But you're here today?"

I didn't like his question, but I answered it anyway. "Yes, we decided to spend the weekend together because we've been busy and barely see each other."

Ethan snorted and looked at Archie. "See? He's already forgotten about his mission to accompany Sophie."

I froze. Sophie *again*? And Peter had to accompany her this weekend?

Archie ignored him and turned to me. He pointed at two avocadoes in a bowl. "What are you going to make?"

"Avocado dip," I said. "It's Peter's favorite."

"You're a good cook?" He smiled.

I laughed nervously. "It's something simple."

Ethan snorted again and looked away, folding his arms. Archie caught my frown before I could force myself to smile.

"Let me call Peter, so he'll know that you both are already here." I reached for my phone on the countertop.

His dad held up a hand. "Don't worry about him. Why don't you sit here with us, Rory?" He pointed to the chair. "We can chat while we're waiting for him."

My throat closed as he settled on a stool at the kitchen island. Slowly, I sat on the chair opposite him. Ethan leaned on the island with his arms still crossed in front of his chest. I felt like I was in an interrogation room.

"Do you need a drink or anything?" I offered.

Archie seemed to notice my nervousness. "Ah yes. Diet Coke would be great. How about you, Ethan?"

His brother gave a dismissive wave. .

I grabbed two Diet Cokes from the fridge and two glasses from the cupboard and put them in front of Peter's dad.

"Perhaps Peter hasn't told you about our relationship?" I asked.

"On the contrary, he has." Archie smiled, leaning back in his seat. "I just wanted to meet you and chat without him around. And it isn't a crime to get to know my son's girlfriend, right?"

My palms were sweating, but I resisted the urge to wipe them on my thighs and nodded.

"So, how long have you been dating?" he asked politely.

"Since last October."

"You said you live in Boston? So, how did you meet?"

"Well," I cleared my throat, "I'd lived in California since my freshman year. Last year, I was looking for a roommate, and Jane answered my ad, but—"

"Jane?" Archie interrupted, surprise showing clearly on his face. "So, you also knew Jane?"

"Just briefly, when I interviewed her and accepted her offer to be my roommate," I explained. "But then she was sick, and Peter came. Later, he decided to continue Jane's rental agreement with me."

"Interesting." Archie nodded, his eyebrows meeting as he frowned. "Jane had a unique personality, , don't you agree, Ethan?" He turned to his brother. "No one could guess what she was thinking. She refused to stay in a hotel because she'd planned to stay in your house." He looked at me and chuckled, shaking his head. "And she agreed to let Peter replace her staying in your house?"

"Yes. If she hadn't vouched for Peter, I wouldn't have accepted him."

Archie nodded again, his eyes on me.

"Kids nowadays," grumbled Ethan. He leaned toward me. "What kind of business do your parents have?"

"Manners, Ethan." Peter's dad raised a hand to stop Ethan from saying anything more. "Let me do the talking."

Ethan scoffed unpleasantly, but Archie ignored him.

The doorbell rang.

"Let me get it." I jumped from my seat and scurried to the door. Whoever had come, I was happy for the distraction.

I opened the door to find Marcus on the other side, and he regarded me with a look of concern.

"Miss Rory, how are you?" he asked, taking my hand and studying my face. "Oh, your hand is cold."

"I…" Pulling up the corners of my lips, I forced myself to say, "I'm fine."

From the way he looked at me, he knew I was lying, but he didn't comment further about it. "May I come in, then?" he asked. "I need to talk to Peter's dad and uncle."

I blinked. "But how did you know they were here?" I whispered as he passed me.

Marcus only offered me a smile when he stepped inside and walked into the kitchen.

"Ah, Master Archie and Master Ethan." He shook Archie's hand. "How are you?"

"Marcus. How are you, my friend?" Archie said warmly, giving Marcus a pat on the back. "It's been months since I've seen you. I hope you and Rosa like living in this warm climate."

"I'll bet he likes it," Ethan grumbled, but he shook Marcus's hand.

"Yes, Master Ethan, my wife and I like it here, and we're happy to help Master Peter," Marcus answered. "Is there anything I can do to assist?"

Archie pointed to his drink. "No need. Rory already gave us Diet Cokes. Just sit down and chat with us."

Marcus smiled, taking a seat. "Master Peter will be here soon."

Archie squinted at Marcus and me, and he gave a small smile.

With Marcus there, Peter's dad and uncle didn't ask me any further questions. Instead, they chatted about how great the weather in California was while I listened to them.

Then I heard someone open the front door.

"That must be Peter." Marcus looked at me and gave a slight nod.

"Yes." I jumped up right away and scurried toward the front door.

When I met Peter at the door, his face was red, and the little artery in his temple throbbed at a rapid beat.

"Are you okay?" he asked, pulling me closer after signaling me to come outside and close the door behind me. His hands were cold.

"You didn't tell me your dad and uncle were visiting today," I said as Peter stared at me, his eyes full of concern. "You should've told me."

"I didn't know either," he said. "When I noticed my dad's car wasn't in the parking lot at the office, I knew he'd tricked me. I called Marcus to come over until I could get back." He stopped, his eyes searching my face. "Did…did they harass you?" he asked.

"No, they just asked me questions, like how long we've known each other and when we met. But why were they asking me without you here? And your uncle wasn't very nice to me. Have I offended him somehow?"

Peter's face whitened. "I'm sorry. Just ignore him. He isn't a pleasant person." He smiled reassuringly. "Now, let's go in and face them."

Holding my hand, he took a deep breath before he opened the door and walked inside slightly ahead of me.

Archie and Marcus were standing in the sunroom facing the French doors when Peter and I entered the kitchen. From their hand gestures, it looked as though they were discussing the door. Ethan was still in the kitchen, drinking his Diet Coke. Marcus nodded to Peter when we joined them. Peter tightened his fingers around my hand when I tried to pull away.

"I didn't know you wanted to have a meeting at my house," Peter said to Archie, his voice cold. There was no "Hi, Dad" or anything. I was surprised at his frank manner. "If I'd known, I would've waited for you here rather than rushing to the office."

Archie smiled. "I changed my mind."

"I don't like that." Peter glared at him.

"I know, but it's your fault too."

"What?" Peter firmed his jaw and his eyebrows knotted.

"You should've brought her to meet me," his dad said, glancing at me.

"I was going to, but I've been doing nothing but work meetings all week and babysitting, just in case you forgot." Peter pulled me closer to him. "I'm offended that you felt the need to barge into my house and ask my girlfriend questions without me here. That's rude!"

Archie gazed at me and shifted his eyes to Peter. "Well, all right, then. I'm leaving now." He gave a smile and thrust his hand toward me. Peter frowned but nodded to me, inching his body aside to let me shake Archie's hand.

"It was nice to see you, Rory. I hope when we meet again it'll be at a better time."

"Nice to see you, sir," I said.

"Just call me Archie, like my son does." He chuckled and tapped Peter's shoulder before walking toward the front door. "See you Monday, Peter."

"Call Sophie. You know how important the deal is," Ethan said to Peter before he ambled toward the front door without sparing a glance at me. I gave a tight smile as Peter placed his hands on my shoulders and stood close behind me.

"I guess I'll be taking off too, Master Peter," said Marcus.

He nodded. "Thanks, Marcus."

"My pleasure. Nice to see you again, Miss Rory," said Marcus, smiling at me.

"Nice to see you too, Marcus." I looked over my shoulder at Peter. "Should we walk them out?"

"No," Peter said flatly.

"Thanks for taking care of the kids, Marcus," I heard Archie say to Marcus as they walked toward the front door

"That's because I like them. They're good together. Rosa likes her too," Marcus responded.

Archie gave a light chuckle. "I bet they are. Goodbye, now, Marcus."

"Goodbye, sir."

The door closed.

Once we were alone, I frowned and turned to face Peter. "I

need you to explain this." I pulled my head away when he tried to touch my face.

His hands dropped to his sides. "Yeah." He took my hand and walked to the living room.

I sat on the sofa as Peter settled on the ottoman in front of me. He licked his lips, lowering his eyes as I looked at him.

"I'm listening," I encouraged him to begin.

Peter scooted his ottoman forward until his knees touched mine. "My family…" He took my hand again and held it. "My extended family is complicated. I have a hard time dealing with them. The seniors set a high standard for the younger generations. I've often felt suffocated, and it has become harder after joining the family business. Tom was lucky because he decided to stay away from them. It wouldn't be this difficult if…" His voice trailed off.

"If what?"

He swallowed. "If you were from their circle."

Scowling, I pulled my hand away, but Peter didn't let it go. His eyes didn't meet mine but were turned down at our hands.

"The last time I brought it up," I said, "you were upset and forced me to stop saying that I'm nobody. This is what I was afraid of. Your family doesn't easily accept people outside of their circle. Why did you do that?"

Peter straightened his back, and his jaw tightened. "Because I love you, and I don't want to be with anyone but you. Whoever I fall in love with isn't any of their concern. My life is *my* life, not theirs."

"But you were afraid, weren't you? Afraid that he wouldn't have let you date me if you'd brought me to meet him earlier." My mouth suddenly felt dry after saying the words.

Peter crossed and uncrossed his legs in silence.

"Peter," I said gently.

He gave a tight-lipped smile when our eyes met. "I'm not afraid of them," he said. "I didn't do anything wrong. I love you. Period.

But I was afraid that you'd refuse to be with me once you knew how stuck-up my family was. You detest snobby people, and I have many in my family." His eyes gazed straight into mine. "Then, you'd leave me."

My stomach twisted. "Do you..." I paused as my voice cracked. "Do you think...we have a future together? Or maybe we should—"

Peter sprang forward and covered my mouth with his hand. His eyes became round as they bored into mine. "Don't say those words. Please don't."

Slowly, I peeled his fingers off and held his hand in mine. The muscle on his neck was pulsing. We looked at each other for a moment, and I gave a sad smile before I could stop it.

Sighing heavily, Peter held his palms up and covered my face with them. "Don't give me that look. It breaks my heart."

I closed my eyes, wondering what our future together would be. Then I remembered what my aunt always told me when I felt uncertain. *"Don't be afraid of tomorrow, Rory. Enjoy the moment and live one day at a time."*

I opened my eyes. Yeah, I should enjoy my time with Peter, no matter what the future offered. Holding his palms, I pushed them gently away from my face and nipped his pinky, just hard enough to make him yelp and flinch.

"What are you doing? Are you crazy?" he cried, cupping his pinky.

I smiled broadly. "Does it hurt?"

"You think?"

"May I see it?" I leaned forward.

Peter cringed and studied his little finger. The tip of it was slightly red, and he pouted at me.

"Peter."

"What?"

Chuckling, I put my hands around his waist. "Let's go to Solvang."

"The Danish Village? The one in Santa Barbara County?" He tilted his head as he looked at me. "Why?"

"I'm not in the mood of barbequing anymore," I said, looking up at him. "Besides, it's stuffy in here."

He ran a finger along my jaw. "Yeah, it's stuffy in here," he nodded, exhaling through his nose slowly. "By the way," he asked as I pulled away, "are you related to wolves?"

I laughed heartily, and, roaring like a tigress, I pretended to claw his face with my fingers.

He burst into laughter and gave me a quick kiss. "Promise me that you'll never leave me."

I nodded, and he stood to get his car keys. I looked at his back and breathed a sigh. If we couldn't be together forever, I hoped he would never forget that I was the girlfriend who had dared to nip his finger.

Chapter 29

I WOKE UP AS THE SUN came through the window, brightening the guest room where I slept. I reached for the bedside table to grab my phone. The screen read 7:15 a.m.

Last night, we'd returned home very late, and I didn't fall asleep right away. I tossed and turned before finally dozing off. The surprise visit from Peter's dad and uncle yesterday had made me feel uncomfortable. Many doubts and fears in my mind had become real. Although Peter had looked aloof, his mind had been troubled too. Many times, I caught him staring into the distance and looking preoccupied. If he hugged me, he would hold me longer than usual, and grief flashed briefly on his face when he pulled away.

Sitting on the bed, I noticed two text messages from Peter sent about fifteen minutes earlier. I opened the first one.

> *I'm cycling. See you in two hours.*

There were two heart emojis next to it.
I smiled and opened the next message.

> *Check the Thanksgiving video and let me know what you think. It's in a red flash drive on my desk.*

Feeling giddy, I threw the blanket aside and went to the bathroom to wash my face. It had been months since he'd promised to edit the video. It would be fun to see all of the things Peter had filmed, including my aunt dressed up in a costume for the Turkey Trot 5K, the traditional Boston race that was held in Franklin Park on Thanksgiving Day.

It was almost eight o'clock when I went up to Peter's office after having my quiet morning coffee in the backyard. It was my first time entering the office without him.

Standing in the doorway, I scanned the inside. It was clean but a bit messy. I noticed some loose papers on the long table, on the working desk, and on the carpet, two document folders on a coffee table and a plush armchair, a stapler on top of a lower bookshelf, and piles of books in the corner. I smiled to see our caricature on the wall and my picture sitting on the L-shaped work desk in front of the three big monitors.

"How could he work with three monitors?" I shook my head, pushing aside some loose papers from the keyboard. A few of the papers fell and landed underneath the desk.

Sitting on the high-back office chair, I began to open the desk drawers to search for the flash drive. I pulled out the first drawer and noticed the red flash drive in the far corner. My hand reached out and stopped as I hesitated, but I took it out anyway. That must have been the one, since there were no other red flash drives around.

Holding the cordless mouse, I moved it around to make sure the monitors were alive, then inserted the drive into a USB port. In a split second, a dialog box appeared on the middle monitor. I clicked around and opened the right drive. There was only one video file in it. I double-clicked on it and pushed my chair away to pick up the papers on the floor while waiting for the video to load.

Then I heard a woman's voice.

"Hello, Peter."

Startled, I hit my head on the desk as I straightened my back. Wincing, I rubbed my head. On the monitor, Jane was sitting on her hospital bed with her eyes straight ahead as if she were staring at me. She was terribly pale and her lips were cracked, with noticeable black color under her eyes. Her sterling gray eyes were dull. I could see the pain on her face, but she managed to smile.

"By the time you watch this, I'm already gone because my surgery failed. I'm sorry I can't be with you anymore. Ah, I can guess you're crying by now. Please don't cry. I don't particularly appreciate seeing people cry. Promise me; don't be a cry baby, okay?" Jane stopped, looking away as she wiped the corner of her eye with a hand attached to an IV line.

I reached for the mouse to turn off the video, since I didn't want to watch it, but the mouse stopped working. Maybe it needed to be recharged. I moved my finger to the monitor to see if it was a touch screen. It was.

In the meantime, Jane kept talking. "Peter, I have a favor to ask you. Please take my position. I've convinced all the elders in the Sandridge families to accept you, and they've agreed."

My finger froze in the air as I was about to close the video. Her words surprised me. Unthinking, I kept watching.

Jane shifted on her seat, leaning forward. "Peter, White Water is in danger. Uncle Ethan has persuaded Grandpa to sell it. As you know, Uncle Ethan thirsts for power and influence. He has forced people to be on his side. If he has more power, there won't be any peace in the Sandridge families. That would destroy our family businesses that were built decades ago. I want to prevent that."

I could clearly see great pain on her face as she took a deep breath. She swallowed and continued. "Please help me and make White Water the most profitable company of our family businesses. Once it becomes successful, it will strengthen Archie's position in the family to control Uncle Ethan. I believe you can do it well. Your wittiness and charming personality could win over the employees and the shareholders. However…" Jane stopped, casting her eyes down as if she wanted to choose her words carefully. "To be successful, you can't be with Rory. I know you'll feel upset to hear this, but please hear me out."

Jane's eyes stared straight at me. "Rory is smart and kind. However, she isn't the right woman for you right now. What if she's the same as your other girlfriends, who only wanted you for money and status? Besides, you met her such a short time ago. I suggest you find a woman of prominent social status and family background to support you. I've overheard that Grandpa has thought to partner with Fournier Enterprises, and I believe you know the meaning of this. Yes, eventually, you would be introduced to Mr. Fournier's daughter, or maybe some other girl from his social circles...."

My vision blurred. My heart was numb as a sudden coldness hit my core.

Tears rolled down my cheeks like rain, creating a small pool on the desk as Jane's words continued until she said goodbye and wished him luck, and the video ended.

Feeling like I'd been hit by a bus, I sat there, staring blankly at the screen. I felt as if Jane was still looking at me and saying that I wasn't the right woman, that I was standing in the way of her brother's success. Her suspicions that I was using Peter to get to his money kept ringing in my ears.

I brushed my damp forehead with the back of my hand. Now I knew why he'd changed since the New Year. Why he couldn't contact me. He was cornered. His grandpa had told him about the plan, which was why he was meeting with Sophie. He'd known that we had no future together because I couldn't meet his family's expectations. He couldn't explain it to me without bluntly saying that I would be the cause of his failure, and breaking up wasn't on his agenda, so he persisted in keeping our relationship going.

However subconsciously, he'd chosen his family over me. Peter had hurt me in many ways without realizing it. He'd stood me up and kept changing our video call times to whenever he felt was convenient without considering my schedule. As much as I loved him, I refused to succumb to being played around with or tolerate his excuses.

My stomach was heavy, as if I'd swallowed a big rock. I closed all the windows and put the flash drive back in the drawer. As I stood up and gathered the loose papers, my finger touched something. Lifting the papers, I noticed an identical red flash drive with the initial *R* written on it. Dumbfounded, I stared at it, then gave a sad chuckle while putting the papers back on the desk. I took the flash drive.

"Well, this is it," I said quietly, gazing at the flash drive in my fingers. Dropping it into my pocket, I scanned the room as if I wanted to memorize it. Then, I shuffled toward the door and closed it behind me.

Peter had returned from his cycling when I was in the loft.

"Rory, I'm back!" he called.

Forcing a smile, I stood and leaned on the railing. "I'm here." I waved. "I've been organizing your new books."

He looked up, smiling. "I'll be there in a minute."

"Hurry up, hurry up," I teased him.

"Thanks for organizing the books. I've had no time," Peter said as he nimbly climbed the stairs. "Did you find a good book yet?" His hair was matted with sweat.

His eyes followed my finger, pointing at the piles of novels as he leaned down to kiss my cheek.

"I've ordered more new books. Once they're here, I'll let you know so you can borrow them."

"Thanks!"

"Oh, have you found the flash drive yet?" he asked.

I took it out of my pocket and showed it to him.

"Great. Now, I'm going to take a shower, and let's have brunch after that."

"Sounds good. I'm hungry." I said.

"Let me know where you want to eat."

Smiling, I nodded.

Peter flashed a smile before turning toward his room. My eyes were misty as I looked at his back. We weren't supposed to be together.

And I wasn't supposed to find that flash drive.

Chapter 30

$\mathcal{T}$WO WEEKS PASSED. ONCE WE returned to normal life, we were both buried in our work. Peter had one meeting after the other, and I was busy with my projects. I stayed busy mostly because I wanted to forget about the video and gradually drift away from him. Deliberately, I never initiated contact with him.

I was about to push the glass door to our client's office when someone called my name. I turned to see Sam walking out of the elevator and sauntering toward me.

"Ready to go home?" he asked.

I nodded. "It's been a long day."

"I hear ya." He chuckled, and we walked together toward the parking lot.

"Hey, Rory, if you're free, let's grab a quick dinner. I know where the best sandwiches around here are."

I glanced at my watch. It was six in the evening. His invitation was perfect because, at this moment, I didn't want to be alone. Besides, I liked talking to him, and we had had meals together a few times in the past.

"Sure." I nodded.

As I slid inside my car, Sam was typing something on his phone.

"The sandwich place isn't far from here," he said, looking at me. "I just texted you the address, and I'll see you there."

"Great," I said, starting my car.

The sandwich place wasn't too packed, and we got a nice spot to sit near the window that overlooked the parking lot.

While enjoying our sandwiches, Sam showed me pictures of his trip to Tokyo and Kyoto, including one where he wore a full kimono outfit—a traditional Japanese garment—complete with the traditional footwear. Without his glasses, he looked handsome, and that navy kimono made his blue eyes stand out.

"How's your aunt doing in Boston?" he asked.

"She's good, and busy with the charity work at her church. That's her passion."

"Yeah, that's really nice, though. My grandma is active at church too, especially since my uncle passed away." His face became forlorn.

Sam had told me that he'd grown up with his uncle after his dad passed away due to drug abuse. His mom had run off and married another man.

"It's sad that your uncle was childless when he passed. Maybe, if he'd had a child, your grandma wouldn't be so sad."

"That's one of the things that made my grandma sad too. His wife left him for a rich man because, at that time, my uncle hadn't become successful yet. He'd just finished law school and was about to take the bar exam." Sam shrugged.

"He never remarried?"

Sam shook his head. "He dated a few women, and he really loved the last one. Unfortunately, they weren't meant to be together."

A tinge of pain hit my chest at hearing his words. *They weren't meant to be together.*

Sam tapped on the table in front of me when I remained silent. "Are you okay?"

"Yeah." I forced a thin smile. "I was drawn by the story of your uncle's love life. It's so sad he didn't have a chance to marry his girl-friend. What happened to them?"

From his expression, I knew he didn't want to share that infor-mation with me, and I didn't try to convince him.

Glancing at my watch, I noticed the time. "Hey, it's past nine. I think I should leave now."

Sam looked at his watch too. "Yeah, let's go. My fault. I was talking a lot."

"Not at all." I shook my head.

We cleaned up our sandwich crumbs and tossed them into a trash bin on the way out. As we walked across the parking lot, the heel of my shoe got stuck in the street drain cover, and I would have fallen forward if Sam hadn't been walking in front of me.

"Ah, women's high-heeled shoes." He held out his arm. "Hold onto my arm while you pull your heel out."

I accepted the offer and wiggled my heel free.

"I can pull it for you," Sam said, bending down.

"No...no...I'm good," I replied. "Wait." I wrenched and wiggled a bit harder. With one giant pull, my heel was free.

"Is it broken?" he asked as I continued holding onto his strong arm to check the shoe.

"No, thank God! I just bought these shoes a month ago," I said, planting my foot on the ground.

"Everything's okay? No pulled muscle or anything?"

I shook my head. "Thanks for lending me your arm."

Sam smiled and together we sauntered toward my car.

"Thanks for the sandwich," I said, sliding inside.

"Don't mention it. See you tomorrow, Rory." Sam tapped the top of my car once I started it. "Sleep well."

"You too. See you tomorrow."

My phone buzzed as I neared my apartment. It was Peter. He had been texting me and had left a few messages but I hadn't responded yet.

Taking a deep breath, I answered the phone.

"Hi," Peter said, his voice coming from my car speaker. "How are you?"

"I'm tired. It has been crazy in the office," I said.

"I see," Peter replied. "Yeah, it's been crazy in my office too." When I didn't say anything, he asked, "Have you eaten dinner yet?"

"Yes, I just came back from dinner with Sam."

"Again? It seems that you've been dining together a lot lately," he said flatly.

I shrugged, although he couldn't see me. "Well, we're working together a lot now. He's experienced in dealer litigation, and I'm the senior analyst for troubled dealerships. Besides, I like talking to him."

Peter huffed, and the line became silent again.

"This weekend," he said, breaking the silence, "can you stay at my house again? I can pick you up tomorrow."

"Hmm…I can't this weekend," I said after thinking about my schedule. "Sam invited Zoe, Sebastian, and me to watch the new Marvel movie together. It's gonna be nice to hang out with my coworkers so we can bond. I did things like that when I was in Boston. Don't you have to entertain Sophie?" I asked, not giving him a chance to express his displeasure. "You said that entertaining her is part of your job now." I poked the sensitive topic on purpose.

"I asked Tom to entertain her because I wanted to spend time with you, but I didn't know you'd have plans with your friends."

"Well, if you'd told me earlier, I wouldn't have made plans this weekend."

"So, I need to make an appointment now?" he asked, his voice rising.

I frowned. "Of course not. Why do you sound so unhappy? I've never complained any of the times you've canceled our plans."

"That's because I already scheduled this weekend to spend time with you," he said. "My schedule is tight, and you know that. So, if I plan something, it means I have to adjust everything else accordingly."

Anger rose in my chest. "That's unfair and selfish! Just because your schedule's tight, it's okay for me to change my plans, but not for you? Just because you're the president of your company with thousands of employees, you assume that your time is more important than mine? Wow, I didn't know you sacrificed so much, Peter!"

"Don't be sarcastic. You haven't complained about that before. Is it because you really want to spend time with your friends? Or with Sam?" Peter said coldly.

"If I haven't complained, it doesn't mean I agree. I've been *tolerating* your busyness, Peter," I protested. "And, yes, I like spending time with Sam. At least he always keeps his promises."

Peter scoffed, and I closed my eyes as my hand clenched the phone.

"I've had a long day today, and I'm exhausted. I don't want to argue with you. Let's talk again when we both aren't too busy."

"Sure." He hung up.

I rubbed my hands across my face and let out a heavy sigh. I sat in the car for a while before getting out, then dragged my feet toward my apartment. The room was dark as I opened the door. Feeling for the light switch, I turned on the light. After dropping my computer bag and my purse on the carpet, I dialed my aunt's number.

While I waited for her to answer, I sat on the sofa and pulled my legs close to my chest. It seemed to take forever until finally I heard her voice on the other end.

"Hi, Rory. How are you, dear?"

Tears welled behind my eyes. I bit my lower lip to keep it from trembling.

"Rory? Are you there?"

I swallowed and answered in a thick voice, "Yeah."

"What happened? Your voice sounds different. Where are you? Are you crying? Wh—"

"Auntie, I can't be with Peter anymore. I think it's time to break up," I said, interrupting her.

There was silence on her end of the line. "When?"

"Soon."

"Oh...."

"And I'm gonna be the one to do it."

Chapter 31

"I'M GLAD WE FINALLY HAVE time to meet today," said Peter, offering Rory a smile. They'd agreed to meet in a restaurant Peter knew Rory would like. On this bright, sunny day, sitting outdoors was the best choice. "We haven't seen each other for, what, two weeks?"

"Three," Rory said without looking at him. Her fingers rubbed her water glass, and her eyes didn't move from it.

A pang of anxiousness jolted through his chest. "Are you okay? Have you slept well?" he asked. "You look pale."

She shook her head. "I'm…just tired."

Peter reached out to touch her fingers, but she moved them away. A flood of nervous energy flooded him, and he noticed that Rory kept looking away. Her shoulders drooped and her eyes were dull, not bright with their usual vigor, and she kept staring down at her hands.

"Rory, are you okay?" he asked again in a whisper.

"Peter," she said.

"Yes?"

"Let's break up."

"What?" Peter almost jumped from his seat, and he felt like his blood was being drained from his body. "Why?"

Pushing her chair back, Rory rose to her feet, her fingers curling at her sides, and he saw pain reflecting in her eyes.

"I can't continue this relationship anymore," she said.

"W—why?" he stuttered, rising from his chair slowly. "I thought everything was fine."

He thought she seemed conflicted. Her lips pressed together in a slight grimace. "Obviously, you and I have a different definition of the word 'fine.' Our relationship is an illusion, Peter," she finally said.

Rory shifted her weight from foot to foot. Her face was slightly red, and it was apparent she was warring with herself. Peter bit the inside of his lip, forcing himself not to hug her as he usually did when she was upset.

"We've deceived ourselves. I've kept telling myself not to worry about the future. It's only temporary. But day after day, I can't see the light at the end of the tunnel. We're *far* from okay, and I know you feel that way too. Don't you?"

Before he could answer, she continued, "You never consider my schedule. You've stood me up many times. You've been busy with Sophie, and you keep saying that her father has a business that will benefit your grandpa. Whatever it is, her role must be significant in that deal, and I can't compete with her. She has become the center of your life, and she's been too important for you to spare any time for me, even if it's just sending me a text or calling me." Rory bit her lower lip. "Because of that, I've drowned myself in work. If my boyfriend doesn't care about our relationship, why should I? Why am I always the only one who keeps adjusting my time for you? And what kind of relationship is it if we can't even make an effort to communicate with each other, even after I moved here? I'm tired of this kind of relationship. You're too selfish." Her voice cracked.

"I can change," Peter said in a whisper. His throat felt sandy.

Her shoulder-length, dark brown hair moved slightly as Rory shook her head. "You can't. You care so much about your company, and you have an obligation to ensure the partnership business with Sophie's father will be successful. You're a responsible guy, Peter. You won't sacrifice them for your own interests because you aren't that kind of person."

His head spun as he listened to her words. "Is that a strong enough reason for you to break up with me?" he asked bitterly.

Rory glanced up and looked down again. "I can't stand living in your world. It's too complicated for me to understand, Peter. You're right—I detest arrogant people, and you have a bunch of them in your family."

"I can't change them because—"

"And I understand that," she interrupted. "And I *won't* change myself either."

For a moment, neither of them said anything.

"Another reason is…I've lost interest in you," she added. "I like someone else."

A fire shot into Peter's stomach. "Is it Sam?" he asked coldly.

"I won't answer that."

Peter's stomach felt like it had dropped into his ankles, and he couldn't believe what he was hearing. "So, you want to break up?" he asked.

Rory's cheeks paled even more, and Peter was afraid she would faint.

She sighed and took her couple's bracelet off her wrist. Looking directly at him, she put it in Peter's hand. Her fingers were icy cold when they touched his palm. "Let's break up, Peter," she said.

Her gentle eyes stared at him for a few seconds before she lowered them. She stepped back and turned, her steps echoing down the pavement as she departed, leaving him alone.

Chapter 32

I'D DATED A FEW MEN before Peter. During past breakups, I'd felt angry for up to a week, but then I moved on.

But that was not the case when I broke up with Peter.

I couldn't forget how visibly torn he'd looked when I left him. His face was pale. His hands were balled into fists. I'd felt his eyes following me until I turned the corner. I didn't know how long he'd stood in a daze. I didn't want to know because I'd left the place in a hurry and didn't want him to catch me sobbing.

My heart felt torn into pieces when I said I was no longer interested in him. It was cruel, because he didn't deserve those words, yet I didn't deserve to be treated the way he'd treated me, as if I weren't his girlfriend. But I had to say something that would make him hate me and move on.

For the whole day after that, I lay curled up on the carpet in the corner between my bed and the wall, weeping until I fell asleep.

To bury our memories, I worked longer hours. The more pain I felt, the more I worked. Zoe and Sebastian noticed the difference, but they thought it was because I wanted to work permanently in California, so they let me be.

Sam didn't like it. He bugged me to leave the office when he noticed my Skype business account online after office hours. When

I turned off Skype to avoid him, he came down to my cubicle to check on me.

I wished I could tell Sam about it. Maybe later, if I could manage not to shed tears over it.

On the sixth day after I broke up with Peter, I was about to take lunch with Ana from the retail department when I noticed Tom standing next to his car outside my office. My heart sank.

"I'm sorry, I have to take a rain check," I said to Ana.

She followed the direction of my eyes, and, noticing Tom, she nodded. "Don't worry. We can go together whenever you aren't busy. See you later."

I nodded and walked to Tom's car. "Hi," I greeted him as cheerfully as I could manage.

"Hi." He gave a small smile and waved, opening the passenger door for me. His eyes were not shining like usual. I sighed softly. Although we were good friends, I knew he would be on Peter's side because he cared about him, tending to protect him as if Peter were his kid brother.

"How are you, Tom?" I asked.

Tom sighed, driving his car toward the shopping center not far from my office. "I'd be better if I hadn't heard the bad news."

"Is Peter okay?"

He squinted. "You broke up with him. Why do you care?"

I shrugged. "I just wanted to make sure if he's drunk at a bar he won't give my number to the bartender."

"Even if he was drunk, I would make sure he called me," he snapped.

"Thank you."

"You're welcome," he said coldly.

My fingers played with the strap on my satchel as we fell into silence.

"Why did you want to break up? I thought you guys were a

good couple." Tom's fingers clenched the wheel so tightly his knuckles turned white.

I swallowed and looked out the window. "Well, maybe we weren't as good as we seemed."

Tom scowled. The silence grew, and I started feeling like I was suffocating, especially when we passed my old apartment where Peter and I'd used to room together. I knew Tom had done it on purpose.

"Do you want to know why we broke up?" I broke the silence.

Tom glanced at me for a few seconds before returning his eyes to the road. "I'm listening," he said, his voice colder still.

My stomach knotted. I liked Tom because he was always kind to me, but I needed to push aside my feelings and focus on my goal, which was to make him hate me too.

"I've lost interest in your brother," I said in a matter-of-fact tone.

Tom's car screeched as it made a sudden turn. He pulled into the entrance of a nearby public park and stopped in the parking lot.

"Because you have a new man?" he asked sharply.

I blinked. "What?"

He scoffed, shaking his head without hiding a disgusted expression. "Are you pretending that you're innocent now?" he asked. "You came out of the sandwich restaurant near Fashion Island with a guy a couple days ago, holding his arm and giggling. Don't deny it, because I was there with my friends and I saw everything."

I blinked again.

"Still pretending you don't remember?" he snapped. "The guy was wearing a white, long-sleeved shirt and driving a silver BMW 8 series Gran Coupe. His license plate read 6SJR890. Ring a bell? And don't tell me that he's *just* a friend, because you both seemed pretty chummy."

I mentally slapped my forehead because Sam had been dragged

into the issue. But if that made Tom hate me, it would be worth a try.

After composing myself, I turned to Tom and gave him a sad smile. "I guess that guy is more interesting than your brother."

What I said worked well, as Tom's face turned red.

"Really?" He studied my face as though trying to determine if I was telling the truth.

"Yes," I said firmly, feeling my nails dig into my palms. "I think we had a connection from the day we met."

"Did you feel a connection when you met my brother?" he asked.

"It felt different this time," I said shortly.

We looked at each other for a few seconds before Tom closed his eyes and turned his face away. "Peter loves you more than you can imagine, Rory, and I feel stupid for encouraging him to tell you how he feels. I thought you loved him and could've been the one. In the end, you're the same as all those other girls who claimed they liked him. You just played with his feelings." He pointed to the door. "I can't look at you anymore. Please get out of my car."

I bit the inside of my lip and nodded.

Before I opened the door, I turned to him and said, "I was thankful for your brother's love, although in the end, we grew apart. However, stop thinking that your brother is a gentleman. He isn't. Goodbye, Tom."

Tom didn't look at me as I closed the door.

"Be brave, Rory," I said to myself as I walked away.

That day, we had a heat wave, but I didn't feel the heat and humidity at all as I walked slowly back to my office. My heart felt like thousands of needles were piercing it every second. I'd never realized that breaking up with Peter meant that I would lose a good friend, but I was right to do this. The more they hated me, the better.

Chapter 33

MY AUNT WAS IN TOWN, but she stayed with her friend on Balboa Island for a few days before staying with me. She didn't say anything, but I could tell that she worried about me. I told her that I was fine, especially as it had already been a month since I broke up with Peter. However, she still wanted to check on me.

"Leaving early today?" asked Sam as we bumped into each other in the hallway. His eyes were on the computer bag on my shoulder.

"Yes, my aunt is here. I need to pick her up at her friend's house on Balboa Island," I said.

"She chose the right time to stay on the island. The weather has been beautiful out there."

"Yup, I heard that too, but she doesn't want to hear it every time I try to convince her to move back to California." I laughed. "Living here is expensive, and besides, she loves Boston."

My phone buzzed, interrupting our conversation.

"See you tomorrow," Sam said as I nodded at him and answered it.

"Hello?" I said, not recognizing the phone number.

"Is this Rory?" a woman's voice asked on the other end.

"Speaking."

"My name is Susan, your aunt's friend. I'm sorry to break this news, dear. Your aunt has had a heart attack, and now…"

I froze. My phone slipped from my hand and fell to the carpet. Panic rose in my chest. My breath became short, and I heard myself wheeze with every exhalation. It was impossible. Aunt Amy was the healthiest person I'd ever known.

In my daze, I heard footsteps approach, followed by a strong shake on my shoulder. Sam must have heard my phone hit the floor. "Hey, Rory. What happened?" he asked.

"My aunt," I wheezed.

Sam picked up the phone and held it to his ear. "Hello?" he said before glancing at me. "Hi, this is Sam, Rory's coworker. Yes, she's still here. Her phone fell. She must have been shocked by the news."

He nodded. "Her aunt. She's mentioned it. Okay. Which hospital? I see. Yes, I know that hospital. Yes, we'll be there shortly. Thank you, ma'am."

Sam ended the call, and I tried to focus on his words.

"Your aunt is in the hospital because of a heart attack. I'll take you there," he said calmly. "Before we go, did you bring your inhaler with you?"

Wheezing, I nodded and opened my satchel. My hand trembled, and it was hard to open the flap fastening the front.

"I'll hold your bag." Gently, Sam took the bag from my shoulder and opened the flap for me. Holding my purse, he searched for the inhaler. Once he got it, he gave it to me.

"Here, take it first," he said.

Bringing the inhaler to my mouth, I put the mouthpiece between my teeth and closed my lips tightly around it before pressing the top down. In less than three minutes, my lungs opened and started to function well again.

"Do you feel better now?" Sam's eyes narrowed with worry.

"Yeah."

"Come on, let me take you to the hospital," he said, signaling me to follow him.

"I can drive there by myself," I said, refusing his offer.

He shook his head. "It's better if I drive you."

I looked at him before nodding and following him to his silver BMW parked in a reserved parking space.

After making sure I buckled up, he put my bags in the trunk and slid into his seat. Then he plugged the coordinates of the hospital into the navigation system.

A tear fell from my eye as he drove the car toward the gate. "She's my only family, Sam. If she passes," I choked on my own words, "I have no one."

He looked at me, his eyes full of sympathy. "Don't torture yourself like that. Just think positively that she'll be okay."

I nodded.

It took us forty minutes to get to the hospital. Susan, my aunt's friend, gave me a hug when she saw me. I was glad that she'd already stopped crying, although her face was still red. A nurse with a low ponytail approached me.

"Are you Mrs. Wakumi Ishida's niece?" she asked, looking at her clipboard.

"Yes." I nodded.

"Your aunt is being prepared for surgery. The doctor is going to perform a coronary artery bypass. Once she's done, you can see her. Now, please follow me because I need you to fill out some forms," she said.

"Rory, wait," called Susan. She handed me my aunt's bag. "Just in case you need her driver's license," she said. "And if you need me, I'll be here for you."

"Thank you, Susan."

She nodded and sat again, dabbing her wet eyes.

I turned to Sam. "Thank you for bringing me here. You don't have to wait for me. I'll take an Uber later."

"Do you need help with the forms?" he asked, ignoring my question. "I could help you read them to make sure you're covered."

I looked from him to the nurse. "Is it okay if my friend helps me? He's a lawyer."

"I think it should be fine," she said.

"Are you sure you don't need to go somewhere?" I asked Sam doubtfully.

"I'm here for you," he assured me.

I gazed at him for a moment and nodded, feeling glad of his offer.

Sam walked behind me as we followed the nurse. His presence was helpful because there were many things to read and sign. He compared and reread the forms with all my aunt's information before I put my signature on them.

After I was done, the nurse brought me to my aunt's room while Sam went into the waiting room with Susan.

My heart dropped when I saw how pale Aunt Amy was.

"I'll be fine," she said as I took her hand. "Don't worry about me, kiddo."

"I know." My voice trembled. Clearing my throat, I said again, "I know you'll be fine. You're a wonder woman."

She gave a light laugh. "Yes, buy me the costume complete with a golden lasso."

I nodded. "Sure, once you're out of the hospital."

Her angular eyes were misty as they looked at me. "Love you, pumpkin."

Pushing my fears to the side, I leaned down to kiss her forehead. "I love you too, Auntie."

"Pardon me, ma'am," said the nurse to my aunt. "She has to leave now."

My aunt nodded.

I braced myself and smiled at her. "I'll be outside," I said again, turning quickly to make sure my aunt didn't see my wet eyes.

Outside the room, my vision blurred with tears. I covered my mouth and tried not to sob out loud. Susan rushed to comfort me. Sam lowered his head and didn't say anything.

THE SURGERY WAS ONGOING. SAM left and promised to come back, although I'd already asked him not to.

Around eight o'clock, he returned with Maxine, his girlfriend. He'd already introduced me to her during what was supposed to have been a double date. But since I'd already broken up with Peter, just the three of us had lunch together.

I liked Max. She and Sam complemented each other. Max was outgoing, and Sam was sometimes a bit reserved.

"Your aunt has been in the OR for five hours now?" asked Sam.

"Yeah, the doctors said it takes three to six hours for that kind of surgery," I said, exhausted.

"Why don't you change your clothes?" suggested Max, taking a T-shirt from the bag she carried. Her olive skin looked perfect in her green shirt. "I lent you my T-shirt because Sam said that you might stay late tonight, so changing your clothes will help you feel fresh. And"—she took out a toiletry bag—"a new toothbrush, a new hairbrush, face soap, and toothpaste."

I was touched by her kindness. She reminded me of Lizzy, my old roommate.

Max let out a laugh as I hugged her tightly. "Go, change into this clean shirt. I'll wait here with Sam."

I nodded and took the bag with me.

"See, you look better," said Max as I came back. I noticed a pillow and a folded blanket on the sofa. Two thermoses, a few bananas and chocolate bars, and two boxes of sandwiches were on the table.

"Hot cocoa and chicken soup." Max pointed at the thermoses.

"You shouldn't have," I said, "but thank you."

"That's what friends are for. Sam told me that you have no

family here. I understand because I have no family but him." Max glanced at Sam. "If you want me to, I can stay with you tonight," she offered. "Don't worry—I'm a detective, so I'm used to sleeping anywhere."

"Thank you, but it isn't necessary. You guys have already given me a lot."

Max sighed and looked at Sam, who shrugged. "All right. But call us if you need anything." Her eyes locked on mine.

"Thank you," I said.

Sam and Max accompanied me for another half hour and then left. I was incredibly grateful for their presence. Their kindness reminded me of Rick and Maggie, our family friends. Rick had passed away two months after I moved to Boston, and since then, Maggie had moved in with their daughter in New Jersey. Otherwise, they would be here for me.

I sighed and looked around. Not many people were in the waiting room anyway. After pouring myself a cup of hot cocoa, I sat down with the blanket around my shoulders. Taking a sip of cocoa, my mind flew to Peter. If he were by my side, I would feel better, but…I shook my head. My decision to break up with him was best for both of us. Closing my eyes, I tried to breathe calmly and control my emotions.

I must have dozed off, but later, a hand gently shook my shoulder. A nurse woke me up. Next to him was a doctor still in his surgery garb. With a jolt, I sat straight up.

"Miss Arrington?" the nurse asked me. "Doctor Lee is the one who performed your aunt's surgery."

"How was it?" I asked, my voice trembling.

"It was successful," Doctor Lee said, giving a reassuring smile. "Everything is fine now, but she needs time to recover. She's still sleeping from the medication and she will be in the intensive coronary care unit for a day or two, so we can monitor her condition closely."

Tears fell from my eyes. "Thank you, thank you."

"You're welcome," the doctor said, shaking my hand. "You look tired, young lady. Why don't you go home and sleep? You need rest too." His expression was one of concern.

"I can call you a taxi if you want," offered the nurse.

"Thank you." I gave them a smile and pointed at my thermoses, pillow, blanket, and food on the table. "I'll stay here tonight."

"Well, make sure you get some rest, then. Have a good night." The doctor gave a nod and left.

The nurse looked at me. "Do you want me to show you where the vending machine or hot water for coffee and tea are?"

"Thanks, I know," I replied.

"Okay, just wanted to make sure." He offered me a smile. "Good night."

A buzz came from my phone just as I sat down. It was a text from Sam.

How's the surgery? I bet it should be done by now.

I texted him back. *The doctor just told me it went well.*

I'm so glad! I'll pick you up tomorrow morning so you can change your clothes and rest before going back to the hospital, he responded.

I was touched by his kindness. *Thanks. Goodnight, Sam.*

Goodnight, Rory. See you tomorrow.

THE NEXT MORNING, A SOFT-SPOKEN nurse came to see me. My heart dropped to the floor when I saw her grim expression. She informed me that my aunt's condition wasn't good. Her blood pressure kept dropping, and her blood count was low.

Noticing how pale I was, the nurse patted my shoulder. "Do you have anyone who can be with you now?" she asked.

"My boyf—" I stopped myself, wiping my damp forehead. "I'll call my friend later."

She nodded. "If you need someone to be with you, let me know."

"Thanks."

Around seven-thirty, Martin called and advised me to take a few days off work to be with my aunt.

"I can work from the hospital if you want," I offered.

"Aurorette Arrington," Martin said solemnly without using his French accent, "let me advise you that a job is a job. Your aunt is your aunt. If you leave this company, you can find another job, but you cannot replace your aunt. Yesterday's already passed, and we don't know about tomorrow. You only have today. To give you peace of mind, take two or three days off, and then we can do something if you need longer than that. Agreed?"

I was speechless. Beneath his harsh words, Martin had a gentle heart.

"Okay. Thank you," I said.

"Good. Don't forget to give me an update, okay?" he asked before hanging up.

An hour later, Sam came to the hospital with two dozen donuts for the nurses. Everybody was happy to get a free breakfast, and they thanked him wholeheartedly. In many ways, Sam was almost as charming as Peter.

"For you," he said, giving me two chocolate croissants. "I'll drive you back to your apartment. I suggest you take a nap before coming back to the hospital."

"I can't go back. My aunt's condition isn't good," I said quietly, looking up at him.

"I know, but your health is important too," he said gently, sitting next to me. "Try to rest for two or three hours and then come back. Your aunt won't be happy if you're sick too, right?" he added.

"I'm afraid of losing her." I looked down, trying to hold back my tears.

Sam placed his arm around me, allowing me to lean my head on his shoulder as my tears fell.

"When my dad passed away and my mom left me, I thought I was the unluckiest kid on earth," he said, sighing. "Now, I want to return to my younger self and tell him that I was actually the luckiest kid. I still had a grandma, an uncle, and an aunt who loved me." He pulled away to look at me. "Come on. Let me take you home."

Sniffing, I nodded and gathered my belongings and we walked slowly toward the exit.

Chapter 34

SAM WAS RIGHT. THREE HOURS of sleep did wonders to refresh my tired soul. After lunch, I gathered some clothes and food for my stay at the hospital.

My phone rang as I was locking the door to my apartment. I frowned. It was Tom. I didn't want to answer, but he used to be my friend.

"Hey, Tom," I said.

"Hi, Rory." His voice sounded hesitant. "How are you?"

"Okay. How about you?"

"I'm okay too," he said slowly.

"What's up?"

"Umm, is it okay if I meet you?" he asked.

"Well, I'm busy and about to step out now. Why?"

"I want to talk to you, and I'm actually standing behind you right now."

Turning around, I saw Tom in his light green shirt and jeans, waving at me as he turned off his phone. "Hi." He regarded the tote bag in my hand and the computer bag over my shoulder. Since I planned to spend the night at the hospital, I wanted to occupy myself by watching or reading something with my notebook. I'd brought food so I didn't have to spend money at the hospital cafeteria. "Are you going somewhere?"

"Ah...yes." I nodded.

"What time will you be home?" he asked.

"I won't be back until late, maybe tomorrow. Why?"

Tom shifted his weight from foot to foot, biting his lower lip. "I wanted to apologize for my rudeness the other day," he said without looking at me. "Breakups are normal. Just...it was my wishful thinking that you and Peter would be together forever since you guys looked great together."

I could feel the smile on my lips. "Thank you, but..." I shrugged.

He looked up, and our eyes met. "You aren't mad at me?"

"I was mad and sad, but mostly sad. However, I understand your sentiment."

He was about to say something when my phone buzzed. I raised my hand to stop him and glanced at the display. It was the hospital.

I cleared my throat and answered. "Hello?"

"Rory?"

"Speaking," I answered.

"Hi, this is James from the hospital. I just want to know when you'll come back to the hospital?"

"W—what happened?" My lower lip trembled.

"Your aunt. Her heartbeat is erratic, and we just gave her some medication, so she should be okay in a few more minutes. But we thought it would be better if you come here soon."

"Yeah, I'm about to leave now. Thanks for letting me know," I said and hung up. Forcing a smile, I spun on my heel to face Tom. "Sorry, Tom. I have to go now. Talk to you later, okay?"

"Rory, what happened?" He held my arm as I tried to pass him.

"Nothing...just...sorry, I need to leave now." I pulled my arm free and scurried toward my car.

"Rory, you look pale. Tell me what happened," he insisted.

With my hand on the car door, I briefly closed my eyes. Without looking at him, I said, "My aunt...she had a heart attack yesterday and open heart surgery last night. I just got a phone call that her condition isn't good. I..." I took a deep breath. Everything inside me felt raw and exposed. "Sorry...."

I widened my eyes as Tom held his hand against the car door. "I'll drive you there."

"What?"

"Have you considered me as your friend?" he asked.

Puzzled, I looked at him and nodded.

"Then you should accept my offer." His blue eyes looked at me warmly, and I needed someone to be with me.

"Okay. Thanks."

Solemnly, Tom took the tote bag and signaled me to follow him to his car. He slid into the driver's seat and started the engine. We didn't say anything. I was too worried about my aunt and just wanted to be there for her.

"I'm sorry about your aunt. It must be tough for you," he said finally.

I looked across the car and gave him a tight smile. "She's my only family." I looked out of the window as my sight became blurry.

Tom tapped my shoulder gently and sighed. "Peter loves your aunt. He must kn—"

"Don't tell him." I whipped my head to face him. "Please don't. I couldn't stand it if he looked at me in pity."

Tom opened his mouth but closed it again. He looked at me for a moment before returning his eyes to the road.

"Did your boyfriend accompany you last night?"

I groaned and rubbed my neck tiredly.

"Sorry, it's hard to believe that you have a new boyfriend so soon after breaking up," he said in an apologetic tone.

"Do you see a circle of light above my head? I'm not a saint, Tom," I responded wearily.

We rode in silence until we reached the hospital.

"Thanks for driving me here," I said as I unfastened my seat belt.

Tom turned his car into a parking space. "I'll go with you," he said.

I shook my head. "That's okay, I—"

"Rory," Tom cut me off. He seemed annoyed. "You're my friend, so shut up and let me help you. I'll leave after I make sure you're okay."

My heart stopped beating for a few seconds, as if Peter stood in front of me rather than Tom. Although they were born from different mothers, I could see a resemblance between them from certain angles. It made me miss Peter badly.

"Thank you," I swallowed.

Tom nodded and opened his trunk to get the tote and computer bag for me, and we walked toward the hospital entrance.

TOM WAS THERE WHEN NEIL, the cardiologist's assistant, explained my aunt's condition in front of the intensive coronary care unit. It turned out he was Tom's old friend from college.

"We've decided to let your aunt stay in the ICCU until she's out of the woods," Neil said. "But she's stable now. We assume she's worried about you, which was why her heartbeat was erratic earlier. But, yeah, if you could stay here for a night, it'd be good for her."

"Yes, I planned to stay here tonight," I said.

Neil nodded. "Okay, I'll come back again this afternoon," he said, turning to Tom and shaking his hand. "Good to see you, man. Let's catch up over a meal one day."

"Likewise, Neil. I look forward to it." Tom offered him a smile.

Neil smiled back and left. Tom's eyes followed him until he disappeared around the corner.

"What?" Tom said, feeling my eyes on him.

"Nothing." I shrugged but gave him a meaningful smile. Then I walked toward the waiting room at the end of the corridor.

"Hey," he said, catching up with me. "What's with that smile?"

"What's wrong? I smile because I want to smile," I said with forced casualness.

He lifted a single eyebrow and gave my shoulder a nudge, then fell into step beside me. When we entered the waiting room, we found Sam and Max already there. They stood in unison as I approached.

"Rory." Max gave me a quick hug and released me. "How's everything?" she asked, her eyes filled with concern.

"Why are you both here?" I asked. "I thought you'd be here this afternoon."

"I was worried about you, so we decided to come earlier because we wanted to make sure everything was okay," said Sam.

"Well, my aunt's heartbeat was erratic, but she's stable now. The doctor said she must've been worried about me and suggested that I stay here tonight and tomorrow, which is exactly my plan."

"I see," Sam said. "Let us know if you need anything. We can bring you some food tonight."

"Thanks, Sam."

Tom, standing next to me, suddenly thrust his hand toward Sam. "Hi, I'm Tom. And you are…?"

"I'm Sam," said Sam. My eyes widened as I watched them shake hands. "Nice to meet you."

"And…?" Tom's head whipped to Max.

"Oh, this is Max, my girlfriend," Sam said, smiling and placing his hand on her shoulder.

I pretended not to see Tom's eyes bore into me after shaking Max's hand.

After Sam and Max left, Tom started drilling me when we were in the hospital coffee shop.

"Max is Sam's girlfriend." Tom shifted a little in his seat, looking straight at me. "Isn't he greedy for having both you *and* Max?"

I sighed. I couldn't play dumb anymore by pretending that Sam was my boyfriend.

"Sam's an attorney in my office." I flipped my hand. "We've been working together a lot because he's the legal representative for us each time we have to deal with our clients who have financial problems. When you saw us, we were having dinner together after working late."

"And...he isn't your boyfriend?"

I shook my head slowly.

Tom leaned forward. "But why were you holding his arm so intimately outside the restaurant?"

I blinked, then gave a nod as I understood his question. "My heel slipped into the street drain cover and got stuck. Sam lent his arm so I could pull it out and then he helped me walk to my car."

"But you're not dating him," he said slowly, as though trying to reassure himself.

"No."

"If there's no third person, why did you break up with Peter?" He looked at me curiously.

"I..." I stopped and looked at Tom. "I lost interest in your brother."

His blue eyes gazed into mine, searching for lies hidden there.

"Come on, Tom. Give me a break," I whined. Without waiting, I gathered my bags and stood.

Tom followed slowly, his eyes fixed on me. "I think...I think you're lying to me about your feelings," he said. "But I'll give you a break *today*."

I almost rolled my eyes. Apparently, persistence was hereditary.

"Thanks for everything today, Tom. I really appreciate it," I said, standing in the hallway before he left.

He stepped forward and gave me a hug. "Don't mention it. See you again, Rory."

"Tom?" I stopped him as he turned to leave.

"Yes?"

"Don't tell Peter, please," I begged.

His lips twitched, but he nodded. "Okay."

Chapter 35

THE NEXT DAY, SAM AND Max took me out for breakfast because they didn't want me to stay in the waiting room and worry about my aunt's condition.

After eating, I agreed to accompany Sam to Corona Del Mar, while Max left us for work. As a homicide detective for the LAPD, she worked different hours than regular office employees. Sam looked at her proudly as she walked toward her car.

"How long have you been with her?" I asked, stepping into his BMW.

"Eight years."

"Wow! That's quite a long time."

He nodded, peering through his windshield.

"Why don't you propose to her?"

Sam didn't answer right away and drew his lower lip into his mouth. "It's complicated."

I chuckled. "When I said my relationship with Peter was complicated, you laughed at me."

"You can laugh if you want to," he challenged me. "I'm not that petty."

"Ha ha ha." I made a face at him.

Sam smirked.

"Seriously, why can't you?" I asked again, sucking my boba milk tea drink.

"Max is a single mother of a ten-year-old boy, and her job is too dangerous in my family's opinion," Sam said, seeming to choose his words carefully. "And…she's five years older than me."

I coughed, splashing some milk tea on the dashboard. "No way! She's almost forty? She looks younger than you!"

Sam smiled proudly and pulled two tissues from the box hanging behind my seat. "That's gonna be sticky if you don't wipe it off right away." He gestured to the mess with his head.

"But age isn't a huge matter, right? Remember Priyanka, who married one of the Jonas Brothers? She's ten years older than Nick," I commented, cleaning the milk tea from the dashboard.

Sam shrugged. "Yeah, blame me for being a coward. Maybe subconsciously I don't want to disappoint my grandma. My dad was an abuser, which is why my mom left him. My uncle divorced his wife. I'm practically the last man in the family. And if my marriage to Max ended, it would break my grandma's heart."

My head bobbed up and down in understanding.

Sam didn't say anything more, and we drove on silently.

"Tell me, why are you going to Corona Del Mar?" I asked, breaking the silence.

"Visiting my uncle's grave. Today is the third anniversary of his death. I want to pay my respects. Usually, Max accompanies me, but not today."

I winced slightly. If I'd known he was visiting his uncle's grave, I wouldn't have joined him. But staying in the hospital wouldn't make me feel good either.

We stopped at a flower shop nearby for a bouquet of yellow roses.

"He liked yellow roses," Sam said without me asking.

"My mom liked yellow roses too," I said.

Sam smiled and put the bouquet on the back seat before sliding into the driver's seat.

Thirty minutes later, we arrived at the cemetery. I took the flowers from the back seat and gave them to him.

"Thank you. Come on." Sam walked in front of me, a backpack over his shoulder and the flowers in his hand.

The land where the cemetery was located was huge and hilly, with flat graves covered by meadowlike, manicured grass. After passing the graves, we walked toward some burial sites surrounded by chest-high limestone walls and small gates. It gave a sense of privacy for the families who visited them.

As we reached a smaller plot next to a red myrtle tree, Sam opened the wrought iron gate and motioned for me to step inside.

"This is a nice site!" I exclaimed in a whisper. "It has a stone bench too." I pointed at the bench near the gate.

Sam smiled and knelt in front of the headstones before placing the flowers on the ground. I scanned the plot, then knelt next to him and clasped my hands in front of my chest to say a short prayer.

Sam pulled a few weeds from the ground as I read the names on the stones.

"Jonathan Pearson Williams," I muttered before turning to read the other one. "Marie Ishida Arr…" I blinked a few times and leaned forward to read clearly. "Marie Ishida Arrington?"

Sam looked at me as my head whipped around to face him.

"Why is my mom…" My voice trailed off. "Is this some kind of joke?" My hand trembled as I pointed at the headstone.

"No, it's not a joke. That's the name of the woman he loved dearly," Sam answered solemnly.

My chest tightened as I clutched the grass at my sides. *It can't be true!*

"I'm sorry if this seems dramatic, because I had no idea how else to reveal it to you without causing you more pain, but I can explain." Sam helped me to my feet and led me to the stone bench. I was dizzy as I sat next to him.

"Are you okay to hear this?" He looked at me gently.

I nodded, clasping my fingers together. My hands were cold.

"In the middle of 1993, my uncle decided to take some courses at the University of Tokyo. It was a year after he'd divorced his wife for cheating on him. When he was there, he met a first-year student named Marie Ishida and fell in love with her. Luckily for him, she felt the same way. They were always together until my grandma called my uncle back to the States because my grandpa was very sick.

"My uncle loved my grandpa and left Tokyo in a hurry. Two days later, my grandpa passed away and left his law firm to my uncle. It took him a year or so to take care of everything. After he was settled down, he went back to Tokyo to find Miss Ishida, but she was no longer at the school. He was shocked and reached out to people who knew her, but they all seemed to hate him. Feeling confused and heartbroken, he returned to the States."

Sam stopped and studied my face. After being silent for a couple of minutes, he continued.

"Five years later, while he was working in his client's office, he bumped into one of Miss Ishida's classmates. Her husband was working in that office as a Japanese expatriate. She happened to be picking up her husband from work that day. From her, my uncle found out about your mom's pregnancy, her dropping out of school, and the fight in your mom's family that caused her to fly to Boston and change her name to Arrington, your grandma's maiden name. That classmate seemed reluctant to reveal more, but she told him that his daughter's name was Aurora.

"Remember our conversation about your name when you'd explained that it was derived from Aurora, the ancient Greek goddess of the dawn, but then your mom changed it to Aurorette because she loved everything about the French?" he asked.

I frowned and nodded slowly. "Yes."

"That day, after I returned home, I double-checked with the notes my uncle and I had collected about you and your mom. I thought it had to be a coincidence.

"I'm not sure how he finally found your mom's address in Boston, but it was too late. The house had been sold to a new owner who didn't know where your mom had moved. The odds were against him because he always seemed to be one step behind you and your mom. One day, he learned that she had passed away, and that broke his heart even more. He felt remorseful and regretted what he'd done to her. A few years later, he fell sick, and his health gradually declined. Before he passed away, he told me to put her name on his headstone, next to his, and then continue looking for you.

"When we met in the café that time, I was following your aunt's trail. My uncle and I had figured out that, if your mom passed away, and your name couldn't be found in any orphanages, it meant someone was taking care of you."

"But how are you sure that I'm his daughter?" I asked.

Sam smiled patiently. "Let me continue. My uncle and I didn't know that your aunt had changed her name from Wakumi Ishida to Amy Ishida," Sam said. "When the nurse at the hospital mentioned her real name, I thought it was another coincidence, but I felt uneasy. I kind of...you know...*tricked* you into letting me help you with the paperwork. I'm sorry, but I had no choice. While helping you, I had a chance to see her identity clearly from the information you wrote down, including her driver's license. Her face hasn't changed much, and that made it easy to compare it with the memory I had from a picture your mom gave to my uncle all those years ago. That's how I was convinced that you were my uncle's lost daughter."

A tear rolled from my eye. Everything he said seemed so surreal. Sam looked at me with sympathy. From his backpack, he took out an old photo album and two books with leather covers. "I can't convince you more, but these are my uncle's diaries. He wrote everything from the day they met to the days he attempted to find you. This photo album contains pictures he took with your mom and a few pictures that your mom shared with him. I hope the diaries and the album can shed some light on the questions you might have."

He stood. "Take your time. I'll wait there." He gestured toward the gazebo overlooking the rose garden.

I didn't respond but gazed at the books he put on the bench. My heart raced as I let my mind soak in the information Sam had just told me. It was hard to believe that the picture of the gray-haired man with gentle brown eyes in Sam's office was my dad's picture.

My hands trembled as I reached for the photo album and opened it. A lump grew in my throat as I saw the picture of my parents standing in front of the University of Tokyo. My dad's hand was on my mom's waist. Sweeping her light brown hair to one side, my mom's head leaned on my dad's broad shoulder, and big smiles covered their faces. They looked happy together. I turned one page at a time to read the notes below the pictures.

On another page, there was a picture of my mom and my aunt with a note: "My older sister, Wakumi, and me. No one would guess that we're sisters."

A small smile crossed my lips as I read it. Since my aunt looked like Grandpa Kenji and my mom looked like Grandma Audrey, no one could tell they were siblings.

My dad's handwriting was legible. From his notes, I got the story of how they met, fell in love, separated, his brokenhearted search, and his attempt to find me. I blinked hard as I read a note that my dad had left for me on the last page of his diary. In the note, he said that he loved me and wished to be with me along the way. He also told me to bring my mom's ashes, if we hadn't scattered them, and bury them next to him so they could be together.

My mind and my heart were numb as I stared at the headstones. Too many secrets were coming to the surface at the same time. I'd hated my dad for abandoning us. But now, I knew that he hadn't abandoned me. We just weren't fated to meet.

Sam looked up from his phone as I approached the gazebo. "Are you okay?"

"Yes, I just feel overwhelmed," I said.

He nodded. "I understand."

I forced a smile. "Can we leave? I don't want my aunt sensing I'm not there."

"Sure. Let's go." Sam rose from his seat and slowly walked beside me, crossing the soft green grass and the graves, toward the parking lot.

I didn't say a word all the way to the hospital, but I looked out the window with my hands clasping the books tightly. I didn't know how to accept the news. Was I happy? Angry? Sad? In disbelief? Mostly, I felt a sense of unfairness for the things that had happened to me.

In the parking lot, I stopped Sam from walking me in. He gave a nod of understanding.

"Thanks for driving me today," I said. "And these…" I lifted the books. "Can I have them?"

"They're yours," he said. "I only kept them until I could find you."

"Thanks." I pressed my lips together. "I don't know how to tell my aunt about this."

Sam thought about it for a moment. "Don't rush. Wait until she's stronger and healthier. She must harbor some hatred for my uncle for causing pain and bitterness in her family, and I don't blame her. Do you have any other questions?" he asked again as I looked down at my feet.

"Did…I have any other siblings? I mean…from other women?"

"No," Sam said. "He dated a couple women because Grandma wanted him to remarry. After meeting your mom's friend and knowing he had a daughter from your mom, he never dated another woman and focused on searching for you."

I swallowed. "Thanks for…you know…never giving up on finding me."

"I owe my uncle a lot. This is only a small part of what I could do for him," he said. "So, can I pick you up tomorrow?"

"Sure."

Sam smiled. "Great. See you tomorrow."

I nodded and turned toward the hospital.

Chapter 36

I WAITED UNTIL AUNT AMY GREW stronger and more stable before delicately breaking the news about my dad. She was shocked at first and then burst into tears of joy. That night, we spent some time together reading his diaries and looking at the photo albums, and we cried again. The anger in our hearts was fading away, replaced by gratitude because my dad had never forgotten my mom. I also told her my dad's last request to bury my mom's ashes next to him. We hadn't scattered her ashes, which we kept in a columbarium in Boston. Initially, my aunt hadn't agreed because we didn't live in California and it would be difficult to visit. However, she'd changed her mind.

My heart drummed in my chest with excitement and joy when my aunt suggested I fly to Japan and visit the University of Tokyo where my parents had met and fallen in love. I'd never wanted to visit the country, but I had a solid reason to do it now. With the pictures my dad had taken and his diary, I could trace the path to my parents' meeting place.

A few days later, Sam met my aunt, who embraced him heartily. Her eyes brimmed with tears upon learning that Max and Sam had accompanied me when she was in the hospital.

I became busy spending my free time with the attorney that my dad had chosen to execute his will and living trust. I signed a lot of papers that identified me as his daughter, legally entitling me to a couple of properties that he'd left for me, his personal stocks, his law firm's stocks, and some antique stuff that I'd never even heard of. My dad hadn't forgotten Aunt Amy either—he left her a generous amount of money for taking care of me. Once my aunt became more robust, she could come to the attorney's office to sign the document.

My eyeballs almost fell out of their sockets when Sam calculated the money that I would receive every quarter as part of the law firm's stock dividend. The amount was more than half of my annual salary. I didn't need to work anymore if I didn't want to.

Sam had firmly suggested that I put all the money into a savings account that I couldn't touch until I reached a certain age. I agreed with him, considering my shopping spree impulse might emerge again, and then all the money would be gone in the blink of an eye. Besides, I'd already signed an agreement to manage the money sensibly. Yup, my dad apparently understood the tendency to shop on a whim.

As for the houses, I continued to use them as rental properties, as they'd been for decades. I didn't like living in a big house, and besides, I didn't live in California. However, I had a plan to buy a single-floor house for my aunt, so she didn't have to go up and down the stairs anymore.

In the office, Sam and I signed a conflict of interest agreement after declaring our relationship, considering that my dad's law firm was a subcontractor for Veles Capital.

Chapter 37

A PANG OF LONGING EXPANDED IN Peter's chest as he caught a glimpse of Rory carrying a bag of laundry to her apartment. Her laundry schedule was always the same—early on Saturday mornings while other people slept in.

"No rush. Just slow down," Peter mumbled as his eyes followed her. "Why are you always walking so fast? See, now you dropped something from your basket."

He chewed the inside of his cheek when Rory didn't seem to realize the missing article of clothing. He wanted to jump out of his car and run to pick it up for her, but he didn't because then she would know that he'd been stalking her. Suddenly, he felt guilty about it, but he missed her. A small smile slowly appeared on his lips when a woman walking her dog stopped Rory and pointed in the direction of her dropped laundry. Rory returned to pick it up and walked back to her apartment.

Peter gazed at Rory as she closed the door behind her. How he wanted to be with her. He vividly remembered how happy he'd felt when they'd been roommates together in their old apartment. She'd taught him how to read the laundry symbols on clothes so he could wash them properly. Almost every day, they'd had breakfast together. If there wasn't anything else to eat, they'd had bananas and bread for breakfast. He could have bought more food for her, but he didn't mind following her more frugal ways. As the sweet memories flooded his mind, he wanted to hug and kiss Rory like he had before.

For once in his life, he'd found pure happiness without their social status standing between them. He'd learned to live a normal life without domestic helpers intervening to help him do even the smallest of things.

But he couldn't be with her anymore.

They'd broken up. Period.

Although she was the one who'd asked for it, it wasn't her fault. Peter had treated her unfairly. He'd stood her up many times and had even been upset when she couldn't adjust her schedule to his. He'd focused on Sophie for the sake of his family business and forgotten that he had a sweet girl to whom he'd promised to be true. Rory was right: he was selfish.

As the warm feelings faded, Peter raised his little finger and gazed down at it. Rory had nipped that finger, and only she would do such a daring thing. That's what he liked about her. She wasn't pretentious or docile like his previous girlfriends.

He brought that finger close to his heart as a heavy lump formed in the pit of his stomach. Sometimes, he sat like that while staring at Rory's apartment. Concurrently, Calum Scott's song, "You Are the Reason," popped into his mind, and Peter wanted to cry. He used to like it because Rory was his reason. Now, the song brought more sorrow than happiness. Furthermore, after tomorrow, he wouldn't see her in the distance anymore. He'd accepted the option offered to him. Although it wasn't the option he wanted, his new life would soon begin. Taking a deep breath, he pressed the brake down firmly and started his car. Shifting the gear into drive, he allowed his car to roll slowly toward the exit gate.

Chapter 38

TOM VISITED MY APARTMENT TO check on Aunt Amy.
"Come with me to a fundraising event next Saturday,"
he said as I arranged assorted fresh fruits in a fruit bowl that
he brought for us on the kitchen counter.

My hand stopped in the air as I turned to him. My eyes narrowed. "Who's the sponsor?"

"Many companies," he said, avoiding my eyes. "It's for a humanitarian project in developing countries, especially in Africa."

"Who's the main sponsor?" I pressed him.

He rolled his eyes but answered it anyway. "Sandridge Group."

"See?" I pointed at his nose. "You lied to me. No, I won't go. I don't want to see Peter there."

"I didn't lie. Peter's company isn't even part of it."

"Still, he's a member of the Sandridge family, and he'll be there."
I scowled. "Why don't you start dating again? You still have one
week to find a date. I know you like Neil, the assistant cardiologist.
Ask him to go with you." I crossed my arms over my chest.

Tom pouted. "I'll tell Peter you lied about Sam."

I pouted in return.

"Please go with me," he begged. "If you don't like it, we can
leave right away. I swear." He held up three fingers in a Boy Scout
salute.

"No, I won't. Besides, I don't have an appropriate dress to wear. You need to find someone else."

"Fine, I'll buy one for you," he said.

I scoffed.

"I'm serious," he said.

"Go with your friend, Rory. Enjoy your life," my aunt chimed in as she entered the kitchen. "I'm stronger now, and you need a break from looking after me."

Tom nudged me, pointing at my aunt with his chin as though to say, "Listen to your aunt."

"I don't have time for a party," I said, glaring at Tom. "Don't worry, Auntie. Tom has lots of friends who can go with him, and he's about to leave now." I almost shoved him toward the door.

"Rory…" Aunt Amy let out a sigh as she sat at the kitchen table. Since her surgery, her voice wasn't as loud as it used to be. "You're still young. Go, be a young person. I want you to be happy," she added.

Tom gave a winning smile and then winced when I nudged him hard in his stomach.

"Okay, I'll go with you," I conceded.

"Great! Let's go shopping for your dress." His eyes sparkled, and he rubbed his hands together. Leaning toward Aunt Amy, he whispered, "Thanks, Auntie."

She chuckled and nodded.

Chapter 39

THE BLACK-TIE GALA WAS HELD in a huge banquet hall in an expensive hotel in Beverly Hills. Comparing myself to the other guests, I thought my dress and textured half-up hairstyle seemed almost too modest. Most of the women wore designer dresses with their hair up. Some of the older women wore high, curly buns, and some younger women had chosen simple, low, classic chignons. Some people sported thick makeup and obvious surgical enhancements.

I knew none of the women or men there, with the exception of Theo and Tom, who were always nearby. If they hadn't been, I would have felt like an outcast.

Theo leaned toward my ear and whispered, "I feel like I'm at a Botox convention."

I snickered at his comment, and Tom rolled his eyes.

"Watch your manners, Theodore." Tom smiled.

"I will, Thomas."

"Should I tell the women that you guys aren't available tonight because you're my dates?" I hissed.

My jaw dropped in disbelief when a woman in her early forties, wearing a dress that showed her cleavage down to her stomach, winked at Tom. My two dates were very handsome men, and attractive women glanced at them when they walked by.

"How dare she wink at you in front of me!"

Tom snickered while Theo pretended to admire the chandelier above us.

"I've never known you to be a jealous person, Aurorette Arrington," he teased me.

"I'm guarding my handsome dates, here. And, yes, I can be a jealous person when I want to be, Thomas Kyle Ryder." I smiled sweetly.

Tom cackled. Our jokes stopped when Theo tapped my shoulder to get my attention.

"What?"

Without saying anything, he gave a signal with his head that Peter was near us.

My mouth dropped. Peter looked handsome and mature with three days' beard growth. When we dated, he'd always shaved his face clean because I liked it that way. His eyes narrowed as they met mine. I swallowed and hid behind Tom to avoid his cold stare.

Peter shifted his attention to Theo and Tom, and they clasped hands and bumped shoulders with each other.

"Now, tell me, why is *she* here?" Peter's question was for Tom and Theo.

Deliberately, Tom drew me closer to him. "She's my date," he said.

"And mine because Emma's sick," Theo said, wrapping his arm around my shoulders.

Peter's eyebrows rose slightly as he looked at us. "I hope you know what you're doing."

Tom was about to say something, but he was cut off when the live music stopped playing. The master of ceremonies, a tall guy with a goatee, wearing a white suit, stepped up to take the stage and welcomed the guests.

Peter glanced at the stage. "Well, enjoy the party," he said, nodding to Tom and Theo. He left us without looking at me.

I felt as if a cold hand had grasped my heart. Looking down and kicking the floor, I mumbled, "I shouldn't be here."

"Ignore him," said Theo. "You're here for us, not him."

"Yeah, just ignore him…although I feel bad for how he treated you," said Tom regretfully.

I let out a sigh and placed my hands on my hips. "Well, we're already here. Why don't we enjoy the expensive free food and drinks? Who knew they'd serve caviar here?"

Theo smiled. "There you go!"

"I'll get drinks for you guys," Tom offered. "Champagne? Wine? Mojito?"

"Champagne," Theo and I said in unison.

"Okay." Tom walked across the room to the bar where drinks were being served by two young bartenders, and Theo and I walked toward the other end. I heard a buzzing sound come from Theo.

"Sorry," he said to me, fishing the phone from his suit jacket pocket. "Hey, Em," he sang, and his smile faded. "What? No, not yet… What? Sorry, I can't hear you. Let me find a spot with a good signal." He held up his finger to me and pointed outside.

I nodded.

He walked toward the French doors, not far from where I stood. After placing some fresh-cut fruit on a small plate, I stood and looked around. People's voices sounded like buzzing bees, and live classical music played in the background. I began to regret accompanying Tom to this event. Now I understood the meaning of "feeling lonely in a crowded room."

My eyes lit up when I saw Tom walking toward me with drinks in hand. "Finally, a familiar face," I joked.

"Where's Theo?" He gave me my drink.

"Oh, Emma called him," I answered.

Just a second later, Theo entered in a hurry, his face tense.

"What happened?" Tom asked. "Is Emma okay?"

Theo nodded. "Yeah, she's okay, but we have a problem." He leaned and whispered something into Tom's ear.

Tom's eyes widened, and he looked at me. "Damn!" he cursed under his breath. Then he nudged my arm. "Uh, Rory, I'm not interested in this party anymore. Can we go now?"

"Why? What happened? The party just started," I said.

Just then, the MC called for Archibald Ryder. On the stage, Archie looked around, and our eyes met. His brows furrowed before his eyes shifted to the crowd, welcoming the guests and mentioning their reasons for gathering. Calm, elegant, and with a small smile on his lips, he captured my attention as if Peter were talking. I could imagine that, when Peter reached his age, he would look like that.

"And now, I'm going to give the stage to my son, Peter, and his fiancée, Sophie Fournier. Please welcome the lovely couple."

Amid congratulations and cheers and clapping hands, I felt like a bolt of lightning had struck me down. My legs turned to jelly when Peter made his entrance. A beautiful blonde woman with green eyes looped her hand on the crook of his elbow. Her nose looked perfect on her oval face. Her long red dress looked perfect on her thin body. She strode next to him with confidence, giving everyone a small wave as she ascended to the stage.

"Tom, d—did you know this?" I stammered, tugging on his arm. "You're his brother."

"I didn't know anything about this. Peter hasn't spoken to me lately." Tom rubbed his temples. "Emma just told Theo to take you out of here, but it was too late. I'm sorry. If I'd known, I wouldn't have invited you to the party. Let me ask him after his speech," he said, and walked toward the stage.

I turned to Theo, who placed his hand on my shoulder and whispered, "I'm sorry, Rory."

As a server passed, bringing a tray of wine in tall glasses, I swiped two and swallowed each in a few gulps. When I wanted to get a third glass, Theo stopped me. Turning his woeful eyes in my direction, he placed his hand on my back, leading me to the French doors and out to the terrace, which overlooked a beautiful rose garden.

A cold breeze embraced us when we stepped outside. Wearing an open shoulder chiffon dress, I shivered as we leaned on the railing.

Theo placed his jacket over my shoulders.

"Thank you," I said, wrapping myself in its warmth.

Theo sighed. "I didn't know everything would turn out like this. It's too fast. You guys just broke up two months ago, and now he's engaged?"

I looked up at the blue sky, its upside-down bubbly clouds like cotton candy that blushed against the warm, reddish-orange color of the sun.

"Oh well," I said, and I didn't refuse when Theo wrapped his arm around me. "We broke up. No, I broke up with him. So, why do I feel sad? Why?" I turned to Theo.

"Because you still love him."

I looked at him and shrugged. "It doesn't matter anymore. In the end, it's better that Peter's with her and not me. Everything is falling into place. Ahhh..." I let out a heavy sigh and looked skyward. "Jane was right. Peter chose the right woman to support him."

Theo looked at me, his eyebrows flying up. "What are you sputtering about?" he asked.

I waved my hand. "Just forget what I said." I leaned over the railing, feeling stupid for saying things I shouldn't have.

Theo held my shoulder and pulled me back. "Okay, you're tipsy. Your face is already red. Let me call the chauffeur, and I'll take you home. Stay out here, but promise me..." He glared at me. "Don't drink!"

Warmth vibrated onto my palms as I cupped my cheeks. Theo

crossed the garden, heading back into the building. Sighing, I leaned my back against the railing.

"I'm not tipsy. I'm sad," I mumbled. The fog in my head became thicker, and at the same time, a sour taste rose in my throat. From the corner of my eye, I saw a party attendant with a tray of champagne in his hands. I turned and swiped three glasses of champagne. Or was it white wine? I couldn't tell. The attendant didn't bat an eye.

I took the glasses to the semi-circle bench nearby, sipping the contents of the first one while gazing at the sky that was becoming redder as the sun fell toward the horizon. I finished that glass in a long gulp and reached for another.

Chapter 40

ASSAGING THE AREA BETWEEN HIS eyebrows, Peter took a deep breath to calm his racing heart. Rory looked wonderful, sexy, and elegant in a light blue, open-shoulder chiffon dress. He'd almost laughed when her surprise showed clearly in her brown eyes as he approached in his stubble beard, something she didn't like because she preferred a clean-shaven man.

Peter couldn't believe Tom had brought Rory to the gala. Didn't Tom realize why he'd been avoiding him lately?

He knew his brother would try to reconnect him with Rory. If everything were different, he would have been happy to accept that because he still loved her.

But she'd chosen her way, and he'd chosen his.

Then something odd had happened.

Earlier, when the MC had announced his presence with his fiancée, Sophie, he noticed Rory's face turn pale, and pain was etched clearly in her beautiful eyes. Why did she look hurt if she was the one who had wanted them to break up?

Regardless, he felt a pang of guilt when Rory swiped two glasses of champagne and gulped them down.

"What are you doing? You can't stand alcohol," he'd said under his breath.

"Did you say something?"

The question had startled him. Archie looked at him, frowning. "No, nothing," Peter said shortly.

His dad had examined his face for a moment and then turned his attention to Sophie.

Peter sighed and saw that Theo had taken Rory out to the garden. "Thanks, Theo," he'd said silently.

"There you are," a melodic voice sang behind him. His thoughts were interrupted by the presence of Sophie, who swayed like a model as she approached him.

Peter gave a small sigh, straightened his back, and forced a smile to his face.

"I've been looking for you," she said, looping her hand around his arm. "Let's meet my daddy."

"Okay." He nodded and walked beside her.

They found Sophie's dad talking to Archie. If Peter were honest, he couldn't stand talking to his future father-in-law, but he politely answered all the man's questions. He was relieved once Mr. Fournier shifted his attention back to Archie.

"It's stuffy in here. I need to get some fresh air," he whispered to Sophie.

"Are you okay?" she asked, concern in her eyes. "I'll go with you."

"No, you stay here," he said. "I won't be long."

Reluctantly, she nodded.

Peter let out a silent sigh as he adjusted his necktie and strode out of the hall toward the garden.

The sun had almost set in the magenta sky, turning the upside-down clouds into purplish-red floating cotton balls. Magnificent. Peter stopped and gazed up in awe.

"What a stunning sky, right, Ror—"

Peter stopped, realizing what he was doing. A sad smile formed on his lips. It was Tom's fault for bringing her here, and he couldn't get her off his mind.

212

Spinning around to go back into the hall, he heard someone sing "Catch a Falling Star" in a low, sad voice. Curious, he followed the singing, and after a few steps, he froze because he recognized the voice.

Tiptoeing, he moved closer to see Rory sitting on the semicircle stone bench. A fire pit lay in front of her, behind the bushes where he stood. Under the lamplight, she gazed skyward, with a fluffy gray cat and three empty champagne glasses next to her.

"How many glasses did you drink?" he mumbled, listening to her sing in a slurred voice.

"For love may come and tap you on the shoulder..." She stopped, sighing while tapping her own shoulder. "His love tapped me on this shoulder, Tubby." She trembled as she caressed the cat's head, evoking a soft purr. "But now, *she* gets his love. Arrrgh." She groaned softly. "He upgraded to someone better and prettier. That hurts. Life is hard, Tubby. Don't you agree? Well, stop whining. Let's find another drink. Where's the drink server again?" She looked around and winced, wrapping her hands around her stomach. "Ugh...my stomach hurts."

"Stop drinking. You're drinking too much tonight."

Peter immediately clamped a hand over his mouth and thought to retreat, but it was too late. Rory had already seen him. Her open mouth formed into a smile that rose to her brown eyes when he walked closer. Almost as quickly, her eyes turned somber, as though she realized something.

"Peter," her voice called sluggishly. Her face brightened, showing that she was intoxicated, or close to it. "Congratulations. I'm happy for you."

Peter detected a note of false cheer in her voice as heat rose in his chest. He almost snapped at her and forbade her saying those words, but he bit his tongue. Calming himself, he stepped forward and stood in front of her. "You're drunk. Where are Theo and Tom?" He was surprised to find out how much softer his voice was.

"He—" Rory stopped and covered her mouth with her hand as two big burps came from her mouth. "Oops." She grinned as her face turned so red. "Sorry. I didn't expect that." Then she giggled.

Peter looked at her, feeling amused by how innocent her face appeared. "Rory, where's Theo?" he asked again.

Her head whipped around. "Theo is—" Her eyes widened, and she pointed at something behind him. "Oh, look who's here. Your pretty bride."

Peter turned to see Sophie walking toward them.

"I thought you just wanted to go out for a moment," she said. Her green eyes fell hard on Rory before she shifted them to Peter.

"That was my plan, but this lady is drunk. I just wanted to make sure she doesn't make a scene," he said. "Why don't you go back inside, and I'll return soon."

"You're pretty," Rory said, smiling lazily at Sophie. "No wonder he wants to marry you."

Sophie raised her tiny nose. "Of course." Then she placed her hand on his shoulder, smiling proudly.

On the contrary, Rory's smile faltered. "I want to be pretty too."

Peter couldn't stand to see her this way and turned to Sophie. "Do me a favor. Please go inside and find my brother or Theo. She came with them." He bent over to take Rory's arm. "And you come with me."

She jerked her arm free. "I can walk by myself—whoops!"

Her footing wasn't right, and she slipped. Peter was quick enough and grabbed her. A second later, he heard a gagging sound, and his nose wrinkled when a pungent, unpleasant smell mixed with something sweet from the champagne spewed from Rory's mouth. Wetness seeped into his pants and socks.

"Ewww!" Sophie moaned, pinching her nose.

"Rory!" two male voices called almost in unison.

Relieved, Peter saw his brother and his best friend running toward them, but Sophie's delicate eyebrows drew together.

"Rory? I've heard that name before," she said, looking sideways at Peter. Then her face brightened as she remembered something. "Wasn't she the one who called you the other day?"

Peter didn't answer but focused on Rory, who was still throwing up. He shrugged when Theo and Tom glanced at his pants and shoes covered with vomit.

"You aren't a good drinker. That's why you threw up." Peter gently tapped his hand against Rory's back.

Noticing Sophie's scowl and her eyes on his hand, Peter pulled it away from Rory's back and turned to Tom and Theo. "You guys better take her home." He gave Tom a long stare as though to say, "Please take care of her."

Tom nodded and wrapped his arm around Rory's shoulders. His eyes were reading Peter's face, but Peter turned around and headed toward the banquet hall with Sophie behind him.

"Is the car outside now?" he heard his brother ask.

"Yes," Theo answered.

He felt relieved that Tom and Theo were there for Rory. And right then, he was happy because he had a perfect excuse to leave this boring party early. If Sophie insisted on staying, she could stay by herself.

Chapter 41

I WOKE UP AND DIDN'T RECOGNIZE the room. My eyes hurt from the light, and my head pounded as I pulled myself to a sitting position. A bottle of aspirin and a glass of water were on the bedside table. I took two aspirin and gulped them with the entire glass of water.

"Where am I?" I looked around. It wasn't my bedroom or the guest room in Peter's house. Slowly, memories of the night before returned: the black-tie party, Botox women and men, Peter's fiancée, the champagne, and my stomach hurting. Then I vaguely remembered throwing up before everything became tangled and blurry.

I looked down to see that my party gown had been changed for pajamas. I couldn't think more because my head felt like it was being ripped apart.

The sound of someone cooking came from outside the room. Dragging myself up, I walked toward the door and opened it. The nauseating smell of chicken soup instantly hit my nose.

"Rory, are you up?"

That's Tom's voice. I'm at Tom's house. "Yeah," I croaked. "I'm up."

"Come down. I'm cooking soup for your hangover."

Slowly, I went down the stairs and into the kitchen. My head pounded with each step I took. My stomach felt like it was boiling, and my mouth was parched.

In the kitchen, Tom placed a bowl of soup in front of an empty chair. Next to it was a plate of eggs sunny-side up.

"Come, sit here." He patted the chair.

"Could you please keep your voice down?" I moaned, sitting down. His voice was somehow too loud in my ears.

"I haven't heard those words for a looong, looong, looong time," he sang.

"Peter?"

He nodded and gave me a spoon. "Eat the soup. It's good for a hangover," he said.

I sipped the broth as Tom settled on the seat in front of me, eating his breakfast of two pieces of toast with bacon and eggs.

"How am I here?" I asked, squinting from the sunlight coming through the kitchen window. "And whose pajamas are these?"

"Emma's. After Theo told her about your condition, she brought the pajamas and another change of clothes because your dress was ruined."

I winced. "I'll thank her later."

"Don't worry about that. Just eat your breakfast," Tom said, buttering his toast.

I continued to eat, but something flashed in my mind. As if stung by a bee, I stood from my seat and slammed back as my head thrashed from the sudden movement. "Oh no! My aunt!"

Munching his toast, Tom flapped his hand. "I called her last night, and she was fine."

"Thanks." I felt relief. Taking a bite of soup, I asked, "I threw up last night, right?"

He nodded. There was clear laughter in his eyes.

"I...threw up on Peter's pants and shoes, right?" I asked again.

"Bullseye." He gave me a meaningful smile, bringing his coffee mug to his lips. "That was an act of *sweet* revenge after he threw up in your car before you guys dated."

"I really did that?" I looked at him, touching my mouth.

He chuckled. "You were wasted last night, Rory." Looking at me from behind his mug, he said, "Do you remember grinning after throwing up?"

I didn't recall that part, but Tom wouldn't lie to me. Closing my eyes, I rubbed my head and dragged my hand down my face. "Oh God. I feel awful now."

"Don't feel that way. I bet he'd thank you for having the perfect reason to leave the party early," Tom said, smiling and pointing at the soup. "Now, be a good girl and eat your breakfast. I barely ever cook for a woman, so you'd better appreciate my effort."

Forcing a smile, I ate another spoonful of soup, and we finished our breakfast in silence.

After eating, I took a shower and changed into Emma's clothes. I wanted to go home because my aunt was alone in the apartment.

Bringing down bags containing my dirty dress and Emma's pajamas, I found Tom in the living room, spritzing his indoor plants with a small spray bottle.

"If you still have a headache, you're welcome to stay here longer," said Tom, eyeing the two bags in my hands. "If you're concerned about Peter, don't worry. I told him not to come while you're here."

"Thanks, I appreciate it, but I have to check on my aunt," I said, tying my hair up with a rubber band. "Thanks for taking care of me, by the way. I shouldn't have drunk like an idiot last night."

He smiled, putting his spray bottle down next to one of the pots. "Well, I wasn't happy to see you wasted like that, but I'm glad you were, because now I know why you broke up with Peter."

"What?" My jaw dropped. "What did I say last night?"

"A lot." Tom winked. "Why don't we talk about that on our way to your place?"

"Why don't you tell me now?"

"I can do that." He shrugged, sitting on the sofa, and I followed suit.

He then repeated the words I'd drunkenly blurted the previous evening. My face must have been blank because Tom narrowed his eyes.

"You don't recall that at all?"

I shook my head slowly.

"Damn, Rory, you've forced me to the next level. You do amuse me." He chuckled and put his iPhone on the coffee table. "Now watch and listen."

I frowned.

"Just do it." He pressed a button.

The light was dim in the video, and in a few seconds, a drunk woman's slurred voice could be heard.

"Why do I feel sad seeing him with another girl? Why? I broke up with him so he could find a girl who supports him the way Jane wanted." She sniffed. "And like magic, now he's engaged to the prettiest girl on earth."

Leaning forward, I squinted to see clearly and gasped. That drunk woman was me!

Tom pressed his lips together, trying hard to control his expression.

"Have you met his dad?" drunk Rory asked. "Oh yeah, you have. His dad is your dad." The drunk me stopped for a second before continuing. "His dad doesn't like me. His arrogant uncle with the crooked nose like...a parrot's beak, uh, nose...no, beak...gave me a disgusted look. I love Peter so much, and I can't let him suffer by dating me, but I'm nobody!"

I grimaced as a heartbreaking cry followed, then there was a honking noise as the drunk me blew her nose.

Tom's face turned red as he continued to stifle his laughter.

"I need more Kleenex," drunk me said before wailing again.

I reached across the table to turn off the phone, but Tom was quick and slapped my hand.

"Don't." He shook his head.

Pouting, I sank back in my seat, wishing the earth would open up and swallow me.

"But Jane was right. There's nothing I can do to help him," drunk me continued. "Sophie Fu…Fu…uh, Sophie something-something is better than me. Her dad's rich…very rich…and fat."

"Could you turn it off, please?" I begged, covering my face in shame.

Tom grinned and turned it off. I landed a few hard punches on his arm, although I knew it was useless, because Peter said Tom boxed for exercise.

"You're mean, Thomas Kyle Ryder." I glared at him. "Videotaping me while I was drunk."

"Rory, my dear," he smiled sweetly, "don't you know that you're the most hilarious girl I've ever met when you're drunk?"

"Shut it," I hissed, my cheeks flaming.

His smile faded, and he looked at me solemnly. "I'm sorry. I shouldn't have recorded you, but I had no choice. I can't deny that I want to see you get back together again with my brother, and I've been curious to find out your reason, especially after I knew there was no third person. After last night, everything is crystal clear. And then I realized that you and Peter are almost the same in that you don't share when you're in trouble. That's bad, you know. You should learn to share with people so you can live stress-free."

"There's no such thing as a stress-free life," I objected, hunching my shoulders.

"Did you decide to break up with Peter after finding Jane's video for him?" he asked after a few minutes.

"Pretty much." I raised my face to look at him.

"What exactly did she say?"

I sighed. "Even if I told you, it wouldn't change the fact that I broke up with Peter, and now he's engaged to another woman."

"It may not change the fact, but it helps me understand the whole story," he insisted.

"Okay." I nodded after considering his words, then began to repeat what Jane had said in the video.

Tom's eyebrows drew together as he pulled at his lower lip with his thumb and forefinger, paying attention to my story. His eyes became red as he suppressed his emotion. He must have missed Jane too.

"And what's the main reason you broke up with my brother?" he asked as I paused.

I sighed, looking down at my fingers. "To achieve his goals, Peter has to find a woman with a strong family background and prominent social status. And"—I shrugged—"I'm not the right one. My background won't fit into your family standards."

Tom shifted in his chair, tapping the tips of his fingers together in front of his mouth while eyeing me briefly.

"Well, Peter has Sophie now." I gave a chuckle, straightening my back.

Tom exhaled. "I'm sorry if you feel offended by the video. My family is…" He lifted a shoulder, his voice trailing off. Shaking his head, he continued. "I wish I could do something to justify the resentment you feel right now. However, if you allow me, my next explanation might give you a different point of view."

I shrugged, leaning on my seat.

With a heavy sigh, he began. "Grandaunt Lily was my grandpa's precious baby sister and had been unwell since she was young. One day, she fell in love with a famous young doctor in town. No one knew that, later on, he took advantage of her, stole her fortune, and ran away. Feeling ashamed, Grandaunt Lily killed herself. In front of her grave, Grandpa swore to protect everyone in his family from the same misfortune." Tom looked at me. "Yes, my families are snobs. However, they aren't simply snobbish people. The adversity had changed everything and made my grandpa callous."

I didn't respond but tucked in my lips, looking down. His explanation wouldn't change anything.

I looked up and blinked as Tom laughed all of a sudden.

"Why are you laughing?" I scowled.

"I'm sorry, but…" His laughter stopped. He raised his hands and clamped them on his head. "I always thought I was a stress-free person, but now I'm stressed out because of my brother." He gave a helpless glance.

I chortled to see his act, and then he chortled too.

"Tom, there's something I have to tell you." I looked at him as we sat in silence.

"Good or bad news?" he asked. "If it's bad news, please save it for our next meeting. I've had enough for today."

"Good news."

"Okay, then, tell me." He waved a hand.

"I found my dad." Biting my lips to stifle my shriek, I widened my eyes at him, waiting to see his reaction.

As I'd expected, Tom's eyes popped wide and his mouth fell open.

"What?" He almost jumped, then his eyes narrowed. "Wait, it isn't a joke, right?"

I shook my head as I felt a big smile spreading on my lips.

"Oh my God, Rory!" Tom hurried over and hugged me as if I were his favorite childhood teddy bear that had been lost and was found again. "What wonderful news! Oh my God. Tell me everything."

"I'm going to." I wheezed, trying to breathe. "But stop squeezing me."

Sitting back on the sofa, he looked at me solemnly as he signaled me to begin.

It was hard to tell the story calmly as my heart started beating triple time from the excitement.

"Wow!" Tom stood after I'd shared the news, only omitting information about the financial benefits I'd inherited from my dad. His head was shaking hard. "Double wow!"

"It is, isn't it?" I said. "I can't believe it either."

"So, Sam is your cousin?" He returned to his seat, looking at me.

"Yes." I nodded and reached out with my hand to stop him standing up again. "Stop fidgeting. My hangover gets worse when you move too fast."

Tom obeyed and looked at me. "I'm so happy for you," he said, his tone thoughtful. "Although you can't meet your dad, at least now you know that he loved you and your mom." Then he pulled me into his arms, and we didn't move for a few moments until my sudden burp forced us apart.

"Oops." I covered my mouth, feeling the heat coming from my cheeks.

Tom's nose wrinkled a bit since the burp had a slight unpleasant smell. It was obvious he was holding his breath for a beat. "That's… loud," he teased me.

"Sorry," I apologized. "My stomach's still gassy from last night."

"I can tell," he winked, standing up. "I'll give you something to ease the gas."

"Thanks," I said, covering my mouth as I felt another burp coming.

THE FREEWAY WASN'T CROWDED, AND it took less than an hour for Tom and me to get to my apartment.

Just as I closed the car door, Tom said, "Rory?"

"Yes?" I leaned into the passenger-side window.

"Thanks for telling me about finding your dad. I'm truly happy for you," he said. "About my dad, I'm sorry if he didn't seem to like you. Most of the time, he doesn't discriminate against people. He cares more than he shows. I hope you don't have hard feelings because of that."

"I appreciate you telling me that," I said. "It won't bother me anymore since I won't see him again, right?"

Tom looked down briefly and raised his eyes to meet mine before nodding slowly. "Right."

"I need to ask you for a favor," I said.

"Sure."

"Please don't tell Peter about me finding Jane's video. I chose what was best for me, and he's already chosen what's best for him. Everything seems to be falling into the right place now, so please"—I locked his eyes—"don't intervene."

It seemed like he wanted to say something, but he stopped himself. "All right, I won't tell him," he agreed. "Take care, Rory. Sleep well, and send my regards to Aunt Amy."

I nodded, waved at him, and walked toward my apartment.

Chapter 42

A MONTH PASSED, AND MY AUNT had already returned to Boston. Before she left, Sam had arranged our first meeting with his extended family, which was now my extended family.

The meeting had gone smoothly, although I'd been nervous and wondered whether my dad's family would accept me. My extended family from my mom's side had shunned my mom's pregnancy, which automatically meant not acknowledging my presence in the world.

But I was wrong. My dad's family had received me wholeheartedly.

My grandma, Lois, had a warm personality. She was genuinely happy to meet my aunt and me, and she even thanked my aunt for taking care of me. My dad's younger sister, Claire, and her husband, Ron, welcomed us enthusiastically. My two grown-up cousins, Kimmy and Jesse, seemed excited to meet me. Jesse was the same age as me, and Kimmy was a year younger.

Aunt Amy seemed to enjoy my dad's family too. Almost immediately, she and Aunt Claire had a serious conversation about baking, even exchanging a marble cake recipe.

I felt drunk on happiness after meeting my dad's family. I had peace in my heart, and my body felt lighter. Although my dad's family wasn't big, it was enough to give me the new experience of having cousins, a grandma, an aunt, and an uncle.

When they found out that Aunt Amy and I didn't live in California, Grandma Lois and Aunt Claire were disappointed, but they seemed happy when we promised to fly back for Thanksgiving and Christmas.

Without my aunt around, I felt lonely and wanted to go back to Boston. My new extended family was helpful, but I had no reason to stay longer in California. Nevertheless, my project wasn't over yet, and it had even been extended for another two months. I should have felt happy for the opportunity to be transferred to California. If only I hadn't broken up with Peter.

The fact that Peter had become engaged to Sophie shortly after our breakup bothered me. It seemed surreal that he'd moved on so quickly. But Peter had chosen the right woman for him, and I should've been happy for him. Maybe I needed to move on also.

My reverie was interrupted by a loud buzz coming from my phone on the coffee table. I picked it up and almost dropped it again when I saw it was Ryan calling. The last time he'd texted was when I was at the Boston airport, a day after he'd kissed me in front of the elevator.

My heartbeat raced. For a second, I didn't know what to do. Calming my heart, I answered right before the voicemail picked up.

"Hello?"

"Hey, Rory." Ryan's voice was still the same, cheerful with a pleasant tone.

"Um, hey, Ryan."

He must have picked up my hesitation because there was a pause on his end. "Did I catch you at a bad time?" he asked.

"Ye—" I covered my mouth and then slapped my forehead. *You said you want to move on, and this is your chance, silly.* "No, of course not. Uhhhh...I'm distracted by something outside my kitchen window," I lied.

"Oh, what happened?" He sounded curious.

"Uh…" I bit my lower lip, thinking hard to make up a story. "You know…my neighbor's cat and my other neighbor's dog—they're fighting."

"Really?"

"Yup." I bit my lip harder.

There was another pause on his end before I heard chuckling.

"Why are you laughing?" I pouted.

"Because you're still a terrible liar, Rory."

After a second, I chuckled too. "That bad, huh?"

He didn't answer, but his chuckling continued.

"Are you still uncomfortable because of…the kiss?" he asked after he'd calmed down.

I scratched my head over his question. He hadn't been so direct in the past, but I liked it. "Well, a little," I said after pondering my answer.

"I'm sorry," he said, "but I thought I should do it, even if only once." Then he paused before continuing. "Hey, I'm in Irvine. Could we meet tomorrow, maybe for lunch?"

"What?" I almost jumped off my sofa. "You're here? When did you arrive?"

"Well…I'm taking a week off and will fly back on Sunday night."

"Why didn't you call me earlier?" Then I stopped myself. He hadn't reached out to me because he'd thought I was still upset with him.

I was right.

"I wanted to, but…" He stopped. "You looked so upset after I kissed you, I didn't want to make you more upset than I did that day. Besides, you're busy at work, and I'd rather ask you to go out with me on the weekend. If you're available, do you want to meet me tomorrow? Could you?" His voice was hesitant.

"Yes, of course," I said, nodding, although he couldn't see me. "Let's meet tomorrow. I'll pick you up."

There was a pause on his end. "Really?"

I chuckled. "Is there any law forbidding me picking you up? Just text me where you're staying, and I'll pick you up at…ten o'clock?"

"Sure."

ON SATURDAY MORNING, I WENT to pick up Ryan. My fingers curled and uncurled as I walked across the hotel parking lot toward the entrance. Regret crawled in my heart for volunteering to come get him. I should have refused to meet him because I didn't know how to act in front of him. The memory of our kiss returned to my mind again last night. No, I hadn't initiated the kiss, but I hadn't refused it either.

"Shut it, he's your friend," I hissed to myself. I must have said it more loudly than I'd meant, because one of two teens walking in front of me glanced over his shoulder in my direction and then rolled his eyes.

Ryan was sitting in a big chair as I stepped into the lobby. His eyes shone when he saw me, and he rose from his seat.

"Hi!" He waved, walking toward me.

"Hi," I said back, clasping my hands together.

His eyebrows knitted while his hand was pointing at my hair. "Did you…forget your hair curler?"

My mouth fell open. I raised a hand to touch my hair, but there was nothing there. Wait. I didn't use hair curlers.

By the time I realized he'd tricked me, Ryan was already outside the lobby, laughing.

I rolled my eyes and marched toward him.

"You tricked me," I complained, half laughing.

"And you fell for it once again, just like in college," he roared as I punched his shoulder hard. When we were in college, he had countless harmless tricks up his sleeve to make me laugh. Back then, he could pull them off with a total poker face.

I glanced at him while we walked to my car. Ryan must have noticed my nervousness, and he'd used a trick to melt away the awkwardness between us.

"I'll drive," he said, extending his palm up.

I hesitated but gave him my key anyway.

"Where're we going?" I asked, putting on my seat belt.

"Our alma mater," he answered.

"Oh, that's great. I haven't been there since graduation," I commented as Ryan steered the car toward the main road.

"By the way, congrats on finding your dad," Ryan said as we hit the freeway. "When Sally told us that Sam's your cousin, no one could believe it."

"Yeah, I couldn't believe it either," I said. "He could've stopped searching and taken all the money my dad left for me. But he didn't. He kept his promise."

"Sam's a reliable man," Ryan said. "You should be proud to be his cousin."

"Yes, I am," I agreed.

Fifteen minutes later, we reached our alma mater. Ryan parked the car in the parking structure across from the student center. Students were walking by us as we crossed the street. Looking at the heavy backpacks on their shoulders, I didn't miss the campus life at all, but I missed the freedom of not having any responsibility except maybe to study.

I was sitting on the grass, watching Ryan join a few students to shoot some hoops. He looked happy and even tagged the tallest student for a three-point challenge. Gazing at him, I realized how much I'd missed our togetherness, and I regretted our growing apart once we chose our majors. Until that moment, I hadn't remembered why.

"Is he your boyfriend?"

I heard a voice next to me. My head whipped around to a ponytailed girl in glasses, looking at me.

"Oh no, he isn't," I answered. "We're friends, and we're here together to walk down memory lane because we used to be students on this campus."

The girl glanced at Ryan and shifted back to me.

"I thought you guys were a couple because of the way he looks at you while he's playing," she commented, nodding slowly.

I pealed polite laughter in response to her comment and observed him. She was right. When he was about to throw the ball to the hoop, he stole a glance at me and was stunned to see me smile. His opponent used the chance to steal the ball and throw it. Ryan spread his arms, shrugging, and we smiled at each other. Then I sighed and looked down. Ryan and Peter. Both were kind and considerate men who loved and cared about me. I wished I could bounce back from heartbreak and move on with Ryan.

Before heading back home, we stopped by the university's botanical garden. I walked behind Ryan, busying myself taking pictures of plants and flowers in the garden for my Instagram account.

"Rory," he called, glancing at me over his shoulder when I stooped to take a picture of a cottontail rabbit.

"Yes?" I answered.

"I quit Veles Capital. Next week is my last week with the company."

I almost dropped my phone, looking at his back. "What? Why?"

Without stopping, he said, "I'm going to be an English teacher in Japan."

I was stunned.

An English teacher in Japan. That was Ryan's dream. When we were in university, he'd taken some teaching courses and some classes to learn the Japanese language. I thought he'd been joking when he said he wanted to go to Japan and be a teacher there. He wasn't.

Sensing I wasn't following him, he stopped and turned around, looking at me in silence.

"When will you go to Japan?" I rose, feeling heavy in my stomach.

"In two weeks."

"That's...fast."

He nodded, giving me a small smile. "Yeah, I was surprised when the company that arranges the exchange and teaching program contacted me sooner than I'd expected, but I'm thrilled. You know how I love teaching kids, and thanks to your Japanese heritage, you piqued my curiosity about learning the culture."

I ambled toward him and stopped a few feet in front of him. "How long will you be there?" My voice was quiet.

"Well, I signed up for a two-year teaching program. Once I'm done, they'll evaluate me and give me a choice to continue the program or come back to the States."

Two years. Wow.

Ryan took two steps and leaned forward to me because I was dumbstruck. "You look sad."

Biting my lips, I said, "I am."

"Why?" he asked, gazing with focus.

"After college, I lost someone I cared about, and now I'm going to lose him again."

Ryan swallowed and nodded. "I'm sorry. This time, I promise you I'll keep in touch, and I won't disappear like last time."

I chuckled sadly because I didn't want to hear any more promises. Forcing a smile, I nodded and said, "Yeah. Okay."

Chapter 43

$\mathcal{J}$ DROPPED OFF RYAN AT HIS hotel and drove back to my apartment. I'd promised to take him to the mini-golf amusement park tomorrow before heading to the airport.

On the way home, I couldn't shake off the heavy feeling in my heart. I liked Ryan very much. However, I hadn't had any thought of dating him. If I had, it wouldn't be fair for him because I couldn't forget Peter yet. Peter had a special place in my heart. Still, the news of Ryan teaching in Japan for two years shocked me.

Getting out of my car, I paused when I heard someone call my name. I turned to notice a lanky young woman walking across the parking lot toward me. I scowled when I recognized her. It was Sophie, Peter's fiancée. *How does she know my address?*

"How...how did you find my place?" I demanded as she stopped in front of me.

Without her thick makeup, she looked very young.

She shrugged. "Peter's phone."

I blinked.

"He let me check his phone," she added quickly.

I could tell she was lying, but I didn't care. "What do you want from me?"

Sophie stood tall, seeming to detect the coldness in my tone. "I know about your relationship with Peter, but I want you to forget him."

I narrowed my eyes. "I broke up with him."

"When?"

I closed my eyes briefly and opened them again. "Why do you want to know?"

She swallowed, and her fingers clenched onto her purse. "I want you to leave him alone. Don't contact him. Don't show up at a party where he's invited. Don't ask for help or sympathy, even if you're drunk. I don't want to see him patting you on the back again as he did when you were throwing up at the gala."

My mouth fell open. I clamped it shut while gathering my thoughts about that day. I vaguely remembered Peter stroking my back while I vomited.

"You should leave him alone," repeated Sophie, her voice rising a notch.

"Listen," I said impatiently, "I'm the one who broke up with him. I haven't contacted him since then. If he helped me that one time, it's not my fault."

Her eyes widened, and she looked alarmed. "He's mine and always will be mine."

She pulled out a yellow piece of paper and a picture from her clutch and shoved them at me. Frowning, I took them from her hand and opened the yellow paper. I felt the ground shake beneath me as I read the contents. It was a disclosure for abortion procedures with Peter's signature on the bottom of the document, dated almost five years ago.

My jaw dropped in shock when I looked at the picture of her, lying on the bed. She was lying behind a man who had his back to the camera. They were naked, and their bodies were covered by a blanket from the hips down. With only her shoulders showing, Sophie looked at the camera, blushing.

"What is this?" I looked at her, my hand trembling. I staggered backward and tried to steady myself.

Sophie raised her chin and said, "To show you that he's mine."

"And...this?" I pointed at the abortion paper.

She nodded. "I found out that I was pregnant two months after we slept together. I told him, but he didn't seem happy about it. Because I loved him, I obeyed and did what he wanted me to do. It was probably the best choice since I was young, only nineteen, and my daddy would have been upset with me if he'd found out."

"You lie!" My voice was weak. "Peter wouldn't sign that paper."

"Don't you recognize his signature?" she challenged.

I stood tongue-tied for a moment. "And the picture? You fabricated this picture, right?" I asked, trying to deny the facts shoved in my face.

She smiled sweetly, but her eyes mocked me. "The birthmark on his left shoulder—does it look familiar to you?"

I looked at the picture again and noticed a tiny birthmark on the man's shoulder, which was as big as a penny in real life. I'd seen it every time Peter wore a sleeveless sport shirt. Deep, piercing pain ripped at my stomach, forcing me to bend over slightly to ease the pain.

"I've loved him since I was young. When he asked me to sleep with him, I was over the moon and decided to take a selfie as a memento of our first night together," Sophie continued.

"You're sick!" I blurted, throwing the picture and the paper at her.

She glared at me and stepped forward, her hand raised in the air. She froze when a tire screeched on the parking lot as a car rushed into a parking spot.

As I glanced over my shoulder, a tall figure stepped out of the car.

Peter.

"Sophie! What are you doing?" Peter cried, running toward us. He touched my shoulder. "Rory, are you okay?"

"Don't touch me!" I brushed his hand away and stepped back. "After what you did to her, how dare you act like a gentleman in front of me?"

"I—I don't understand," he stammered.

"*Those* are evidence of your ill manners." I pointed at the paper and the picture on the ground.

Peter picked them up, scanning the contents. "Oh my God," he whispered, his hands shaking as he dropped them.

Emotionless, Sophie knelt to pick them up. She folded the paper and put it and the photo back in her clutch. Then she stood still, watching us like a little girl expecting something exciting.

I couldn't stand to see Peter's face, so I rushed toward my apartment.

"Rory, please, I can explain!" he cried behind me.

"For what?" I screamed, turning to him without stopping. I clenched my fingers hard and winced as my nails dug into my palms. "Pretending to be innocent after you asked her to sleep with you and then forcing her to abort your baby? You're a sick coward, Peter!" I turned back.

I heard a painful sound escape his mouth. I stumbled to a halt and turned around to see Peter bent forward with his hands on his knees, groaning.

I'd never seen him like that. For a second, doubt crept into my mind, but I pushed it back. A beautiful girl from a notable family like Sophie's wouldn't tarnish her reputation that way. All the good things I'd thought about Peter were gone.

Gritting my teeth, I turned and let myself into my apartment without looking back, slamming the door behind me.

Chapter 44

"CAT GOT YOUR TONGUE TODAY?"

Startled, I looked at Ryan, who was swinging his putter to hit the golf ball, aiming for the cup near the wacky windmills. The ball rolled straight to the cup, but it stopped a few inches from it. He groaned about his unsuccessful swing and walked toward the windmills to give a last little stroke that pushed the ball into the cup.

We were in the mini-golf park as Ryan wanted to spend his day here before going to the airport. I was doing my best to focus on him and hide my feelings after learning the shocking truth about Sophie and Peter yesterday. I laughed and bantered jokes. However, it wasn't enough.

"What happened?" he asked, retrieving the ball.

"Nothing, I just…" I shrugged. A wisp of my hair blew in the afternoon breeze. I tugged it behind my ear. "I have a lot on my mind. I'm sorry."

He observed me silently, and then he signaled for us to go to the next hole.

"Breakup hurts. I told you a bunch of times that a long-distant relationship isn't easy."

My head swiveled toward him. "We didn't break up."

Ryan tsked, shaking his head. He took my wrist and lifted it.

"No couple's bracelet." Then he lowered it and let his fingers linger around my wrist before he released it. "I didn't see it yesterday either," he added. "I assume that you 'didn't break up' recently."

It was useless to hide it any longer. I gave a shrug. "Yeah, I broke up with him more than three months ago."

Ryan didn't say a word. As we reached our next hole, he put his golf ball down between the edge of the green and the start of the brick that lined the hole.

"Let's play truth or dare," he said, standing next to the ball.

My eyes narrowed. "Now?"

"Why not?" He shrugged, grabbed his putter, and hit the ball.

I frowned and slowly nodded. "Okay. Sure."

"Truth or dare?" he asked.

"Truth."

His lips curved, and he cast his eyes down for a few moments before straightening his back. "Have you ever liked me, Rory?"

I blinked at him, caught off guard, and wanted to dodge the question, but I'd chosen to play the game. After hitting my golf ball, I turned and looked at him. "Yes."

Ryan's face brightened. His eyes bounced between mine.

"Your turn," I challenged him.

"I choose...truth." A smile formed on his lips.

"Why did you stop contacting me after we chose our majors? I thought we were best friends."

He looked at me for a long moment before answering. "Because of you."

"What?" I raised my eyebrows. "What did I do?"

Ryan tsked again and walked toward the hole. I walked beside him. "Don't ask more questions because now it's your turn."

I thought for a second and said, "Truth."

"If you'd never met Peter, would you have fallen in love with me after we met again in the office?" he asked. I could see hope in his blue eyes.

I nodded. "Yes. Your turn."

His eyes sparkled a little bit before dimming. Picking up the golf ball, he mumbled, "I wish you'd never met Peter." He turned away and walked across to the café, passing by the next hole.

"Hey, our next hole is over there!" I pointed.

"Game's over," he said.

"That's tricky." I followed and grabbed his elbow to stop him. "Tell me, what is it? Why are you suddenly upset with me? Because I almost beat you in this game?"

Ryan let out a sigh and turned to me. "I'm not upset with you."

"Okay." I looked at him, waiting for further explanation.

"I'm upset with myself," he said.

"Oh." I stiffened.

He dropped the putter on the ground and placed his hands on my shoulders. "I've been in love with you since college, Rory. Since the day I left the Toblerone bar in your backpack. I..." He swallowed, shaking his head. "I didn't have the confidence to ask you out, to be my girlfriend. So, I sent you lots of hints, but you didn't respond to them." Ryan squeezed my shoulders gently before releasing them. "It broke my heart that you chose a different major than mine, and I took it as a cue that you didn't like me, especially after I saw you get out of Mike's car, and you both seemed buddy-buddy. Of course, a pretty girl like you would find a handsome guy like Mike rather than someone like me, a lanky, unattractive boy who only wore black clothes. That's why I chose to stay away from you."

I felt a sudden heat behind my eyes and looked away.

"Stupid Ryan," I said quietly. "You *are* stupid."

"Huh?" He blinked.

I heaved a sigh and turned to him. "Didn't you realize that you'd been nice not only to me but also to other girls? You'd helped them with their homework, invited them to ride in your car while I was in there too, or when we planned to watch a movie together? Now, tell me, how could I tell if you had any feelings for me?" I gave him a sad smile. "I gave *you* a hint too."

"You did?" he asked.

I nodded. "The Pokémon GO umbrella with Pikachu on it, remember?"

Ryan furrowed his eyebrows and then nodded slowly.

"You gave it to—" I stopped, trying to remember the name. "Uh…I forgot her name. Anyway, it took me two hours to create that umbrella because I remembered you wanted to have one of the Pokémon GO accessories. But I had no money. So, I made it for you."

His lips parted.

I shrugged. "Even though you liked wearing black clothes and you were very skinny, I liked you, Ryan. You are a good guy, but I was afraid to tell you."

Ryan looked stunned for a moment and then moaned and ran his hands over his face. "Oh God, how stupid we were."

"Yeah." I nodded, looking down at my wrist where the couple's bracelet used to be.

"Rory."

"Yes?" I looked up at him.

"If I weren't going to Japan, would you mind going on a date with me?"

I looked down in silence, scratching the ground with my toe. "But you knew you'd be going to Japan since you'd applied for the program, right?" I said, gazing at him. "That's your dream, and you wouldn't cancel it just because we were dating."

Ryan was dumbfounded and shook his head. "No. I wouldn't."

The gentle breeze was blowing through the flower bushes nearby, teasing his hair on his forehead.

Since we weren't in the mood to continue playing, Ryan asked me to drop him off at the airport. It was an hour earlier than what we'd planned.

I nodded, and we left the mini-golf park after handing in our balls and putters.

The Los Angeles Airport was crowded as always, but I got a nice parking spot near the elevators. After taking his luggage from the trunk, we strolled into the terminal.

As we were walking toward the security line, Ryan put his hand on my elbow. I looked at him with raised brows. He lowered his head and inserted his hands into the pockets of his cargo pants.

"Rory, I want to offer something. Want to hear?"

I nodded.

He took a deep breath. "Let's say, if, after I return from Japan in two years, and both of us are still single, would it be possible for us to go on a date?"

I looked down as I felt his eyes boring into my skull.

"I can't beat Peter financially, but I've already paid off my student loans, and I always pay my credit cards monthly," Ryan continued. "I don't have a mansion, but I have a small, decent condo to live in. I don't have a fancy car but a reliable car for work. I can't promise you anything but to give you my heart, love you, and do my best to make you happy for the rest of my life."

That was the sweetest promise a man had ever made to me.

"You just proposed to me." I chuckled.

"Is it possible?" he asked solemnly.

I swallowed and nodded. "Yeah, it's possible."

His face broke into a smile. He raised his hands as if he wanted to hug me, but then he let them drop.

"Ryan," I said, studying him. "Do me a favor. Let's say you find a good woman before we meet again. Please don't hesitate to ask her out. Please don't be shy like you were in college. You're a good man, Ryan. Someone worth fighting for."

After saying those words, I threw my arms around him. Ryan seemed startled, but he hugged me back. I wiped tears with my finger.

"Thanks for liking me, Ryan, in college and now." Sniffing, I pulled away from him and stepped back. "Enjoy your time in Japan, and good luck there."

"Yeah," he said. "Goodbye, Rory, and take care of yourself."

"You too," I said. "And keep in touch."

Nodding, Ryan turned and sauntered to the escalator, giving his passport and boarding pass to the TSA employee. I waved to him when he looked at me while ascending to the second floor. He smiled, waving back before joining hundreds of travelers queuing in front of the security checkpoint.

Spinning on my heel, I walked across the ticketing area to the parking lot.

Chapter 45

"SOPHIE SHOWED THE PICTURE AND the consent form to Rory?" Tom's jaw dropped. Peter had called to tell him about what happened in the parking lot of Rory's apartment building, but Tom couldn't come to his brother's house until two days later. "Why did she do that?"

Peter shook his head. "I can't believe it either. She even told Rory that I *forced* her to have the abortion." He groaned. "God, how stupid I am!"

Tom gazed at Peter, sensing a fight inside him. His brother stared at his feet. Occasionally, he paused and drew his eyebrows together as he internally debated something.

"Are you okay?" he asked, nudging his brother's arm.

Startled, Peter raised his eyes. "I've been thinking over and over about Sophie's behavior. I didn't understand why she kept the form and the picture after everything happened. As for the picture, well, I could understand if she kept it for sentimental reasons. But the consent form? If you were having an abortion because you'd done something stupid, would you keep it? If I were her, I would've burned that form after I came home from the clinic. It seems to me that she kept them on purpose, like she wanted to be prepared for this kind of situation."

"What do you mean by that? Like using them to blackmail you?"

Peter nodded slowly, feeling nauseous. "That's my assumption."

Tom's hand flew to his mouth as he looked at Peter. "No way." He shook his head. "It can't be. Sophie's a spoiled girl because her dad loves her dearly. I don't think she has the backbone to do such a thing."

Peter looked at him. "Then can you explain why she kept those things for years and showed them to Rory?"

Tom didn't respond. What Peter said made sense, but he couldn't comprehend why Sophie would keep the items. It didn't match her character.

People changed. Although Sophie was beautiful and seemed meek, perhaps she wasn't as submissive as she let on. Tom wasn't sure what to think, as he knew his sense about women was never accurate.

He didn't know Sophie very well. He'd left London when he was eighteen and had only met her briefly on Jane's birthdays. From even those short meetings, he could see that Sophie loved Peter and seemed jealous if any other girl got close to him. But to blackmail him? That seemed impossible!

"What will you do now?" he asked.

Peter shrugged. "The damage is done. Rory hates me. You should've seen the misery and shock in her eyes. I'll never, ever forget the look on her face." He hunched his shoulders. "If I'd known back then that I would eventually meet Rory, I would've behaved better. I wish I could turn back the clock."

Tom's expression turned thoughtful when Peter pressed his hands to his face and groaned. From his teenage years to his early twenties, Peter had been a wild young man who loved partying, drinking, using drugs, and racing cars. But sleeping around with women? That wasn't his style because he didn't want to be like Archie, their dad, who had slept with numerous women and suffered the consequences.

"Tell me your plan so I can help you," Tom said.

Peter dropped his hands, shaking his head. "I don't know. But I want to see that picture again to make sure it's me because, I swear to God, I don't recall anything about that night. I just know I woke up naked with her next to me."

"Think again," Tom urged.

Peter scratched his chin, thinking hard. "Well, I remember clearly up to when I entered the living room. I was kind of realizing that the living room wasn't mine. And she led me to the bathroom because I threw up again. I must've passed out because I don't remember anything until the next day." He swallowed, pausing.

"And?"

"As I told you last time, I woke up naked and rushed to get dressed. Then I left her alone."

"Was she awake when you left?" asked Tom.

Peter buried his head in his palms. "I don't remember. Maybe she was still sleeping."

Tom moved and sat next to Peter. He tapped his brother's shoulder gently. "I'll help you find the picture."

"How?" Peter asked without raising his head.

Tom was silent because he wasn't sure. "Well," he cleared his throat, "I'll find a way. Maybe I know someone who can help me."

Peter glanced sideways at him. "Thanks."

Tom scoffed. "Do you think I'm doing it for *you*?"

"What?" Peter blinked, not believing his ears.

Rubbing the corner of his lips with his thumb, Tom said, "I'm doing it for Rory because I love that girl."

A wry smile broke on Peter's face. "Still, thank you."

Chapter 46

ALMOST TWO WEEKS AFTER I had dropped off Ryan at LAX, I took an Uber to the airport for my flight to Tokyo. I was going to spend ten days there, but I hadn't told Ryan because I wanted to be alone while tracing my parents' footsteps to the university where they'd met. I even forbade Sam and Max taking me to the airport because they didn't want me to be alone, especially after I shared with them the sudden visit from Sophie and how she'd shown the consent form and the picture to me.

"Warm towel, miss?" the flight attendant offered, holding it with tongs.

"Thank you." I took the towel and wiped my face and hands with it.

I'd bought a ticket in premium class, one level above economy class. Although I had extra money from my dad and could afford business class, I decided not to. If I splurged, Sam would be upset. I wanted to be a woman who could control her money wisely.

After an over-ten-hour-long flight, I finally arrived at Narita Airport and took the Narita Express train to my hotel near Tokyo Tower. Sam had stayed in the hotel on his last trip and recommended it to me. Its location was perfect for sightseeing, recreation, dining, and getting around.

On my first day in the city, I went to the University of Tokyo, where my parents had met. With guidance from my dad's pictures, I found the bench where they used to spend their time reading books or chatting. I visited the students' dorm where they'd stayed, and I strolled the campus on paths lined with cherry trees on both sides. The whole area must have turned pink every spring from the beautiful clusters of cherry blossoms.

Tokyo was amazing. Wherever I turned, I saw an ocean of people in every direction. They swarmed like ants, and their footsteps rumbled under my feet when they passed me or when we crossed the intersection together. Despite how fast they walked, amazingly, there were no collisions. It was as though they had built-in radars in their bodies, detecting any obstacle in front of them. Once, when crossing the busiest intersection in Japan, called the Shibuya Crossing, I deliberately walked into people, and they swerved effortlessly. I had to admit that it would have been nice to have someone with me on this trip, but I enjoyed my time alone in Tokyo, spending my days visiting parks, shrines, temples, shopping centers, and museums, including the famous futuristic Digital Art Museum.

But Peter's image kept coming into my mind, regardless of how hard I kept reminding myself what he had done to Sophie. Every word he'd said, every smile he'd offered, and every kiss he'd given me were as clear as if he were standing next to me. My heart jumped in delight when someone called his name while I was queuing in front of the Edo-Tokyo Museum, and that ticked me off.

On my way to Shinjuku Gyoen National Garden, I took a train and happened to be in the car where an elderly drunk man was passed out on his seat. His body leaned sideways to the right, and his legs were spread open. My nose immediately wrinkled in disgust because of the horrible odor of liquor, urine, and vomit. Together with other passengers, I squeezed myself tightly to the other side of the car, away from the man.

What could have forced him to drink like there was no tomorrow? I wondered. I couldn't take my eyes off him. An image of Peter when he was drunk last year flashed in my mind. It was exactly like this, minus the urine smell. My chest tightened, and I closed my eyes briefly to shake off his image. I jumped out of the car at the next station with the other passengers who couldn't stand the smell. I sat in an empty chair on the station platform and hugged myself. Forgetting Peter wasn't easy. How I wished I'd never met him.

Chapter 47

"**H**OW DID YOU GET THIS picture?" asked Peter, staring at the photo of the two naked bodies.

"Isaac," said Tom from inside the fridge. Sulking, he straightened his back and turned to Peter. "Hey, what happened to your fridge? Why can't I find a single bottle of beer in here?"

"I'm trying to keep alcohol out of the house," Peter responded impatiently. "Tell me, why did Isaac help you?"

"Peter Ryder," called Tom, "I know you've attempted to stop drinking. But seriously? No beer? And what is *this*?" He took a bottle out of the fridge to read its label. "Apple and peach green tea? Do you drink this? I thought only Rory drank these." Clicking his tongue, he returned the bottle and closed the refrigerator door. "Ugh, this house isn't interesting anymore. Wait…" He stopped, grinning. "Maybe Marcus has some beer. I'll go next door."

Peter grasped his elbow. "Be serious. *Please.*" He frowned, waving the picture in front of his brother. Tom seemed overly ecstatic today. "Now, focus. Why did Isaac help you? Wouldn't he want to protect his sister? Remember, he was the one who sent the pictures of Rory and me to the Sandridges, because he wanted to be on his daddy's good side."

"Dude, do you know you're the most boring person on earth?"

Tom shrugged, headed to the sunroom, and dropped onto the sofa, pouting.

Peter rolled his eyes and followed behind him, feeling his patience wane.

"Thomas Ryder, please tell me," he pressed on, sitting next to his brother on the sofa.

Tom took time to answer. "Isaac," he said finally, "owed me a lot of money because he has a gambling issue. I don't know when he started that habit. I didn't even know that he's lived in Los Angeles for three years now. One day, I met him in Vegas, when I was there for the Cirque du Soleil show, and he asked me to loan him some money. Since I thought of him as our childhood friend, and his father was our family friend, I lent him some, but he never paid me back. Last year, he was arrested for being involved in a bar fight and a DUI, and I bailed him out.

"Isaac has a weak personality, and he's afraid of his dad. He's nice to me because he wants to hide his gambling and drug issues. You know, if Mr. Fournier knew about that—oh boy—he'd disinherit Isaac from the family fortune," Tom scorned. "So, he owes me...*a lot*, and it's time for him to pay me back little by little."

Peter narrowed his eyes at the satisfied smile on his brother's face. Tom was kind and loyal, but he could pull some stunts that surprised the hell out of him.

"And he agreed to steal the picture from his sister?" Peter asked.

With a smile on his lips, Tom nodded and snatched the picture from Peter's hand.

"Hey!" cried Peter, attempting to steal it back.

"Chill, bro," Tom said. "I'm going to give this picture to a good friend of mine in the LAPD. You can come with me if you want."

Peter's jaw dropped. Curiosity grew in his light brown eyes. "Since when do you have a friend there?"

Tom pointed his nose into the air. "You don't know me at all."

He made his voice sound deeper than usual. "I know a bunch of people in the underground. Do you know my nickname? Tom—"

"Be serious!" Peter kicked his brother's shoes. He wondered how many times he'd used those words with Tom today.

"Thanks to Rory," Tom answered, moving his feet away.

"Rory? How is she involved in this?"

"Well," Tom scratched his chin with a tip of the picture, "Rory's cousin is dating an LAPD detective. And—"

"Rory's cousin?" Peter talked over Tom. His eyebrows flew up. "Wait, I didn't know Rory had a cousin."

Tom grimaced slightly. "There've been a lot of things happening since you broke up with her. I'll let you know later. But now," he raised his palm at Peter, "let me continue."

Peter rubbed his neck and nodded.

"Rory's cousin is dating an LAPD detective, and I happened to meet her when I accompanied Rory to the hospital after Aunt Amy had her heart attack."

Peter jumped out of his seat, pulling his brother up by his shirt collar.

Tom's eyes widened at his sudden aggression.

"What did you say? Aunt Amy had a heart attack? When? Is she okay?"

Tom pushed his brother's hands down, shoved him aside, and smoothed his T-shirt with one hand. "You ruined my shirt," he said, pouting.

Peter glared at him and curled his fingers, ready to beat him up if he kept joking around.

His eyes fixed on Peter, Tom said, "Aunt Amy had a heart attack a month after you and Rory broke up. Yeah, thanks to you, who's always busy and never has time for people who care about you."

"Hey, do you think I'm playing marbles in the office?" Peter asked, offended. "I have a responsibility to—"

"Knock it off, Peter," Tom snapped. His face flushed crimson.

"I'm tired of your excuses. You've been hiding behind your busyness. I understand that you have a huge responsibility on your shoulders. You accepted Jane's position at White Water because she wanted you to prevent the company being sold.

"Yes, I know that Uncle Ethan persuaded Grandpa to sell the company because, if White Water became financially strong, Archie's shares would be worth more than his, and he doesn't want that. Ethan wants to control the Sandridge Group and is selling the family's businesses one by one because he isn't interested in managing them. He's greedy and only wants the money.

"But Jane could predict his movements, which was why she hoped you could make the company successful. Furthermore, if you succeed, Archie's position in the family becomes stronger than Ethan's. Yes, you dislike Archie for neglecting us when we were young, but you chose to help Archie rather than Ethan."

Peter widened his eyes, shaking his head slightly. "Wait...h— how do you know all of this? No one but Jane, Marcus, and me knew anything."

Tom narrowed his eyes, seemingly annoyed by the interruption. He blew out air but answered the question anyway. "Rory found Jane's video."

"She...what?" Peter jerked his head back.

Tom shrugged as if saying, "You heard me."

"And then she...she told you?" Peter stammered.

Tom's lips twitched. "Indirectly, when she was drunk. After she sobered up, I confronted her, and she told me everything. I also confirmed it with Marcus." He paused, studying his brother's face. "Rory decided to break up with you because she didn't want to be an obstacle to your saving White Water, and she was aware that you would fulfill Jane's last request because you loved her. She was hurt after Ethan and Archie came over here and gave her a hard time, and then she listened to Jane on the video saying that she wasn't the right one for you and that she might be using you for your money. On top of that, you were spending your time with Sophie because"—he shrugged—"you care about our family businesses. Rory didn't want to succumb to the unfairness you subjected her to."

Tom exhaled and looked straight into Peter's eyes. "You *hurt* the girl who genuinely loved you. And that's your loss."

Peter's cheeks turned pale. He groaned, covering his face. "I can't believe it!" His voice was muffled against his palms. "I thought she hurt me, but I've hurt her even more."

"Yes, you did—well, our family did," Tom said flatly. "You stood her up. You didn't have time for her. You focused your attention on Sophie and your businesses and ignored the people who love you. You even avoided me and Theo. You *are* a jerk, Peter. Yes, you are. If I can say it bluntly, as a brother who loves you: you are as bad as Archie. Well," he clicked his tongue, "minus sleeping with all those women."

Peter's face remained white as a sheet, but he didn't say anything.

"And Aunt Amy. You ignored her too," Tom said matter-of-factly. "I didn't expect you to contact her often, but at least calling her once in a while to say hi wouldn't have killed you, would it?"

"How was Rory when her aunt had the heart attack?" Peter asked quietly, feeling ashamed and wishing he could vanish from the face of the earth.

Tom scoffed, walking across the sunroom back to the kitchen. "What do you think? She only has Aunt Amy, and she was freaked out when it happened. But Rory is a tough girl, a fighter. She handled herself well and had good, supportive people around her."

Something flashed in Peter's mind as he turned to Tom. "You mean her cousin?"

"And his girlfriend, the LAPD detective," Tom added. "Speaking of which," he took his car keys from the kitchen table, "I'm leaving now because I want to give this picture to her. The faster we solve this issue, the better."

"I'll go with you."

Tom nodded.

"And please fill me in about everything that's happened since Rory and I broke up, especially about her cousin," Peter pleaded, following Tom.

"Sure, you got it."

Chapter 48

TIME FLEW BY. AFTER TEN days in Tokyo, I returned home to California.

Dragging my luggage, I strolled to immigration as people rushed around me. I didn't have a reason to rush despite my flight having landed more than an hour earlier.

It didn't take long, since the immigration line was short.

"Hi," I said, giving my passport to the officer.

She smiled, took my passport, and scanned it.

"How was your trip to Japan?" she asked, her eyes reading her screen while comparing it to my passport.

"It was great, but I'm glad to be back," I said.

The officer smiled and handed my passport back to me. "Welcome home."

"Thank you." I took my passport and walked toward the exit.

I looked at my cell phone to find an Uber. If I couldn't find one, I thought I might stay overnight at the airport. Sam had told me to call him if I needed a ride, but I decided not to bother him.

As I approached the exit, my eyes once again tricked me into imagining I saw Peter, this time standing near the automatic door. I groaned inwardly, rubbed my eyes briefly, and continued walking. *I must be going crazy! Why do I keep seeing him?*

"Do you hate me so much that you don't even recognize me anymore?"

"Okay, this isn't good. Now I'm hearing his voice in my mind," I told to myself. Usually, his image made no sound. "I should make an appointment with a psychiatrist this week to get Peter out of my mind," I murmured, shaking my head.

"Do you hate me so much that you don't recognize me anymore?" the voice repeated, becoming louder and sounding all too real.

Stunned, I halted. Spinning on my heel, I noticed that Peter's image was still there, looking at me sorrowfully.

Desperately, I shut my eyes tightly and opened them. The image was still there, walking closer toward me.

Is it... real?

Peter, not his image, stopped in front of me with his hands in his jacket. He seemed taller than the last time I'd seen him. Standing closer, I didn't see the usual mischievous twinkle in his eyes. The frown lines on his face were more pronounced. He looked a decade older than he had the last time I'd seen him.

"Do you really hate me that much?" he asked in a lower voice, but I heard the bitterness and sadness underneath the words.

I frowned. The tips of my fingers went numb as I clenched my luggage.

Peter was silent too, but I felt his eyes on me.

"Why are you here?" I asked. "How did you know I was arriving today, at this hour?"

Twisting his wrist, he glanced at me and then lowered his eyes, his Adam's apple bobbing in his throat. I sighed and pushed past him. Peter stretched out his hand to take my luggage. I wanted to jerk it free, but something in his eyes stopped me. I swallowed. His hand clutched the luggage handle, only a couple inches away from mine.

"Finally, you found her!" a deep voice boomed behind me.

Startled, I released the handle and turned to the speaker. A sturdy black man in a security uniform and a Tony Stark mustache approached us. He smiled at me and gave a nod of acknowledgment to Peter.

A tight smile broke out on Peter's face as he nodded. "Yeah, finally."

Then they exchanged a fist bump.

Pointing at Peter, the man said to me, "You *are* a lucky girl, you know. This man has been waiting for you since, what, three nights ago? If I were a girl, I wouldn't let him go. Man…too bad I don't have a sister. If I did, I'd introduce her to you, brother."

"Three nights ago? What's he talking about?" I wondered, but I kept silent.

"Good luck, bro! Hope you can resolve your issues with her. And, please, don't stand in the middle of people's traffic, lovebirds." He winked and left us alone.

Peter gave a light chuckle as the man walked away. I took that chance to jerk my luggage handle free from him and scurry toward the exit.

"Rory!" he called.

I ignored him.

"Rory, please." He caught up to me and wrapped his fingers around my elbow.

I turned and jerked my arm free. "What do you want, Peter?" I snapped, anger rising inside me. "Why do you keep pestering me? You and your fiancée? For God's sake, stop bugging me!"

I marched away, but Peter was faster than me.

He blocked my way. "The baby wasn't mine," he said, breathing hard and fast. "Sophie lied to me and fabricated the picture. The man in the picture was her real boyfriend, who looks similar to me from behind. She alter—"

"That's none of my business!" I glared fire and tried to move around him.

Peter blocked me again with stubbornness in his eyes. "At first glance, no one can tell that the man isn't me. She only knew about the birthmark on my shoulder because it's noticeable whenever I'm not wearing sleeves. But there's another birthmark on my right lower back. It should be visible on the man's back from his position in the picture, but there's no second birthmark on him. You can check for yourself." Peter pulled the photo from his back pocket and pushed it into my hand.

I refused to accept the picture but took a look at it without saying anything and then walked around him.

Peter followed like a persistent puppy. "Sophie couldn't let her dad know that the baby was her boyfriend's, the son of his executive assistant, who was lower on the economic ladder than her family. When I was wasted, she plotted with him to use me, thinking her dad wouldn't hesitant if the baby were mine. Rory, she showed you the picture to push you away from me because she knows that I...I still love you."

I stopped and faced him. "Don't lie to me, Peter. You forced Sophie to abort the baby."

"No, that's not true. The consent form is about an abortion method that the doctor *had* to perform on her."

"That's the same thing," I snapped.

"It's different!" He sounded as though he was about to cry in frustration and caught my arm to stop me. "That night," he said, continuing to ignore my glower, "she called me because she said she was in pain. When I arrived at her apartment, I found her lying on the living room floor with blood everywhere, and I rushed her to the hospital. The doctor there said she'd had a miscarriage at eight, nine, or ten weeks along. I don't remember exactly. He said it could be done naturally, but Sophie didn't want to wait. She wanted to make sure no one would find out. As you know, before the procedure, she had to sign the consent form. Then, when she asked me to sign it too, I did it right away because I thought the baby was mine, and I felt guilty for making her suffer."

I was beginning to feel dizzy. Biting my inner cheek hard, I studied his face.

"With Isaac's help, Tom got the picture to see whether the man was me, because I didn't remember anything about that night. Then, Max blew up the picture to see it clearly, and my gut was right. There's no second birthmark on the man's back."

I raised an eyebrow. "Max?"

"Yeah, your cousin's girlfriend," Peter said, as if I didn't know who Max was. He released my arm. "Tom asked for her help."

I closed my eyes briefly, my breathing heavy. "Please leave me alone, Peter," I said wearily.

He nodded. "Yes, I'll do that. I just wanted to tell you the truth so you wouldn't misjudge me."

"That was why you waited here for three nights?"

"Yeah, because no one would tell me exactly when you'd arrive."

I looked down, feeling sorry for him. Clenching my jaw, I looked up. "Thank you for clearing things up, but I won't change my mind. Goodbye, Peter."

"I know you won't." He quickened his pace. "But it's late now. Let me take you home for the last time, and then I'll disappear from your life forever."

"I'm going to take an Uber," I said over my shoulder.

"Stop being stubborn, Rory. It's almost eleven o'clock. Are you sure about taking an Uber to Irvine from here? From LAX?"

I stopped. He stopped alongside me, his eyes pleading. "Okay, I'll go with you," I said after giving a second thought to his offer.

He looked relieved and took my luggage from my hand. For a few seconds, I didn't want to release it, but I let him drag it from me as we walked toward the parking lot.

Peter was quiet, knowing I didn't have any desire to catch up.

Looking out the window, I wanted to be home soon, because

sitting next to him was torture. Unfortunately, the odds weren't in my favor. The traffic was heavily backed up due to a car accident.

After almost an hour and a half, we finally made it to my apartment.

"Thank you for the ride," I said politely as Peter took my luggage out of his trunk.

"Don't mention it," he said. "Oh, I almost forgot."

He took a paper bag from his trunk. "Before picking you up, I stopped at a Japanese supermarket and bought food you'd like. For some reason, I felt like tonight was the night you'd arrive." He handed me the bag. "Just heat it up in the microwave."

"I'm not hu—"

"Please," he interrupted, his voice sounding tired. Beneath the flickering streetlight, I saw the puffiness under his eyes.

"Thank you." I took the bag from his hand.

Our fingers brushed and I took a step back instantly, and so did he. His mouth settled into a thin line after he took a deep breath and slowly let it out.

"Please drive safely. It's very late," I said quietly.

"Yeah, I will." He nodded. "Goodbye, Rory."

"Goodbye, Peter."

For a few moments, we just looked at each other. My stomach twisted and I bit my lower lip to stop myself from crying. Then, almost in unison, we turned our backs. I walked toward my apartment, and he walked to his car. As I was about to unlock my door, I heard his tires rolling over the loose gravel of the parking lot as Peter turned toward the exit. Through the crack of my door, I watched his left taillight blinking in the dark when he turned, and slowly the light faded before finally disappearing.

I closed the door silently and leaned my forehead against it. A tear dripped down my face, and I stood there, motionless, for some time.

Chapter 49

It was Saturday morning, a few days after I'd returned from Japan. With our close friends and my dad's family, my aunt and I gathered at my dad's burial site to honor his request to bury my mom's ashes. Her ashes had been kept in the columbarium in Boston since she'd passed away, and my aunt had brought them with her to California yesterday.

I was sweating through my kimono as I stood next to Aunt Amy. Wearing a kimono for midsummer wasn't the right decision. My aunt had insisted on wearing a black one, the traditional Japanese dress for the ceremony. I respected her request and agreed to wear it for the first time. Tom gave me a sympathetic glance as I kept fanning myself with a small fan.

As the ashes were lowered into the earth, my aunt cried and tapped her hand on her chest while saying something in Japanese. I couldn't speak the language, but I assumed she must have been talking to my mom, telling her to rest in peace next to the man she'd loved. Her body shook as I placed a hand on her shoulder. My aunt was one of the most emotionless people I'd ever met. But today, she showed such strong emotions that my heart ached to see her like that.

After the ceremony was over, we rented a room in a nearby restaurant for some refreshments. I felt relief as the cold air from the central AC hit my body. It would have been nice if I could go back home and change into my regular clothes, but that was out of the question.

I'd just finished two mini burgers when Theo approached our table and whispered to me, "Rory, can I talk to you for a second?"

"Sure." I wiped my mouth with a napkin and leaned toward Max, who sat next to me. "I need to talk with Theo. Please let my aunt know if she's looking for me."

"Sure." She nodded. "Is everything okay?" She looked at me, concern written in her eyes.

"Yes. Be back in a sec."

Theo was waiting on the rear patio as I pushed the double doors open.

"Sorry to keep you waiting. I had to tell someone where I was just in case my aunt was looking for me. So, what's up?" I asked.

Adjusting his glasses, Theo cleared his throat. "I hope you won't be mad at me for what I'm about to say."

I narrowed my eyes. "What's it about? As long as it isn't about Peter, I'm fine."

Hesitation showed clearly on his face, but he set his jaw and said, "Peter canceled his engagement with Sophie."

I huffed and raised my hand to stop him. "See, this is why I've tried not to talk to you or Tom, because you guys keep bugging me to go back to Peter. This is unbelievable! Whether he broke the engagement or not, it's not my problem."

Theo bit his lip and nodded slowly. "Yes, that's right. It's not your problem. But I can't stand to see his gloomy face since you broke up with him. He's practically a zombie, doing what people tell him to do. No smile. No energy. Just work, work, and more work. Marcus told Tom that his bedroom light is on throughout the night. Peter's gotten thinner and looks different. That's why"— he pressed his palms together in front of his chest—"I hoped you could talk to him as a friend. I know you wouldn't want to be with him again, and that's okay. He'll listen to you. He doesn't listen to anyone else."

I stared at him. "No."

Theo was stunned by my answer. "But please be his friend," he begged.

I shook my head. "Once we met, I'd cross the line I've marked between us, and I can't do that. It breaks my heart to hear about his condition, but he'll snap out of it. He doesn't need me. Besides," I swallowed, shaking my head again, "I don't want to deal with his complicated family. I won't forget the condescending look his uncle gave me or Jane's opinion about me. I've had enough. No, I'm sorry. Let's say we were dating again; his family wouldn't accept me because I'm not suitable for Peter's future. He'd better find a woman his family will approve of. My family and I couldn't beat that."

Theo's face reddened, and he pressed his lips together tightly as he looked at me.

"I'm sorry for disappointing you." I looked at Theo's eyes behind his glasses. "Well, I think I should go in now, just in case my aunt needs something from me."

Without waiting, I walked toward the doors. When my fingers touched the handle, I turned to Theo. "I'm really sorry."

Theo nodded slowly.

I offered him a small smile before walking through the doorway to the assembly room.

Chapter 50

"HOW DO YOU LIKE MY pancakes, rascal?"

Looking up from his plate, Peter gave a small smile to Rosa, Marcus's wife, the only person who called him "rascal" because of the mischievous things he'd done in his childhood.

"They're delicious as ever," he said.

Last night, Tom had informed him about the burial ceremony for Rory's mom's ashes. His insides wrenched because, if they hadn't broken up, he would have been next to her for that momentous day. He was happy that Rory had found her dad and that the handsome lawyer he'd felt so jealous of was her cousin, but how he wished to have been the first person to receive the good news.

This morning, he didn't want to be alone, and so he'd invited Rosa and Marcus to have a late breakfast with him. As usual, Rosa made him his favorite soft, fluffy pancakes, the ones he'd made for Rory too.

"You should eat more, rascal," she commented, putting two more pancakes on his plate. "You're getting skinny. I don't like it."

"I'm planning to eat more." Peter forced a smile, noticing Rosa's knitted brows, and added more fruit to his plate.

Rosa seemed unsatisfied and exchanged a glance with her husband. She widened her eyes at him, pointing her head toward Peter as if to say, "Give him some advice."

As expected, Marcus sighed and called him softly.

"Peter, you should take care of your health. Don't lie to me that you've been working hard morning and night, and, anyway, that's not good for your health."

Peter chuckled, putting his fork on the plate. "Are you spying on me now, Marcus?"

Marcus smiled at him. "Yes, because I have to. Since you broke up with Miss Rory, you haven't taken care of yourself. That's why I decided to step in again and look after you like I've done since you were a baby."

Peter glanced at the gray-haired man and his wife, who were sitting to his right and left, concern clear in their eyes. It was the same look they gave him every time he was depressed. "Don't worry. I'll rebound soon."

The doorbell rang, interrupting their conversation.

"I'll get it." Rosa got up and walked across the front hall to open the door.

Peter was about to bring a blueberry to his mouth when Rosa scurried back.

"It's Sophie," she said flatly. "She wants to talk to you."

Heat rose instantly from his stomach as he glanced up to see Sophie standing in the living room.

"Be calm, Peter," Marcus reminded him as he rose from his seat.

"Yeah," Peter said over his shoulder and walked toward the living room. His ex-fiancée looked down, avoiding his eyes, twisting her hands together. There was none of the haughty manner she usually showed.

"What do you want to talk about?" Peter said coldly as he stopped in front of her.

"I want you to reconsider your decision to end our engagement, Peter." Her green eyes searched his.

"What? Why?"

"Because..." Sophie shifted her weight from one foot to another, "I love you and I can't live without you."

Peter furrowed his eyebrows. "Or because you're afraid your daddy will disinherit you?"

Sophie gasped and took a step back.

Peter sighed and smiled sadly. He pressed his hands down inside his pants pockets and looked hard at her.

"Do you know why I accepted the betrothal plan that was offered by my grandpa?"

Sophie shook her head.

"Because I'd always thought you were a considerate girl. Remember the words you said after kids bullied you at my parents' party? When I tried to comfort you?"

She shook her head again.

"You begged me not to tell anyone about the bullying because you didn't want your dad to become upset, and his reaction would be overboard and ruin my parents' party. I never forgot that moment, and that's why I thought I could learn to love you after we were engaged. But," Peter shrugged, "you changed so much. You've become selfish and greedy. You even conspired to trap me in guilt for a crime I didn't commit."

Sophie's lips trembled. "But...at that time, I was afraid."

"Don't you think I *wasn't*?" Peter's voice rose. "For five years, you never revealed that your boyfriend got you pregnant. For five years, you made me think I was the cause of your affliction and abortion. *Five damn years!* And you don't even say sorry to me!"

Peter's face flushed red hot, and he felt the pounding in his ears as his body shook to control his anger. How he wanted to scream at her for all the miseries he'd endured.

"Now, please get out of this house because I can't stand to see your face anymore," Peter said, pointing at the door.

Sophie swallowed. "If you don't reconsider, the partnership will fail. Your grandpa will be upset, and he'll disinherit you from his will."

"Really?" Peter scoffed. "Your father spoiled you, but he's a sensible man. In fact, I got an email from my grandpa that Fournier Enterprises just signed an agreement for partnership. You'll see it on the news tomorrow morning."

His ex-fiancée turned pale.

Peter maintained his eyes on Sophie, although it was hard for him to do so without feeling nauseous. "And do you think I'm afraid of my grandpa cutting me off from his money? You underestimate me, Sophie."

He pulled the door open. "Please get out."

Reluctantly, Sophie moved toward the door. In the doorway, she stopped and glanced at him for a few beats, and then she stepped outside the house.

Peter almost slammed the door, but he didn't. Closing his eyes, he leaned his back on the door, feeling heavy in his stomach.

"Peter," a soft, gentle voice called him.

He opened his eyes to see Marcus and Rosa, gazing at him with sympathy.

A wave of grief, remorse, and anger hit his chest. Tears streamed from his eyes as he saw Rosa spread her arms widely. For a split second, Peter felt as if he'd turned back into a lonely five-year-old boy. Without hesitation, he trudged to the middle-aged woman and cried on her shoulder one more time.

Chapter 51

LOOSENING HIS TIE, PETER WALKED down the corridor after giving a presentation about White Water's quarterly financial report to the board of directors. The meeting was held at the headquarters of Sandridge Group in London. For a few seconds, a smile appeared on his lips, and he felt great satisfaction in watching the board of directors' reaction regarding his company's performance. He'd been working hard to reach the revenue objective that his grandpa had set for the company. Over the last six months, the company's revenue had increased exponentially.

Peter stopped walking and looked skyward, through the transparent dome ceiling, to see the night sky. "Are you happy now, Jane?"

No one answered. Not even a star blinked.

He sighed and took out a long, thin pouch of red ginseng supplements from his jacket pocket. After tearing off the top, he tilted his head and drank the liquid in one gulp. The corner of his mouth twitched as his taste buds caught the bitter taste after the sweetness. He didn't like it, but Rosa had given him a box of red ginseng after she'd returned from her trip to South Korea.

She'd told Peter that the supplement would help fight fatigue and stress, something that Peter needed for his health. Before he'd flown to London, Rosa had stopped by his house and put a dozen of the supplements in his luggage. If he hadn't loved and respected her, he would have thrown them away.

As he tossed the empty pouch into a nearby trash bin, someone called his name. He spun to see Archie walking toward him.

"Congratulations, Peter." His dad patted his shoulder. "In the last six months, you've made White Water's revenue higher than it has ever been. Even Jane couldn't do that. Your grandpa is happy and has canceled his plans to sell the company. You've saved your employees."

"Congratulations to you, too, for your new position as a member of the board of directors. Your position is secured because you hold more stock than your siblings, and Ethan won't bother you anymore," Peter said, offering a thin smile.

Archie shrugged. "Well, Ethan is the bad apple in the family. He loves to launch scheme after scheme against everyone who stands in his way of being the wealthiest one among your grandpa's children. He wanted to control the board of directors by forcing people to take his side. This isn't a new thing for me. I know him well, but because he's older than me, and I don't want to hurt your grandma's feelings, I won't do anything to retaliate against him."

Peter nodded, taking off his jacket and draping it over his arm. "Yeah, I can see his true character now. The longer I've been in the Sandridge family business, the clearer I've seen our family members' true characters."

"I'm glad you can learn from it." His dad sighed. "Ethan is evil and slimy. I was surprised that he worked with Sophie and Isaac. He even encouraged Sophie to blackmail you in front of Rory because he knew how strong Rory's influence was in your life. You changed a lot after living with her for such a short time. I was amazed when you dared to take the lead for White Water. That's how strong her love was, that she was able to change an unruly man into a responsible one. Rory brought a sense of responsibility out of you."

"I should thank Isaac, who came to his senses and helped me

steal the picture so Tom and I could investigate it even more," Peter said.

Archie nodded. "Hey, have dinner with me before you fly back to California tomorrow," he invited his son.

Looking at his dad, Peter shook his head. "I'll take a rain check. Maybe next time. Enjoy your meal, Archie."

Without waiting, he turned and strode toward the elevator.

"Peter!" his dad called.

Peter ignored him.

"Peter, what did you do to my spirited son?" His dad's voice echoed in the empty corridor as Peter pressed the elevator button.

Frowning, Peter whipped his head toward Archie, who hadn't moved. "What did you say?"

With his hands in his side pockets, Archie sauntered forward and stopped in front of his son. His body straightened tall as his olive-green eyes locked on Peter's.

"I'm asking what you did to my spirited son," he repeated.

Peter raised his brows. "I don't understand."

"Have you seen your reflection in the mirror lately?" Archie asked, slanting his head. "You've been going about like a robot, doing everything people tell you to do. Your eyes don't have any life in them. You look pale and aloof. How long do you want to be like this? I miss my spunky, energized, rebellious son who gave me a headache. I'd rather have him than this." He pointed at Peter from head to toe. "You're only twenty-seven. If you don't die because of drug abuse, an accident, or illness, you have a long road ahead of you. But you seem bored with life."

He put his hand on Peter's shoulder and said, "I hate to see you like this, and, honestly, I blame Jane for asking you to take her position."

A deep crease appeared across Peter's forehead. "What do you mean by that? Didn't you expect me to work for Sandridge Group to secure our family's position within?"

The elevator made a soft ding. Archie stepped inside after the doors opened. Motioning to Peter, he said, "I'll tell you the truth. Come and eat with me. I'm starving."

The restaurant was gorgeous. The lighting wasn't too bright nor too dim, but comforting, with a sense of intimacy and soft, melodic music. The artwork displayed on the walls and at each corner was tasteful and set a peaceful mood. The dining tables had a good amount of space between them. The servers seemed to glide along each aisle while gracefully carrying food to the diners.

Peter felt the tension in his shoulders ease as he sat and enjoyed his red wine. The clinking of glasses and cutlery, along with the guests' muffled conversations, created a relaxed and natural atmosphere. Initially, he didn't care where Archie took him for dinner. Once he knew where he was heading, it surprised him that his dad had remembered his favorite restaurant.

"So, what did you want to tell me?" he asked, swirling his wine and sniffing the fragrance before he sipped it slowly.

A gentle smile appeared on Archie's lips as he put his glass of wine on the table, looking at Peter. "I love my children, but I never expected all of you to follow your grandpa's orders. When Tom decided to move to the States, I let him. His mom used to be a famous model there, anyway, so I knew she could help her son find a place to work. I wanted you to follow Tom, but I didn't realize that Jane had chosen you to replace her if her third surgery failed." Archie's face flushed red, and his Adam's apple bobbed as he repressed his sadness. For a few moments, he didn't say anything.

Peter gazed at his dad and waited for him to continue.

"I'd hoped your rebellious personality would kick in—that you'd refuse the position, run away, and never come back here. But you didn't. It forced me to change my opinion about you. Jane was smart and could foresee your talent, something that I missed. But now…" Archie exhaled loudly. "Seeing you like this—it breaks my heart."

Peter raised his hand to stop his dad, his neck tense.

"Why are you suddenly telling me this? Since when have you cared about your children? You haven't bothered to tell your kids anything. I learned most of what I know about life from Marcus. Don't spew things like that just because I'm already successfully leading the company that indirectly helped secure your position."

Archie took his glass of wine and sipped it slowly, ignoring him. His lips smacked against the delicate dry wine that Peter knew his dad had purposely chosen, knowing he enjoyed it. Leaning back into his seat, Peter sampled his wine while the server brought their orders.

"*Bon appétit,*" the server said.

"*Merci,*" said Archie, lifting his knife and spoon.

For a few moments, they ate in silence. Peter glanced at his dad a few times, nearly losing his patience as he waited.

Finally, Archie swallowed his food and said, "Our family has dark secrets that I don't wish my children to be involved in it. I want my kids to have a good life beyond the Sandridges' opulence and power. Yes, I admit that I'm a lousy husband, but a lo—"

"And a lousy father," Peter talked over him. "If you weren't lousy, you wouldn't have had so many kids from so many women and let us grow up with nannies."

Archie raised an index finger. "Don't cross the line, son. That's my personal life."

Peter huffed and put a big piece of meat into his mouth.

"Since you chose to follow Jane's wishes, I decided to train you hard. If necessary, I wanted to break you, so you'd give up and leave the company. But you're stronger than I'd expected. I'm so proud of you, son."

"But I paid the price. I lost someone I loved dearly because of this job," Peter muttered. "Don't be alarmed. I've already sent a resignation letter to Grandpa."

Archie scoffed. "Did someone put a gun to your head and tell you to take Jane's position or break up with Rory?"

Peter's mouth dropped in disbelief. "You don't like her. Ethan doesn't like her. Jane even suggested I break up with her. None of the Sandridge elders like her because of her unknown family," he snapped.

"Who said I don't like her?" Archie wiped his lips with a white napkin.

Peter almost smashed his knife to his plate, but he remembered where he was just in time. "You interrogated her behind my back!"

His dad shrugged. "Son, you're terribly naïve. Don't you know that Ethan has been watching our movements ever since you began working for our business? Your uncle thought that you would fail. After watching your first public speech, he knew that he couldn't underestimate you. In such a short time, you'd turned into a responsible, charismatic, smart man. Later, after Isaac sent your pictures to us, he dug more and found out that Rory was the key to your turnaround. That's why Ethan wanted you to be with a woman who wouldn't be as strong an influence on you as Rory was."

Archie paused, took a sip of his wine, and continued. "I had to interrogate Rory to show Ethan that I was indifferent to my son's girlfriend and let him think I was on his side."

"Wait...I thought Sophie's position was stronger than Rory's in terms of making the company successful?" Peter asked.

"Sophie's dad is a billionaire and well-known. That's a plus," Archie said, cutting his steak into small pieces. "However, it won't guarantee that her influence would be stronger than Rory's because, when you love someone, you want to be a better man for her. And you don't love Sophie."

Peter was stunned. For some time, neither of them said a word.

"Peter, do you really care what the Sandridge elders think about Rory?" his dad asked.

Peter blinked. "What do you mean?"

"My son, look at me." Archie opened his arms wide. "If I cared about their opinion, I wouldn't have slept around and driven your grandpa crazy. He couldn't do anything to me because my performance was good, and I'm smart."

Peter was silent for a few moments before opening his mouth to speak, but Archie beat him to it.

"I know you think I'm selfish and don't care about your mom, or Jane's mom, or Eliza's mom. Yes, I am selfish, but I didn't abandon them. Many men have kids with different women and decide to leave them behind. I was sorry for hurting your mom and those other women, so I decided to stick with Tom's mom. So, stop judging me. I'll be judged later. Now, focus on *your* issue," said Archie, leaning forward. "If you love Rory, go find her. I'll support your decision if you want to be with her."

Peter shook his head. "She hates me."

"Are you sure?"

He nodded, giving his dad a sad smile. "Tom and Theo tried to suggest that she come back to me, but she refused."

His dad rolled his eyes. "Peter, be a man! You're the one who tied a knot, and only you can untie it. Why do you need Tom or Theo to solve it for you? That's ridiculous!"

Completely taken aback, Peter felt his face redden.

"If she refuses you after you ask her, that means she isn't interested in you anymore, but you should meet her like a gentleman." Archie gazed at Peter. "I only met her briefly, but I could see that she loved you. You should try to win her back."

Peter chewed his bottom lip, considering his dad's words carefully.

Archie broke into laughter, and wrinkles appeared at the corners of his eyes. "My God, look at my son. He's more innocent than I thought. At his age, I knew how to win women's hearts."

Peter scowled at his comments but without hard feelings.

"Is she in Boston or still in California?" Archie asked.

Peter shrugged. "I'm not sure. Perhaps she's already returned to Boston since her project was completed a few months ago."

"Great." Archie slapped his own knees. "Go to Boston, then. If you fail to win her back, don't tell people that you're my son, okay?"

Peter chuckled at his dad's joke. "Thanks, Dad...for..." He stopped himself, his cheeks warming uncomfortably. It had been two decades since he'd called Archie "Dad."

Archie's eyes widened, and Peter caught his misty eyes before he looked away. His dad lifted his glass of wine and drained its contents in two long swallows. "Go get her, tiger." His voice was little more than a croak.

Peter smiled and nodded.

Chapter 52

SUNDAY MORNING FOUND THE WEATHER overcast with a ten percent chance of rain. Since I didn't have anything exciting going on, I decided to visit my parents' graves. After packing lunch, a blanket, and an umbrella, I stopped to buy a big bunch of yellow roses, their favorite flowers.

The cemetery was quiet, with only a few visitors milling around. I didn't mind, preferring the tranquility to finish a book I'd been reading.

After cleaning the graves of the fallen maple leaves, I arranged the yellow roses in the vase, then sat on the blanket. Sam preferred the bench, but I liked sitting on the grass. I imagined sitting with my dad and mom at my sides, with their arms around my shoulders. Sighing, I pulled my legs to my chest, hiding my feet under my long skirt.

The autumn wind blew softly, playing with my ponytail with its invisible fingers. A few yellow leaves from nearby maple trees floated down and landed on my parents' graves. I picked them up, piling them near my feet with the rest of the leaves.

I picked one up, admiring the color. The foliage in California wasn't as beautiful as in Boston. I missed the rich array of yellows, reds, and golds of the leaves along the freeways, against the city skyline, the ponds, and around the parks. I missed hearing the crunch of dry leaves under my shoes on afternoon walks. The night before, my aunt had sent a few pictures of the foliage from Walden Pond. That made me envious of her East Coast autumn.

Exhaling softly, I closed my eyes.

It was last year to the day that Peter and I had experienced our first long kiss in front of the equestrian statue of George Washington in the Boston Public Garden.

"I think the foliage here is beautiful compared to England," Peter had said as we strolled toward the parking lot.

"How so?" I'd asked.

"Hmm…" He hadn't answer but smiled.

"You don't know because, deep down, you'd say that the foliage in England is better than here," I'd teased him.

He'd shaken his head. "No. It's better here."

"Then tell me why here is better."

Peter had stopped in front of me and said, "Maybe because you're here."

As I grinned, he'd leaned in and kissed me. With my hand on his arm, I'd kissed him back. For a few moments, we kissed again until my ungrateful stomach growled in protest. We'd giggled.

"I don't think kissing can satisfy your stomach," Peter had said, chuckling. "Let's go eat so it won't bother us again."

I'd laughed, and hand in hand, we'd left the garden.

My stomach pulled as the memory flashed behind my eyelids. It had been more than six months since we'd broken up, but the more I attempted to forget him, the more his memories emerged, like a movie constantly running in my mind.

"Arrrgh! Why can't I forget you?" I leaned my forehead against my knees. Sighing hopelessly, I turned my head and stared into the distance, beyond the gravestones.

Drowning in my thoughts, I didn't realize someone had opened the small gate and stepped into the lot. The soft thump of the gate closing startled me.

It must be Sam, I thought, glancing over my shoulder.

But the sight I found shocked me, and I jumped up.

Peter stood in front of the gate, holding a bucket of yellow roses. A dejected smile formed on his lips.

My heart hammered hard in my chest.

"Wh...why are you here? How do you know about this place?" I stuttered.

Stepping forward, Peter placed the flowers on my mom's grave. "I'm here to congratulate you on finding your dad. And I'm sorry that I'm late for the happy news," he said, facing me.

He held his hands behind his back, standing awkwardly as I stared at him without saying anything. He looked thinner, and his cheeks were sunken and pale.

I swallowed and nodded. "Thanks."

For a few moments, the only sounds I could hear were the gentle swishing of leaves from the trees and squirrels running up and down the trunks of the pines nearby.

"How are you?" Peter finally asked.

Almost at the same time, I asked, "Why are you here?"

That was enough to make us look at each other with small smiles on our faces.

"You go first," he said softly.

I looked at him solemnly. "Why are you here?"

"Because I miss you."

"That's not funny," I said, my voice strained.

"I'm not joking."

My chest ached as he regarded me ruefully. Clenching my jaw, I walked toward the gate and opened it wide. "Thanks for the flowers, Peter. Now, please go home."

He moved closer to me. I frowned and took a step back. Every time he took a step forward, I took a step back, and we waltzed like that until my back hit the wall behind me.

"Do you hate me so much that you don't want to talk to me or even see me?" he asked, not hiding his forlorn tone.

That question was like a needle that pricked my skin.

Curling my fingers to control my emotions, I looked at him. "I don't hate you. We already broke up and…and…there's nothing to say."

He took one step closer, his eyes locked on mine.

I swallowed and looked away. "Please go away, Peter," I said shakily. "I don't want to see you anymore."

"Is that so?" he asked. He reached out, touching my chin and turning my face to look at him. His fingers were both hot and cold. "Rory," he said, looking into my eyes. "Now, look at me and tell me for the last time that you don't love me anymore—just one more time. And then, I'll stay away from you for good. I'll even tell Tom and Theo not to mention me in front of you. But, please, say it one more time."

With my back pressed against the wall and his hand holding my chin, I felt helpless. My chest tightened, and it was hard to breathe. Something inside me inflated and swirled like a cyclone mixed with anger, sadness, disappointment, resentment, and remorse that I'd been suppressing my whole life.

Those feelings weren't only directed at Peter but at Jane and her video, at my dad, at my mom, at Sophie, at Peter's dad, at his uncle, at my aunt, at my classmates who had jeered at me for being an orphan, at my first boyfriend who had mocked me, at the bully ex-manager from my previous company, and at everyone who had ever caused me pain.

Then I felt a sudden *pop!* inside me. The pressure of pain that had been building up for years rushed into my veins.

"Leave me alone!" I screamed, pushing against Peter's chest with my palms.

He jerked his head back because of my reaction, but he didn't budge an inch.

Tears streamed down my cheeks as he caught my wrists and held them tightly. "Go away! Please leave me alone. Go away!" I was struggling to yank them free, but he didn't let go.

The wind blew gently as I stopped struggling, panting hard, my blouse clinging to my back with sweat. I breathed deeply, and Peter looked at me with concern and...love.

I would have fallen to the ground if he hadn't wrapped his arm around my waist and helped me sit on the blanket. Leaning on him, I covered my face and sobbed.

"Shh...it's okay. Everything will be fine," he said, gently caressing my back. "Everything will be fine."

"Why do you keep coming back?" I sobbed. "You don't know how desperately I want to forget you. But wherever I go, I always see your face. Why are you doing this to me?"

He didn't answer, but his hand continued caressing my back.

"Please leave me alone, Peter. You've known clearly that we can't be together. We shouldn't have fallen in love, and I shouldn't have let you stay in my apartment last year. I...please...just leave."

Before I could continue, he tightened his arms around me and buried his head on my shoulder. I was stunned at the feeling of dampness.

"Peter?" I pulled away, but he held me.

"Don't say a word. Just let me be like this," he said, his voice breaking.

We sat in each other's arms and cried in silence.

I looked up when Peter gently pulled away. His eyes were red, but they weren't dull anymore. There was a spark in his light brown eyes. It wasn't as intense as before, but it was there.

"I'm sorry for all the trouble I've given you since we met. I wish I could make your life easier. You can scream at me or punch me in the face, but Rory, please don't push me away." He gently pushed a strand of hair away from my face. "That hurt me so much."

"I can't be with you. Your world is cold and scary, Peter. I'd die if I stayed there." I sniffled.

He tucked some hair behind my ears. "If you can't go to my world, I'll come to yours," he said in a low voice.

A tear splashed out from my eyes as I shook my head hard. "You can't. I've known you can't. You'll do everything to help your family businesses as Jane had wanted you to."

"I sent a resignation letter to my grandpa," he said.

My eyes narrowed, examining his face. With his eyes focused on me, Peter fished his cell phone out of his pocket and showed me the email he'd sent.

"And he refused it." He shrugged, scrolling the reply so I could read it too.

Dropping his phone on the blanket, Peter sighed and took my hand. "Rory, my world is scary, even for me, but we can get through it together. In fact, my dad likes you, and he was the one who suggested that I try to win you back."

"No. You're lying."

"I'm not lying." Peter shook his head. "If you allow them to meet you, I believe they would love you. My grandma and Aunt Helen would love you. Also Tom's mom. Please stay with me," he said again. "Will you?"

My body shook. "What happens if, in the end, you find out Jane was right and I'm using you for selfish reasons?"

"I'm confident you aren't using me. If that was the case, it would've been easy for you to forget me and move on to someone else. But you didn't." Peter squeezed my hand. "Please stay with me, Rory. We can get through this. Don't you still love me?"

I looked down, not knowing what to say. Half of me screamed to say yes, but the other half screamed to say no.

Peter looked at me, his posture stiff, waiting for my answer.

"I do love you, but"—I shrugged—"I don't know, Peter."

His shoulders slumped.

A sharp prick stung my heart to see him like that. I pressed my forehead against his chest, inhaling his scent, as I wanted it to stay in my memory forever, just in case.

"So…we can't be together, then?" he whispered.

"I don't know." My voice cracked. I wrapped my hands around his waist.

Peter let out a heavy sigh as he enfolded me in his arms.

"Rory," he said after a long silence.

"Yes?" I looked up at him.

"I never thought I'd fall in love like this. Let's get back together. Give me a chance to prove to you that I'm the right person for you. I want to fix the things I've broken." Peter put his fingers over my mouth when I was about to interrupt him. "Hear me out. How about you give us a chance for a year or so? If you really can't stand my world, I'll come to your world, and we'll stay there," he offered.

I searched his eyes as he searched mine. "Are you sure? You've been living a glamorous lifestyle since you were born. Working outside the family business isn't easy either. You should be aware that you can't have a job in the same position or the same salary. Y—you may even have to downgrade everything."

He shrugged. "If Tom can do it, I can." A determination was clear in his eyes. "Please give me a chance."

Peter gave a light smile as I brushed his hair with my fingers. I missed seeing his eyes, his nose, his lips, his chiseled jaw. Sighing, I straightened my back to gently kiss his lips.

He leaned in and kissed me back. "Does that mean…yes?" he asked as I pulled away.

I nodded with my eyes.

His lips parted, and his eyes blinked a few times. Then Peter cupped my face, gave me a big kiss, and enfolded me in his arms again. With a wide smile, he released me and offered his hand.

"Let's sit on the bench. It's more comfortable than on the ground. Besides, I want to show your parents that I'm a gentleman."

I chuckled. Holding his hand, I stood, and we sat together on the bench.

"I thought you were in Boston," Peter said, brushing some grass away from my skirt.

"Martin extended the project for another month. This Friday, he told me that he'd asked Sally to transfer me here because my skill is more useful for his clients than hers."

His face glowed. "Really? Wow, that's awesome!" He squeezed my fingers lightly. "I'm proud of you."

I squeezed him back and tilted my head, frowning. "*Did* you think I was in Boston?"

Crimson color rose from his neck and up to his cheeks. He looked away.

"Really?" I almost jumped up from my seat. "Oh my God, Peter. Why didn't you ask Tom?"

He gave a bitter smile. "He's more loyal to you than to me."

"Aw man. I hope my aunt wasn't too surprised to see you standing on her doorstep."

Looking at his awkward smile, I could almost see what had happened. I covered my eyes with my hands. "What did she say?"

He shrugged. "She slapped me in the face and kicked me in the groin. She—"

"Hey, hey, hey…stop it. She wouldn't do that."

He grinned. "She was surprised, but she let me sleep on the couch as usual and fed me with her delicious food."

"That's good." I couldn't believe he'd flown to Boston while I was in California.

"Come here." Peter opened his arms and held me to him. His heartbeat was strong and steady as I pressed my head against his chest.

"How did you know I was here, by the way?" I asked.

"Um, Sam told me," he said vaguely.

"But my parents' gravesite isn't easy to find unless you're familiar with the surroundings or someone else brought you...." My voice trailed off as I gazed up at him. "How did you find your way here?"

His eyebrow flicked up as it usually did when he felt guilty.

I sulked. "Peter?"

Letting out a sigh, he said weakly, "They're here."

"What?"

Standing, I spun around to the direction he pointed. My mouth dropped. I saw my aunt, Sam, Max, Tom, Emma, and Theo sitting under the gazebo. They waved at us, smiling.

Heat rose to my cheeks, and I sat back, covering my eyes. "Oh my God! You brought the cavalry?"

"Actually, no," defended Peter. "I returned here with your aunt yesterday. This morning, when we met Sam, he happened to be with Max, and, uh...Tom, Emma, and Theo happened to be with her. They agreed to show me the way here."

I glared at him.

"Rory, I swear I told them you'd be upset if they came with me."

"Oh nooooo." I dropped my head onto his shoulder. "They were watching us the whole time."

"Not when you were screaming," he comforted me.

"God, I can't believe it! Everybody must think I'm a crazy woman."

"Trust me. They weren't here when you were screaming."

I smacked his arm. "You're crazy! Oh God, Peter, you are crazy!" I smacked him again.

He winced, rubbing his arm as I scowled.

"Hey, can we join you now?" Tom yelled from the gazebo.

"Can they?" Peter gazed at me.

My cheeks were warm, but I nodded.

He flashed a smile and stood up to signal his cavalry to join us.

My aunt hugged me tightly and kissed me before she released me. Emma squealed and congratulated me while Sam smacked

Peter's shoulder hard enough to make him wince before shaking his hand.

"If you make her cry again, I'll get you," I heard him say between his teeth while smiling.

Max wrapped an arm around Peter's shoulder, grinning. "You heard him, big guy." She released him before standing next to Sam.

Theo and Tom laughed, giving Peter a group hug. "Should we feel proud of you for winning her back?" Theo teased him.

I cackled and took Peter's hand.

"Aww... Come on, Peter. Kiss her," said Tom, shoving Peter toward me.

With a smile that went all the way to his eyes, Peter grabbed me around the waist and bent me backward with his other hand, holding my back and supporting my body while kissing me in such an awkward position.

I heard cheering and laughing. I'm sure my face was red when Peter pulled me back up and grinned at me.

Sam started singing, "*L* is for the way you look at me. *O* is for the only one I see...."

Max joined him. "*V* is very, very extraordinary. *E* is even more than anyone that you adore can...."

I covered my mouth and giggled when my aunt and Tom joined them. "Love is all that I can give to you. Love is more than just a game for two...."

"Do you know that song?" I asked Peter, who hugged me from behind.

"My grandpa has sung this song often for my grandma," he answered.

"It's catchy. We should learn it."

"Sure, and I'll sing it for you." He smiled before giving me a quick kiss on the cheek.

AFTER WE'D LEFT THE CEMETERY and had lunch together, I dropped off my aunt at my apartment and then went with Peter to stay overnight at his place. We wanted to catch up on everything that had happened after we broke up, and Peter was eager to learn about my dad and Sam.

That night, we lay on the bed near the window and stared at the sky. As he'd promised months ago, Peter behaved well, and so did I. It might have been strange for some, but we didn't care because we did what was right for us.

Holding my hand, Peter listened as I talked, his eyes on me the entire time.

"Don't you ever get tired of looking at me?" I asked, moving my thumb in a slow circle on the back of his hand.

"No," he said sleepily. "Why should I feel tired of indulging my eyes with the beauty in front of me?"

I snickered. "Okay, I'll let you, then."

"That's my plan."

So, I continued. While I talked, out of the corner of my eye I saw a faint streak of light in the dark sky.

"Peter," I whisper-shouted, sitting bolt upright, gawking in the direction of the tiny light. "Another shooting star!"

He didn't respond.

I looked down to see him snoring gently, his body curled up sideways like a baby.

"You missed the shooting star again."

I smiled and pulled a blanket up to his shoulders.

Lying sideways to face him, I softly sang my mom's favorite song. "Catch a falling star and put it in your pocket, never let it fade away. Catch a falling star and put it in your pocket, save it for a rainy day. For love may come and tap you on the shoulder..." I tapped his shoulder gently and smiled. "Good night, Peter."

I sighed, holding his hand, and let myself drift into a sweet dream.

Acknowledgement

Gratitude is not only the greatest of vir-
tues but the parents of all the others.
– Marcus Tullius Cicero

I have to start by thanking my parents for everything they've done for me. Without them, I might not be the person I am today. When I felt hopeless and failed, they encouraged me to stay focused and keep fighting. Now I know where my fighting spirit comes from. I love you both!

To my better half and forever boyfriend, Steve, for your patience and love. Since March 2020, you've been working from home because of COVID-19, but we barely met during the day because I locked myself in writing this book. I love you, babe! If I had two hearts, you would have both.

To my sisters and brother for keeping my spirits up. Thanks for always putting me in your prayers.

To Rick K, my neighbor in MV. Rest in peace. You are no longer in the world, but I won't forget your kind advice. You understood the struggles and the pain of writing a book, but each time we met, you always said, "Listen, writing a book isn't easy, and you'll feel down. But don't give up. I have faith in you, and I know you can do it." Thanks for your positive affirmation. It made me feel good about myself. I won't give up. Thanks, Rick! Till we meet again.

To Mr. and Mrs. B for sparing your busy time to have dinner with me and my better half. You answered my questions patiently, especially after knowing that I needed that information for my book. Thank you. We should have dinner again soon.

To my in-laws, Ana and Fernando, Mr. and Mrs. Patterson, Leslie, Asun, Irma, Olin, Joy, Odi, Cayung, Dina, and Tepi. Your mental support is essential to me.

To my readers who asked for the sequel. Without you, this book can't go anywhere.

And last but not least, I thank God for giving me the strength to finish this book, for your blessings and graces every day. I love You!

Author's Note

Dear readers,

Whew! Finally, the sequel is done.

I have to admit that writing this sequel was more challenging than the first book. After spending countless hours writing up to sixty chapters, I had to delete half of them and start over because I didn't feel satisfied with the storyline. Sentence after sentence was deleted and rewritten. I never felt confident because I always felt something missing in the story. One morning, I had a burst blood vessel in my left eye from staying up the whole night. I almost gave up and stopped writing.

As many people have experienced, the COVID-19 pandemic made my mind unsettled, and it wasn't easy to stay optimistic. On top of that, I lost two good people I'd admired. One was my lecturer, and the other was Rick K, my neighbor in MV, who inspired me to create a father figure in Rick Perkin for Rory in the first book. Their passing affected me emotionally as though I lost a brother and a dad. May they rest in peace.

Despite the conditions, I kept writing, especially after receiving a few notes from readers who asked for the sequel.

Slowly but surely, the storyline was established. It was getting better once I got pointers from my editor. It meant more long hours spent in front of the computer, but I knew I wouldn't regret it because I always wanted to give my best.

Now, while writing this "author's note," my heart is filled with joy because it meant all the struggles and tiredness have paid off, and my book is ready to publish.

About the Author

Kana Wu, an autodidact author, has loved writing since her childhood. Her debut novel, *No Romance Allowed*, was published in October 2019, and it received two awards as Finalist in the 2020 International Book Awards and Reader's Favorite Awards. It was also a winner in the Romance category for the 2020 TCK Publishing Readers' Choice Awards Contest.

She lives in Southern California with her husband and her two rescued Jindo dogs.

Be the first to know when Kana has a special offer or a new book by checking her website or following her on social media.

https://www.facebook.com/kanawuauthor
https://www.instagram.com/kanawuauthor
www.kanawuauthor.com